The Sword of Cnut

Book 5 in the Danelaw Saga

By

Griff Hosker

The Sword of Cnut

Published by Sword Books Ltd 2024

Copyright ©Griff Hosker First Edition 2024

The author has asserted their moral right under the Copyright, Designs and Patents Act, 1988, to be identified as the author of this work.
All Rights reserved. No part of this publication may be reproduced, copied, stored in a retrieval system, or transmitted, in any form or by any means, without the prior written consent of the copyright holder, nor be otherwise circulated in any form of binding or cover other than that in which it is published and without a similar condition being imposed on the subsequent purchaser.
A CIP catalogue record for this title is available from the British Library.

Contents

The Sword of Cnut	1
Prologue	5
Chapter 1	9
Chapter 2	19
Chapter 3	30
Chapter 4	41
Chapter 5	50
Chapter 6	60
Chapter 7	72
Chapter 8	81
Chapter 9	91
Chapter 10	99
Chapter 11	110
Chapter 12	120
Chapter 13	132
Chapter 14	143
Chapter 15	155
Chapter 16	162
Chapter 17	175
Chapter 18	187
Epilogue	200
Glossary	203
Historical Notes	207
Other books by Griff Hosker	210

The Sword of Cnut

Real People used in the book

King Sweyn Forkbeard - King of Denmark
King Æthelred – King of England
Edmund Ironside - his son
Ælfheath – The Archbishop of Cantwareburh
Abbot Ælfmaer – Abbot of the Augustine monastery in Cantwareburh
Harald Sweynson – the eldest son of the King of Denmark.
Cnut Sweynson - second son of the King of Denmark
Eadric Streona – A Saxon leader mistrusted by all
Eirík Hákonarson – Eorl of Northumbria
Emma – widow of King Æthelred and wife of Cnut
Lady Ælfgifu – a Saxon noblewoman and later Queen of England
Lord Ælfhelm – her father
Thorkell the Tall – Jarl of the Jomsvikings
Hemingr – Thorkell's brother
Æthelstan - the son of King Æthelred
Oswy - the son-in-law of Eorledman Byrhtnoth
Thurbrand the Hold – A Northumbrian lord who controlled southern Northumbria
Uhtred the Bold - A Northumbrian lord who controlled northern Northumbria
Ealdred – the eldest son of Uhtred
Findláech – Mormaer of Moray (the father of Shakespeare's Macbeth)
Eadwulf Cudel - Uncle of Ealdred of Bebbanburg

The Sword of Cnut

Prologue

The battle with the Mercians had cost me dear. I had lost one of my hearthweru, Faramir. After we had buried him, we began our lives again. He was the only warrior we had lost when the Mercians had attacked my home, Norton, but it had been a grievous loss. Such men are irreplaceable. The cost was necessary for this was my home and we had been forced to defend it. My wife, Mary, had been more than happy to return to her home for Agerhøne had been a foreign land to her. Now that she was back and endured the attacks of our enemies she knew that a life of peace did not await her. However, it was in her Christian nature to accept her lot and she resigned herself to a life of danger. Now living in the place of her birth, she threw herself into making our new home, at Norton, both happy and prosperous. My eldest son, Steana, was now hersir of Agerhøne. He had not come with us across the sea. Bersi, my second son, had grown into a warrior. He was not yet old enough for the shield wall but he had led the boys and youths of Norton in our battle against the Scots and the Mercians. He was a leader and would be the heir to Norton.

Gunhilde, my daughter, was now of an age to be married and already young men were seeking her favour. They were all wary of me for I was an important lord who was close to the King of England, Cnut. I smiled at some of the devious ways they sought to catch her eye. She enjoyed toying with them much as a cat does with a mouse.

As for me? I now had only one of my hearthweru left, Gandálfr. He was, as I was, getting older. We both had grey hairs and the scars of battle on our bodies, but we both had more skills on the battlefield than any other warrior within a hundred miles. The two of us now trained and organised the men who would fight under my banner, the banner with the Oathsword, sewn by my wife and her women, upon it. The men who would fight for me all lived within ten miles of my home but that still meant a trek to train. Now that we had a priest and a church I used Sunday as my training day. They came for the service and then, while my wife held a sort of court with the wives, I would train with the men. We provided food and it strengthened the bonds we had begun to build in the battle we had just won.

We had work to do. The weaknesses of Norton had become apparent when we had been attacked. We were lucky for the Eorl of Northumbria, Eirík Hákonarson, was a friend and a good warrior. He guarded the far north and Edward of Billingham, whilst a Saxon, was

The Sword of Cnut

also a friend and protected the other side of the marshy land that bordered the river. The border lands were dangerous, and the proximity of the river enabled enemies to sail close to my walls. Indeed, I had done so when I served Jarl Sweyn Skull Taker, my foster father and uncle. Mary had been one of the captives we had taken back to Denmark with us. The work we had to do was to make our home safer from enemies.

The first six months saw us working every hour that we could. My men now had farms to tend and crops to grow. There was plenty of land to be farmed but we had to clear trees and roots first. Animals that were raised for food were vital to our survival. The pond that lay between the church and the hall was extended and we added young fish. We would have winter food. Walls were built to join the church and the manor as well as the other large houses. I never stopped and all the time I had Bersi and Gandálfr at my side. When I went to seek the new shaft for Saxon Slayer, my spear, I used the expedition to explore my land. We found the sapling that was perfect at the same time as I realised the potential of the beck that ran to the river. Our drekar, *'Falcon'* was moored in the river. It was isolated and if there was a storm inland then trees, hurtling down a river in spate, could be a danger to her hull. I pointed at the beck. "It would take work but we could widen the beck and drag the drekar to shelter beneath our walls. The wider beck would be an added obstacle and the drekar could be safer."

Gandálfr nodded, "If we took her from the water then we could take down the mast and clear her hull of weeds. We will not need her until next summer. She could spend the winter on land where the worms cannot get at her."

It was a good plan and while it would mean more work for every man and boy, we would be safer. Our drekar was our lifeline to Denmark. She was the only warship, so far as I knew, on the river. It took three months, but by the time we had finished the beck was wide enough for the drekar to sail within a hundred or so paces of the path to the village and the land on either side was now swampy. The only way from Norton to Billingham was now by the causeway beneath which the beck passed. I visited with Edward and Osgar in Billingham and we arranged for men to watch both ends of the causeway. We built a signal tower so that we could warn each other of danger. When that was done and the mast taken down we dragged the drekar up the slope and inverted the ship. There was no need to hurry, cleaning weed from a hull and applying pine tar was a winter job. It was best done slowly and carefully.

The Sword of Cnut

I had a horse I had taken from the Mercians. Verðandi seemed to be a horse that was cleverer than most and I enjoyed riding the animal. I rode, once a week, to visit with the others who lived close by. It was to remind them that King Cnut had made me their lord and that I was the justice who would uphold Cnut's Law. I always rode to Stockadeton first and worked my way back. Some of the people were Saxons and some were my men while others were Danes who had settled here long ago. The battle we had fought had made them all my people and I was welcomed when I visited. I saw that they had all improved their defences. As we had discovered, the Scots like to raid and take from this fertile land and I knew that the Norse, Swedes and even some Danes, still raided. Their lands were, in the main, less fertile than the land of which I was lord.

When I returned from my ride I was always gratified to see the two men on my gatehouse and the shields hanging from spears outside the homes of my people. They were the signs that we were not sheep to be sheared by others. We were warriors who would fight for that which we held.

The Sword of Cnut

The Sword of Cnut

order for there are those who dissent. His brother Harald ruled in a different way to King Cnut."

I paused with the horn halfway to my lips, "England is secure?"

The slight frown told me that it was not but Tofti, like all his oathsworn, was loyal to King Cnut. "Streona is dead, and King Cnut has divided the land into four. Eorl Eirík Hákonarson rules Northumbria, Thorkell the Tall commands East Anglia, Leofric has Mercia and the king rules Wessex. Tovi the Proud commands Lundenwic. The king feels that the land is secure. Archbishop Wulfstan is ensconced in Jorvik, and all is well."

I drank some beer to assimilate what I had been told, "But if the king is in Denmark, then who will rule Wessex? It is the heart of the old kingdom."

The frown on the warrior's face gave away the doubt in his mind, "Earl Godwin of Sussex is now seen as a loyal Saxon and he will command in the king's absence."

One advantage of speaking with an old shield brother was that there was honesty between us, "Tofti, I still mistrust Thorkell the Tall and I do not know Earl Godwin. It seems to me that the only lands that King Cnut truly commands are those here in the north."

"And that is why I am here. He wishes you to inform Eorl Eirík Hákonarson of his plans. You two are seen as his rocks and will guard his land."

I shook my head and gave a wry laugh, "We are many hundreds of miles from the English heartland, and we have few warriors."

"I did not say I thought it was a good idea, Sven. I am merely the messenger. The visit to Denmark will not be a long one. Between you and me I think that the king wants to make sure that Denmark understands that it is he who is now their king. He sees England as his home."

There was some relief in his words. Perhaps England would be safe. That was the last of the talk of politics. When we ate my wife was more concerned about the new Archbishop of Jorvik and his plans. She quizzed Tofti hard and I think, made him retire as soon as he could. When Tofti left only I had the doubts in my mind. Of course, I had been commanded and so I obeyed. The day after Tofti left I headed north with Gandálfr and Bersi. We rode to meet with the Eorl of Northumbria and the only man I truly trusted. I had no idea which of the strongholds the eorl would use and so we took a fourth horse with food and blankets. We headed for Dun Holm and, miraculously, he was there at the tomb of St Cuthbert. The eorl was a devout Christian despite his

The Sword of Cnut

Norse roots. It was a lucky meeting and, once more, I could not help but think of the webs and spells of the Norns.

I liked the old Norse warrior. He was a throwback to the time of the Vikings who had raided and ruled the seas. He had mellowed, I think, for he was an old man. When he had become a Christian, he seemed to prefer England to Norway. For King Cnut that was a good thing.

He greeted me warmly, "It is good to see you alive, Oathsword. The evil of Streona is ended and that makes England a safer land for all, Saxons, Danes, everyone." He waved at the newly built church, "You are fortunate that I am here. I came to supervise the building of the tower on the White Church. The Saint now has a home. Would you care to come in and pray?"

I could not lie to a fellow warrior and I shook my head, "My wife is a Christian. I still adhere to the old ways."

He sighed, "That is sad. I hoped that when we died, we would both be in heaven together."

"I will be in the heaven that suits me, Eorl, Valhalla."

"Without your wife."

That was a thought I always kept hidden in the dark recesses at the back of my mind. I had yet to resolve it. I passed over the moment and changed the subject, "I am here with a message from the king."

He became business-like, "Then let us withdraw within. This is a day for warmed ale and a fire."

We entered the wooden stronghold and thralls brought us wine and fuelled the fire. I told him what Tofti had told me. I was honest and gave him my own assessment of the situation. He nodded his agreement. "Archbishop Wulfstan is a good man and Jorvik is safe in his hands. As for Thorkell the Tall…he betrayed the king once before." He smiled, "I am an old man and it will be down to you, once I am gone."

"Gone?"

"I have years on you, Sven, and I know I have outlived most of those alongside whom I have fought. I should like to go to Rome before I die but that will now have to wait until the king returns."

I was relieved and said so, "Yours is the only force north of Jorvik should we be attacked. I command less than one hundred men." I was being optimistic when I said that. I assumed that Edward of Billingham would fight alongside me if we were threatened. He had not done so when the Mercians attacked but I hoped he would in the future.

"The problem we have, Oathsword, is that I have a large area to protect. My own oathsworn are my best warriors and they are here with me. You should know that Uhtred's brother, Eadwulf Cudel, who is

The Sword of Cnut

Lord of Bernicia and commands Bebbanburg, lost a battle to King Malcolm of Scotland last year. The Battle of Carham has cost us Lothian, not to mention the men who died in the battle. Your one hundred men are important, Oathsword." He shook his head, "The defeat was a grievous one and eighteen priests, as well as many warriors, died in the battle on the Tweed."

"You are saying that I will be on my own if we are attacked."

He sighed, "I am saying that I will come to your aid if you need me, but I cannot promise to arrive in time. You are lucky that I am here today. If I was in the north, at Bebbanburg then it would take me a week to reach you and that would involve a forced march. If I was in the west then it would take even longer. Send to me but rely on your own devices. For my part, I will send word to you if my lands are threatened."

I did not stay overnight. We headed back quickly having exchanged secret words that would be used to ensure that no message was sent by an enemy. I told my son and my lieutenant all as we headed home.

Gandálfr had been in low spirits since the death of his friend, Faramir. He was unmarried and the two warriors were the last of my hearthweru. The others had stayed in Denmark with my eldest son. Now he showed his depths of despair, "We have but fifty men, Seven Saxon Sword, and we were lucky when the Mercians attacked. If they come again..." He shook his head, "If every man in the valley came to fight for us there might be a hundred but you and I know the quality, or lack of it, amongst the farmers." Being hearthweru Gandálfr had a low opinion of farmers.

Bersi was the opposite. Since the battle, he had grown in stature. He had moved beyond the shadow of his brother, "Gandálfr, we have made our home stronger. The walls we have made are now higher, our ditches deeper and my father's idea of widening the beck has given some protection to the land that was weaker, the north side of the village. The slingers I lead will soon be ready to become warriors. I am hopeful that we can withstand any enemy who comes to our valley."

Gandálfr smiled. He liked Bersi who was popular with all the warriors, "And that is good. Let us hope that an enemy takes a long time to attack us so that you and your slingers can become real warriors and join our shield wall, but if they come sooner..."

"Let us take baby steps, Gandálfr, my son is right. We have made a good start to strengthening our defences but it is not yet over. We need more weapons and mail shirts. When we reach home, I will visit with the leaders of Stockadeton, Askelton, Pers' Track, Rus' Worthy and Rag's Worthy. They need to know what is expected of them."

The Sword of Cnut

Gandálfr sighed, "And we have enemies who could come from anywhere. They could be Scots, Frisians, the Norse, why even some of our countrymen are not to be trusted. Thurbrand the Hold is no friend of yours, Sven."

He was right for I had taken King Cnut's first wife from under the nose of Thurbrand the Hold. Ironically the only men I thought we could rely on were the men of Billingham and half of them were Saxons. I would need Edward and Osgar on my side. Mary was concerned when I told her the news. "When I was a child, we were often raided by the Scots. I fear that without defences to the north, our lives and those of our people will be at risk."

I nodded, "And that is why we will work even harder on our walls and ditches. If the Scots do come then the eorl will send us word. It is many days from the border, the Tweed, and we will have time to prepare."

Mary was eager for news that was not of war. She was as interested in the new church at Dun Holm as she was in the eorl's words. When I had finished, she nodded, "It is good that the Scots live so far from us. They have hurt us in the past. My father told me of raids that took slaves but I thank God that the eorl is there. With St Cuthbert's bones, we shall have better protection. And as for us…"

I told her my plans. My wife was a clever woman. She could read and she understood strategy. She was also a Christian and did not like war but understood that men must defend themselves. "It is a shame that we have to expend so much time and effort on defending ourselves. That time could be better spent raising crops and animals."

I agreed with her and went further, "If we could guarantee peace then I could use my ship as a trader. The land has riches we could trade."

She frowned, "Riches?"

"Just a few miles south of the estuary, close to the abbey that was raided by Vikings, lies the port of Hwitebi. There is jet to be found there. In some places, it is as precious as gold. You are right, my love, we make our home strong and then put every person to working on the land."

She smiled. My wife had a number of smiles and over the years I had come to learn to understand them. This one was the smile of a cat that has just managed to devour the carcass of the fowl, left to cool. "My ladies and I have been working, since the attack, and I now have a gift for you."

The Sword of Cnut

I was intrigued. She rose and went to the small chest where she kept her sewing. She took from it a black sheet and handed it to me. "What is this?"

"You are now a lord of this land and you need a better banner than the one I made for you in Agerhøne. We can fly it from our gates and when you go to battle then it can be carried. Father John has blessed it."

I unwrapped the banner. Like my shield it was black and, like my shield, in the middle was a white sword, my sword, Oathsword. It looked similar to the one I had always used. The difference was that while the painting on my shield looked identical to my sword, my wife had made the crosspiece on the sword on the standard far longer so that it looked like a cross. It was also bigger. It was no wonder that she had smiled. She was making me fight beneath a cross. Even though I knew her reasoning, I was touched and said so, "This is a wonderful gift. It will inspire my men, should they need to be inspired."

I assiduously avoided any comment about the Christian elements she had incorporated. Half of my people were Christian and even some of my warriors wore the cross of the White Christ about their necks but it did not matter. The sword was there and it was the sword that bound us not only together, but also to this land.

I left Gandálfr to continue working on the defences and I took Bersi to visit the headmen of the settlements. Stockadeton was the largest and the first place I visited. I thanked Alfred for the rider he had sent with the warning. "If we are attacked then that sort of reaction might save us. I have widened the beck that runs between Norton and Billingham. It means your people could join us if they wished."

Alfred shook his head, "St John's Well cannot be abandoned to an enemy, lord. It is a holy place. We have heeded your advice. Thanks to the weapons we took in the last battle we now have men who are armed. We have made our village into a burh. We can defend it."

I admired his courage but I did not want to lose the people of Stockadeton, "If you have to, then come."

Persson at Pers' Track was more practical. He nodded at my suggestion, "If an enemy comes by land we will take to the river and sail to Norton. If they come by river we will have plenty of warning for there is a long loop that has to be negotiated. We will see them and I promise that we will make haste." Pers and his people were fishermen. I knew that they went, sometimes, beyond the estuary, and if an enemy came by sea they would be our early warning.

Eadric commanded the hamlet of Askelton and he was also a practical man. "Stockadeton is closer to us than Norton, Lord Sven. We would head for there." I understood both Eadric and Alfred but knew

The Sword of Cnut

that their decisions would cost me a third of the men available to me. The other farmers promised to join me. Each place we had visited had honoured me with ale and food. It meant that it was almost dark as we neared my home. The new banner fluttered in the late afternoon breeze from the sea and the cross seemed to come alive. Now that it was flying it was clear that it was more of a cross than a sword but the white against the black, as with my shield, was an effective combination.

"Tomorrow, Bersi, we make our last ride. We go to Billingham. I hope to persuade Edward to fight with us this time."

"Do we need his men?"

"If Alfred and Eadric do not bring their men then, aye." I waved a hand at the trees which surrounded the manor. "We have more land we can cultivate but not the people to do so. We need more people from home, settlers who can make this land ours. You did not raid Wessex but there the people are like sand on the beach. They have hewn forests and make the land produce great quantities of food. We have much growing to do."

Seara and her two siblings, Anya and Karl had been survivors from the first attack by the Mercians. They had chosen to live in Norton and my wife, kind, Christian soul that she was, insisted that they stayed with us in my hall. Seara was growing quickly in a home where she was well fed but she was the most practical-minded child I had ever met. She had insisted that the three of them work as servants. She did not want them to be seen as helpless. When we entered the hall, she snapped out orders, "Karl, take Lord Sven's cloak. Anya, take Bersi's." She beamed at me as her brother and sister obeyed her orders, "Lady Mary is preparing food. I can bring ale, my lord."

She was a delightful child who was almost a young woman, with blue eyes that sparkled. "Thank you, Seara, that is most kind."

Mary had made sure that the thralls apart, everyone ate together in my hall. She said prayers and made certain that every platter was full. We had no warrior hall yet and so Gandálfr lived with us. He was the one who was most uncomfortable with the prayers and, during meals, the most silent. The rest chattered like magpies. The talk that night was of the other settlements. Bersi had been with me and the others wanted to know how they fared. He was happy to regale them with the tale. I could not help but reflect that he was the one most like my cousin, Sweyn One Eye. He could tell a tale and conjure a saga like no one. Bersi was showing that he had some of Sweyn's qualities. It was as they all spoke to each other that I realised I did not miss Ribe and Agerhøne. I missed people, like Steana, Siggi, Sweyn Skull Taker and Sweyn One Eye but I was happy here. Despite being in a perilous position I liked

The Sword of Cnut

that I had no lord to answer to. I was the one who commanded. Edward of Billingham was not my vassal but my liege lord was Eorl Eirík Hákonarson and he had made it clear that he would not be commanding me. All that I needed was time to make Norton as secure as had been Agerhøne.

Billingham was the same size as Norton and had a stone church but there was no wooden wall around it. Edward had not made it into a burh. As we rode over the causeway and headed up the slope to the hall I saw men and women tilling the fields. Their houses were slightly different to ours. We had built ours in the Danish style. When first we arrived at Norton we had found a burnt-out village and all our houses were new ones built in the Danish manner. I spied Osgar. He was Edward of Billingham's captain. He commanded the fyrd when they fought. He waved and went to the hall to call within.

Edward was there to greet me when we dismounted. Thralls took our horses and we entered the hall. His wife had died, and he had two sons: Edgar and Ethelred. Both were younger than Bersi although Edward was much older than I was. Osgar had told me that Edward had married late in life. Edward was not a warrior. He was a Saxon who had inherited the land from his father and, it seemed to me, lucky in that he had not had to fight to defend it. It was not that he had soft hands, he did not. He worked but he had the comfortable look of a man whose body was unfamiliar with the wearing of mail. Mary had told me that I had the lean and hungry look of a wolf.

For all that, Edward was a clever man, "So, Lord Sven, what danger brings you to my door this time?"

I told him of the defeat of the men of Northumbria at the Battle of Carham. "With the king abroad, it puts us all in danger. Eorl Eirík Hákonarson cannot promise to come to our aid. If an enemy comes then we have to defend ourselves."

He smiled, "We have not been raided for many years. The last time, before this Mercian attack, was more than twenty years ago and then they did not bother with us but sacked and destroyed Norton."

I nodded, "I know, I was on that raid and it was our ships that destroyed Norton."

The smile left his face and even Osgar looked shocked, "But you have returned here."

I nodded, "Mary, my wife, was taken by me as a thrall. We married and King Cnut, knowing of my connection, gave it to me so, you see, I know how lucky you were. That luck may not last. I have made the beck navigable. What if raiders came up that waterway? Would they choose to attack my walls or simply take your people?"

The Sword of Cnut

"But King Cnut is king of the Danes now."

I laughed, "And there are still men in Denmark who see England as a place of plunder. I sailed with such men. Besides, there are Norsemen who live in a land where little grows. There are Frisians who squat in swamps. Both are fierce warriors and may see the absence of a king as the perfect opportunity to raid. If the Scots come we shall have warning but if it is pirates…"

An awkward silence descended. Osgar broke it, "It is what I have been telling you, lord. Billingham is not made up of one people. We have Saxons and men like me, Viking settlers who sought land here. I have heard, each Sunday, the men of Norton as they train in the shield wall. I fought with Lord Sven when the Mercians came and know both his worth and that of his people. If a ship came up the river then we would be taken and devoured like a lamb by a wolf. None would survive. There would just be the dead and the enslaved."

I saw Edward look at his sons. He had been duped by the Norns. They had left him alone and he thought himself protected. His eyes moved from his sons to Bersi. Bersi wore a leather byrnie. Even when visiting a neighbour, he was ready for war. A short sword hung from his waist. He was already muscled. Edward's sons were like young girls in comparison.

He sighed, "What would you have me do?"

Osgar gave the first answer, "We can join with the men of Norton when they practise. We can make a bell such as they have. Our men have grown complacent, lord." It was a criticism of Lord Edward.

I said, "I am happy to train your men but we need a plan should we be attacked."

The lord of Billingham was out of his depth, "But they could come from anywhere. By sea, the river, across the land. We cannot keep watch all the time."

I sighed, "But we have to try. You are closer to both the sea and the north. Your farmer at Belasis can see the estuary. Ask him to be observant when he tills his fields."

Edward brightened, "That would work and we have those who pick the sea asparagus from the shore where the seals congregate. The women who do that could watch."

Osgar said, "There are some fisherfolk who live close to the sea, Seaton has but three houses. I could ride there and ask them to watch."

I was more hopeful at Osgar's words. He was a positive man and he was beginning to enthuse his master.

The Sword of Cnut

As we left Osgar accompanied us and walked us to the causeway. "Lord Edward is a good man, Sven Saxon Sword, but he is not a warrior. Look to me to lead the men of Billingham to war."

I clasped his arm, "We have fought alongside one another before, Osgar, and I know your worth. I am happy that it is so."

I had been a raider and knew that raiders, Norse, Danish, Scottish, or Frisians, would not attack in winter. There was, however, a time when they would choose to raid. That would be when the days were long and they could sail the seas or cross the land in daylight. They might attack at dawn or in the night but the bulk of their journey would be under the sun. I had almost dismissed the Scots as I knew that they had two forces opposing them before they reached us. First, they would have to pass Bebbanburg and Eadwulf Cudel and then the eorl and his men. Neither were huge armies but we would have a warning. It meant we had time to plant as much as we could. I had trees hewn and their stumps burned so that we would have new fields. We needed bullocks to pull the ploughs and that would mean travelling to an animal market. That was for the future. We had the animals we had brought from Denmark, Siggi's gift was most welcome, and the animals had taken well to their new home. We had more offspring. It was a start. My men had also taken wives and while it would take time, their children would add to our clan. We were not the clan we had been. I had decided that we would be the clan of the horse for the animal we had first taken, Verðandi, had been sent by the Norns and it did not do to upset them. The name seemed to please the warriors especially as Verðandi proved to be such a good animal.

We had brought with us a weaponsmith, Haraldr, and although it had taken time we had managed to build him a workshop. It was far enough away from the houses so as not to be a fire risk but it was within our walls. We had melted some of the damaged armour from the dead Mercians and Scots to make a bell but we had enough left to make spearheads. When we had cleared the trees we had found enough wood to make many spears and axes. We did not have enough iron to make too many axes but we had plans. Osgar had told me of iron in the hills to the south of the river. There were few people there as it had been raided and attacked many times. It was too close to the mouth of the river for that. There was, however, an old hill fort that told me that before the time of the Romans, it had been a defensible area. I decided that, in the autumn, we would launch the drekar and sail across the river. A month of mining would give us iron for weapons and tools as well as jet to trade. I was already planning ahead. This was my land and I had the power to shape it to my will.

Chapter 2

Raiders and the Battle of Billingham Beck 1019

The messenger, when he came, was not from Edward of Billingham nor Persson, but from the eorl who had sent word south from Northumbria. It was stark news. The Norse were raiding once more. Some of the towns in Northumbria had been attacked from the sea. Slaves had been taken. The Norwegian Vikings were taking advantage of the absence of the king. The Scots, it seemed, had suffered too and that was good news. If they were being attacked then they could not attack us. As we had not been raided yet we had time to prepare our defences, but it was a warning and one which I passed on through Bersi, who became my messenger, to all those who commanded close to us. I asked Osgar to come to speak to me. I sat with Osgar and Gandálfr while we planned our strategy.

"If we allow the Norse a free hand then our people will suffer." I had my own ideas but I wanted the two of them to come up with their own.

"What else can we do? We do not know where they will strike." Osgar sounded as though we were defeated already.

Gandálfr shook his head, "If they bring any more than three ships then we are doomed for we have few men who can face and fight the Norsemen."

I smiled, "Gandálfr, you and I have been raiders ourselves. If we were raiding this river, where would we raid?"

He rubbed his beard as he thought. I saw Osgar smiling as he realised what I was doing. "The river has many bends and twists and turns. The nights are becoming shorter and they might fear to be seen. I would land closer to the mouth of the river, west of the beck and then march across the land."

"And?"

"And what, Lord Sven?"

"Which place would be the first one you would come to?"

I saw him close his eyes to visualise the river, "Either Billingham or here."

"But we have widened the neck and the ground is boggy."

"Then Billingham."

I allowed myself the hint of a smile, "And Billingham has no wall to protect it. Once the Norse see that they will race to get at the sheep."

The Sword of Cnut

I waited until Gandálfr had taken in that information. "If we squat like toads behind our walls, then the men of Billingham will be slaughtered and their families enslaved. My plan is simple. Once they are sighted then the men of Norton and as many from the other settlements as can be spared will wait until they attack Billingham and then fall upon the rear."

"But you do not know how many men will be attacking."

"It is of no consequence for no matter how many men there are we have to fight them, and we have something that will, I hope, inspire fear in them."

Osgar spoke for the first time, "Oathsword."

I nodded, "Like it or not the sword has a reputation in the Viking world. King Sweyn coveted it and its history is well known." I drank some ale, "You are right, Gandálfr, we do not know how many men will be coming but we can guess. Each drekar will carry between thirty and forty men. Osgar, the women who collect the eggs and sea asparagus will need to count the ships. Even if there are five or more ships and we are well outnumbered we will have to fight them. We have no choice, but the actual number of men we face might help me to make a better battle plan. Osgar, how many men can Billingham field?"

He sighed, "You need honesty?" I nodded, "Then we have fifteen boys who can sling. There are ten men I would call warriors and another fifteen or so who have a weapon and a shield or helmet."

"You have something we have not, a stone church. When they come put the women and children in the church. Defend that and when we attack we will not have to work out the direction."

"And how many men will you be leading, Lord Sven?"

"If we leave the other settlements out of it for the moment then fifteen slingers, five archers and twenty-five men who are warriors. I am not sure how many from Pers' Track, Rag's Worthy and Rus' Worthy. I will try to persuade Eadric and Alfred to send some men. Even an extra ten might make all the difference."

"And if we lose?"

I turned, "Then, Gandálfr, you and I will be in Valhalla and my wife shall be a slave for a second time." I saw him pale. "We cannot fail."

It is always hard to wait. We knew that at some point we would be raided but knew not when. I spoke to the leaders in the settlements and told them my plans. I said that when we knew the raid had begun we would let them know. I was gambling but I told them that we would have hours only before an attack began. I also explained all to Mary. She was vital to my plans. The women would have to defend our walls.

The Sword of Cnut

We had weapons for them and they had done so once before but Norsemen were a more dangerous foe than Mercians.

She smiled, "Fear not, husband. Gunhild and I will not be taken as slaves." She smiled, "I would see my daughter wed. Perhaps this danger will encourage her to choose a suitor."

I was happy that my wife was being so optimistic. She was assuming we would survive and that boded well. Gunhilde had been the object of many an amorous glance from young men and so far had not shown an interest in any of them. We had eaten well from the gifts they had brought to the hall in an effort to woo her. She had enjoyed the attention. My wife was right. Many younger than my daughter were married and had borne children. This might be the jolt she needed.

I knew that Edward of Billingham had been forced to become more of a leader but Osgar was the real leader of the village to the north of us. However, he had no power, save the natural power of a warrior whom men would follow. The messenger who galloped in on the pony at the end of Harpa came from Billingham with the news that three dragon ships had been seen in the estuary. "When were they seen?" I knew that if they had been seen the previous day then we could be too late."

"The women who pick the birds' eggs saw them at dawn this morning when the sun rose. Lord Edward had told them to get to the beach by sunrise. The women said the ships were highlighted on the horizon."

"Good. Ride back and tell your master that we will be ready this night."

I had the horn sounded and my men came rushing in to meet outside the hall. Some already had weapons. They would not need them yet but it was good that they came armed. It showed that they were ready to fight and to defend.

"Ships have been seen out to sea. It might be that they sail down the coast but let us take no chances. Bersi and Haraldrsson, ride to the settlements and give them the news. Tell them that I need warriors here to fight."

My son and the son of the weaponsmith ran to mount their horses. I knew that my son would mount Verðandi. He saw himself as a future leader. It was good that he did.

I turned to Falmir, he was a fisherman, "Take your boat and fish at the mouth of the beck. Keep watch for the ships. As soon as you sight their mast tops then return here." I smiled, "Any fish that you and your son catch will be a gift."

"Aye, lord. Come Ulf, we have been given great honour this day. We are to be the warriors who will spy out the enemy."

The Sword of Cnut

"The rest of you, we have a day to prepare. Finish all the urgent work and return here an hour before the sun sets."

I was left with Gandálfr. We both knew that this was not only a test of us but the bonds we had built with the other villages. Success might come if we all did as I had planned but if one part failed then the whole could crumble. Would King Cnut have made a mistake in trusting me?

"Three drekar means anything from ninety men to more than one hundred and fifty. They did not say what size of ships they saw."

I laughed, "And would they know a snekke from a threttenessa? What will be, will be. I am content that my plans are in place, and they were soundly made." I lowered my voice, "The Norns spin, Gandálfr, we both know that." I patted the legendary sword that hung from my belt. "You and I know well the power of this sword. It has yet to let us down." He nodded. I had said the right thing. "We also know what the drekar will be doing for we have done it. It will take them all day to negotiate the river, longer than we would for they do not know the channel and they will not wish to risk a grounding." I pointed to my banner which fluttered from the gatehouse. "The wind is against them. At some point, the tide will be too. They will have to step the mast and row. The river is not as wide as some and they will need caution." I was feeling pleased with myself for I had predicted that they would need daylight to sail the river and, thus far, I was proved right. "Come, you and I will examine the beck. That is our ally. Let us examine it in daylight."

We did not wear our helmets or mail. We had no need but we took our spears for they would give us support on the boggy and uneven ground. We headed down the slope to the newly widened beck. The farms all lay to the northwest, west and south of the manor. To the east and the northeast, the land had always been boggy. We had merely used that to make an obstacle. We poked the ground with our spears when we neared the marshy parts to test where the firm parts lay. Puddles from recent rain remained and we avoided those. Even so, mud sucked at our boots. We stopped when it became too difficult to move. We looked at the beck. There was a clear channel. We had used it to bring up the drekar that now lay below our north wall. It had taken all the men in the village to do so as we had been forced to drag it over some of the shallower areas. If the Norsemen made the mistake of attempting to sail up it at night when the tide was not high then they were doomed. Satisfied, we went to the causeway. We had made two crude bridges over the two becks, the one we had widened and the one closer to Billingham. It had not been hard and we had used stones so that the water could still pass beneath the causeway. There was a pond, we

The Sword of Cnut

called it a tarn, to the north of the causeway. The burnt-out mill was now partly underwater.

I jabbed the butt of my spear into the causeway. It was firm. Both our people and those of Billingham maintained this vital link. Had we been enemies then we would not. Gandálfr nodded his satisfaction. "We can make a wedge and march up here, lord." He was right. It was made of stone and solid.

I pointed my spear towards Billingham. I spied Osgar and his men, in the distance, as they planted briars and brambles as well as embedded stakes. They would slow an enemy down. "If my thoughts have been guided well then the Norse will disembark and come along the north side of the becks. The land is marginally drier there and the land is less uneven than closer to our land. Osgar's defences will spread them out." We reached the northern part of the causeway. I risked stepping off. The ground was solid but the difference in height and its unevenness was a problem. I rammed my spear into the ground, "Let us extend the causeway here."

The two of us sought rocks and stones. We only had to make the causeway wider by eight paces. It took an hour to do so and when we were finished I went to a lone blackthorn tree and hacked, with my seax, a branch as long as a spear. I sharpened the end and then placed it in the ground where the widened causeway began. I shaved the bark from it so that it would stand out at night. I had a marker and no matter how dark the night I would know where we could stop.

"Let us speak with Osgar."

Taking our spears we walked across the uneven ground to the defences of Billingham. Both of us studied the ground as we did so. If all went as I expected it to then the next time we did this would be in the dark of night. Osgar was stripped to the waist and he stopped as we neared him. I saw that his forearms were cut and bleeding from the thorns. He gave a rueful smile. "This will make them think."

I nodded and pointed to the slope. "They will be tired too. That slope will suck energy from their legs and if they wear mail..."

Osgar smiled, "There is the problem, eh, Lord Sven? If they wear mail then that will slow them but they will be harder to kill and if they wear no mail then this may not be the obstacle we think it is."

"Aye, a man cannot foresee everything, can he?"

"Your plan is still the same?"

"My men and I will be in position on the causeway by dark. When we know that the Norse are committed to an attack then we will come. There will be no horn until we have drawn first blood."

The Sword of Cnut

"And if they do not come this night?" My hearthweru was pessimistic.

"Then, Gandálfr, I will have cost our men a night of sleep and I expect to be roundly cursed. I am a leader, and I will lead." I turned back to Osgar, "We will leave you to your work, Osgar."

We headed back to the causeway. I noticed how much easier it was going back. By the time we reached Norton the men from Rus' Worthy and Rag's Worthy had arrived. They had wisely fetched their animals. A short while later my two messengers rode in.

Bersi slipped easily from the back of Verðandi. Unlike his brother, he was a natural horseman. "Persson is sailing his fishing boats and bringing his folk here. They will be here before dark. Alfred and Eadric are sending ten men each. They both asked me to implore you to go to their aid if the Norse do not do as you expect."

I nodded. The two leaders had given me men who might otherwise have defended the walls of Stockadeton. I felt the weight of responsibility upon me.

Mary had provided food for all. It was a mixture of the fish caught the previous day and the birds and animals trapped close to the walls of Norton. It was not grand food but it was filling. Our ovens were still lit and bread would be baked all day. Once darkness fell they would be doused. It would be a sign that war had come to our valley. We would have stale bread until the threat was gone.

Persson and his folk arrived in the middle of the afternoon. They had not been idle and had fished as they had sailed. Their boats were shallow drafted and negotiated the beck easily. Their muddied feet showed the effect of the bog.

"We have drawn our boats up and they are close to the drekar."

Mary pointed to the trough, "There is water for you to wash your feet. Our people will give your people shelter although I fear that few will enjoy much sleep this night. Persson's wife looked tearful. "Take heart, Gytha, wife of Persson, for Father John is here to give comfort to all who need it. God is with us this night."

The sun had begun to set and Falmir had still to return. I began to fear that he had come to harm. We had the gates closed and men stood watch on the walls. It was Lars who shouted, "I see Falmir and Ulf."

"Open the gates."

The gates swung open and the father and son entered. I saw that they had fish with them. "They come, Lord Sven. There are two large drekar and a threttenessa. They have anchored close to the north bank of the river. We waited until we saw them tie up before we returned."

"They saw you?"

The Sword of Cnut

Falmir's face fell, "I suppose so. I am sorry, lord."

I shook my head and hid my fears with a smile, "It is of no matter."

Persson was close by and he said, "They will know that the beck is navigable."

"Good, then let them raise their anchors and try to sail up them for the tide is on its way out." Persson realised what that would mean and he grinned. "Now we will see the mettle of these Norseman. Falmir, how many oars are in the three ships?"

Silence fell as we all waited for the news. Each oar meant at least one warrior. "One hundred and twenty."

"Then we know, roughly, the number of warriors. Good. Eat, make your peace with your God and arm yourselves. I need every warrior outside the gates within the hour. We wait for no one."

I went into my hall. Bersi followed. I donned my padded undershirt and Bersi helped me pull on my byrnie. That done he donned his leather byrnie. He had been using a bow for some time and now had enough skill to use it. He put on an arming cap and then his pot helmet. With his short sword at his waist and his seax in his belt, he was ready.

"I will go and ready my men."

I smiled at the term. They were boys but I remembered going to war with Siggi, all those years ago, and we had been boys. Boys became men in a short time. Left alone I put on the arming cap Mary had knitted for me. I placed my helmet on my head and fastened the leather strap under my chin. The baldric and sword around my waist felt heavy. Norse Splitter was in its scabbard. I went outside and took my shield from the spear and slung it around my back. I would not have the banner with us. We had decided to let it fly from our walls but Haraldrsson carried my horn. He had inherited his father's broad chest and while not yet a warrior he would be able to blow the horn that would be our only means of communicating on the battlefield.

I joined my waiting men outside. Less than twenty of us had mail. The others wore ox hide or leather. Every warrior had a shield and a spear. Some shields were smaller than mine but it mattered not. Our formation meant that the mailed men would be at the fore and we all bore large shields.

Gandálfr and I would be at the front of the wedge. Haraldrsson would be behind us between Persson and Ragnar. Behind them were four warriors. It meant that the front of our wedge had seven spears. The rest of the wedge was four men wide. Once we left the causeway my plan was to order the wedge into a line but I had to keep my mind flexible. Until we knew what the Norse intended then I had to think on my feet. The gates closed behind the last man and I raised Saxon Slayer

The Sword of Cnut

in the air; my spear was the signal to march. We strode purposefully towards the causeway. We did not sing even though I knew that the singing of a song would not only put heart in the men but would also keep us together. We would be silent and hidden.

When we reached the blackthorn marker, I raised my spear and we stopped. I turned and whispered, "We sit."

The message hissed down the column. We had less than the crew of a couple of small warships and most of those lacked mail. It was a small number to face the Norse warband but the Norns had spun and we had no choice. We waited and Gandálfr and I stared south across the darkness. Waiting is hard. I heard men leave the causeway to make water and some to empty their bowels. I understood the need. War was terrifying even for hardened warriors and less than a quarter of the men I led could be so described. Time passed and even I began to doubt myself. When I saw the false dawn in the east I wondered if the night would be a wasted one and then Gandálfr pointed. In the darkness, shadows moved. These were not foxes for they were too big but they were creatures of the night. The Norse were here. I stood and my men rose with me. I swung my shield around as did the others. Hefting my spear, I pointed it and we left the causeway. Gandálfr and I followed the path we had walked that morning. Would we walk back or would our bodies lie on the ground before Billingham? Gandálfr and I had worked out the best place to spread into a line earlier. I had to force myself to keep to the plan in my head for, suddenly, the night was riven as Osgar's sentries saw the Norse and gave the alarm. I could not help smiling. I had raided at night and the last thing you wanted was an enemy who was waiting for you.

I took another ten steps and then waved my spear to the right. Gandálfr waved his spear to the left and the men spread out into two lines. Haraldrsson was behind me and ready for my command. He held the horn in his left hand and a sword made by his father in his right. The shapes of the Norse became clearer as we neared them. Dawn was still an hour away but it would become lighter soon. I saw mail and heard the cries of the Norsemen. They used their voices and cries as weapons. We had done so when we had raided Wessex. They thought to terrify the sheep of Billingham. They were unaware of us. I could see that they had spread out in a line and were attacking Edward of Billingham's land from the south and west. The new obstacles were a barrier but the Norse with swords were hacking through them. Osgar's slingers and archers sent their missiles at the Norsemen but mailed, helmed and with good shields the raiders were well protected. The shock would come when we struck. While the Norse had their shields on their left and were

The Sword of Cnut

therefore protected, their weapons were on their right which meant that they would find it hard to strike back until they turned and turning on a slope risked a fall. A fall in battle could be fatal. Gandálfr and I had drilled into our men that this first strike was vital. We had told them to aim for flesh. A wounded man was always weaker. A blow to the shield would merely warn them of an attack. Bersi and his slingers were to our right. They would attack the rear of the Norsemen. If they had to, they could skip down to the beck. Any such move would inevitably weaken the attack on Billingham. I hoped we had thought it through well.

The left side of our line would have few men to fight but they would give solace to the defenders who would see their allies coming to their aid. It was those in our centre and to our right who would make the first strikes. As we neared the raiders I saw my target. He was a Viking with battle bands on his arms. His face, for we were close enough to see, was heavily tattooed. He had a shield with a skull upon it and his helmet was a simple one with a nasal. He was shouting orders and his attention was on the defenders ahead of him. His spear was already thrusting through the hole made in the brambles by the man before him. His left arm was well protected by his shield but I knew my own skill and I used Saxon Slayer overhand. I rammed it at the tattoo of the wolf on his cheek. My spear had a sharpened head and I was strong. Not expecting the blow his shield was already at his front. He must have died almost instantly as my spear smashed through his skull. He fell at my feet. Bersi had ordered his slingers and archers to attack as soon as he saw me thrust. His small band were slightly behind the Norsemen and they reaped a fine harvest. There were no shields for protection and men could try to avoid the arrows and stones if they could see them. Unseen ones felled them. As much as our spears would be effective, the contribution of Bersi and his band was a major one.

Gandálfr was just a pace behind as he slammed his spear into the arm of the Norseman who was raising his shield to his front. Persson, on my right, chose the knee of his opponent as his target and the third mailed Norseman fell. In the case of my comrades, they had to make a second blow to kill the already wounded man but I stepped on the skull shield of the warrior with the wolf tattoo. I now had a little extra height and when I used my spear next I was able to thrust it down and into the neck of the next warrior.

The Norsemen were now aware of our attack and I shouted, "Haraldrsson, now!" The horn sounded three times. It was to alert the men of Billingham more than anything else.

The Norse now saw the trap and as the men of Billingham, encouraged by the horn, renewed their attack to their fore the Norse

The Sword of Cnut

broke. I heard their horns give the signal. They had needed surprise and they did not have that. There would be other targets. The reason for the horn was clear, their leader, or one of them lay dead. I had been a raider and knew that the ones who broke first would be the weaker ones, new warriors on their first raid who had expected an easy time. The better warriors, the veterans, would lock shields and move back to their ships steadily. The problem that they faced was that they had enemies on two sides and by turning to face our threat, they exposed their right sides to the men and women of Billingham. I thrust and I blocked with my spear and shield as the tightening band of Norsemen steadily moved down the slope. Here the ground aided us and not them. It was slippery and sucked at their feet and they were walking backwards. We could see the ground. We were always above them and when a man slipped there was a spear ready to strike. The man who slipped at my feet was an easy kill but he wore a byrnie and as the head of Saxon Slayer entered his body his hands grasped behind the head and his dying hands tore it from my grip.

I drew Oathsword and could not help but shout its name, "Oathsword!"

All around me, men took up the shout. The cry was a weapon we used and the Norse fell back in fear. Perhaps they had heard of its name or it might have been that the wall of words terrified them. Whatever the reason the next man I slew just held his sword up for protection and my sword smashed it away as though it was made of wood. It hacked into his helmet and skull. My blade would need to be sharpened but the Norseman had a warrior's death. We had slain their better warriors and the rest took to their heels. Bersi, his slingers and his archers, had easy targets. As the light became better their strikes were more accurate. It was when we reached the beck that the slaughter really began. No quarter was sought and none given. The Norsemen died, drowned or were swallowed by mud as they slipped and fell. As the sun rose we saw that there were none left to kill but the threat remained.

"Haraldrsson, sound the horn and recall the men." I was aware that the tide was returning and that soon the land on both sides of the beck would become the river,

As the men left off giving the enemy a warrior's death, I turned to Bersi, "You and your band have done well. Now take the mail, helmets and weapons from the dead before they are taken to the sea. We will march and make sure that they have departed."

"I will and I will retrieve Saxon Slayer, too."

"Wedge!" I chose the wedge formation as it was an efficient way to move and we headed along the drier ground above the bog. Some of

The Sword of Cnut

Osgar's men joined us. As the light became brighter we found wounded men. They were slain. By the time we reached the river, we saw that one drekar, a threttenessa, was burning. The other two were being sculled down the river with, from the few oars we saw, depleted crews.

One of the Saxons from Billingham asked, "Why did they burn their own ship?"

Gandálfr answered for me, "They do not have enough men to sail all three back to Norway and they do not wish their vessel to fall into our hands."

He shook his head, "What a waste of a fine ship."

I shook my head, watching the drekar as it sank into the water, "I do not know but I am guessing that there is an important warrior aboard. They have given him a funeral worthy of such a man." I raised my sword and shouted at the two remaining ships, "This is the land of Oathsword and I am Lord Sven Saxon Sword. Any who tries to take from it will meet this fate!" My voice carried over the crackling of the flames and the hissing of the water. The other two ships were less than two hundred paces from us. I knew that they heard my words. There might be some who would return, for vengeance, but I had done all that I could. I had warned them.

The Sword of Cnut

Chapter 3

Lord of the Valley 1019

There was a euphoric mood amongst the men as we marched to Billingham. Behind us, the drekar sizzled and hissed as it sank beneath the waves. It would be a hazard for ships using the river but also a stark warning of the perils of this particular valley. Our mood evaporated when we reached the site of the battle. Many of the men of Billingham who had fought had either been killed or wounded. I could see that my men had suffered just two deaths and four wounded. Edward of Billingham had paid the price for his lack of defences.

I saw him and his sons ministering to the wounded. Osgar had a bloody byrnie and his helmet had a new dent but he was grinning. "Your plan worked, Lord Sven."

I nodded, "But there was a price to pay."

He was an older warrior than me and he stroked his grey beard, "Let us say that you had not planned your attack as you did. What would have happened?"

"I do not know for I did plan and we cannot undo the past. It is done and cannot be changed."

"I will tell you what would have happened. The Vikings would still have come and I would now lie dead with my lord and his sons. What you did was to win the battle. We were a sheep waiting to be sheared."

Edward of Billingham must have been listening for he rose and came over, "Osgar is right. Your preparations were good ones and mine were not. We need walls and we have none. I need to have my warriors ready to fight as were yours." He knelt and held his sword to me, hilt first, "You are my lord. You are Lord of this Valley and we will obey you in all things."

"Rise. No man bows to me. It is good that you have learned from this and we will help you to make your home stronger. Your men can join mine at the wapentake on Sunday. If they train with my warriors then we will all benefit."

It was late in the afternoon when we headed back across the causeway laden with booty taken from the dead. Many of the enemy had fallen in the beck or the river and the ones who were not were burned. The stink of flesh pervaded the air for many days. It was a stench that was a reminder of man's mortality.

The Sword of Cnut

The women were waiting with smiles on their faces as we marched through the gates of Norton. Those from Pers' Track and the other settlements were torn. They wished to stay and celebrate but they all wanted their own beds. They left but each of them begged me to visit with them so that they could honour me with a feast. I did not understand it. They had fought just as I had. This was their victory as much as it was mine. Bersi could barely be contained, that night, as he regaled his sister and mother with tales of the battle. I saw my wife wince at some of his descriptions but she smiled. Gunhilde was thoughtful.

When Bersi finally subsided I said, "Gunhilde, what is bothering you?"

She smiled, "It was only today that I realised the danger we are in. At Agerhøne I felt safe. We were not attacked and life was easy. Here is different. We are strangers and our lives could have ended had you made the wrong decision."

Mary's voice was firm, "Gunhilde, we were attacked in Agerhøne, but you were too young to remember. Your father saved the village there too; it is what he does. As for being strangers, this is my home and I was born here. You are of my blood and so it is yours too." Gunhilde shrank a little for my wife's voice was harsher than she meant. Mary smiled, "Look at this as a warning. No one is guaranteed a long life. You have enjoyed being a pretty flower with all the bees buzzing around you. If you want to be happy then choose your bee and choose well." She put her hand on mine, "I know I did."

That evening saw a change in my daughter. She heeded the words.

The next day was my first as Lord of the Valley. I wrote a letter and sent it with Bersi to the eorl. Haraldrsson went with him. The two had been close before but the battle seemed to have joined them at the hip. I went to speak to Alfred and Eadric. I knew that their men would have told them of the battle but it was important that they understood the full implications of our victory.

"We have warned our enemies that we are not weak but all that means is that an enemy in the future will not take us for granted. They will come with all the force that they can muster. We must not relent. We need to be vigilant and men must continue to train and to train hard."

They needed little convincing.

A couple of weeks later, I wrote a letter to Archbishop Wulfstan to inform him of the attack. I did not send it with a rider but with the captain of a knarr that arrived from King Cnut in Denmark. The captain had brought a letter for me and the knarr captain was clearly unhappy at

The Sword of Cnut

having to navigate the river to deliver it. As well as the letter were two families of settlers. They were not from Ribe but from Zealand. There had been a blood feud and the two families were the last survivors of a clan. To keep the peace King Cnut offered them the chance to go to England as settlers rather than raiders and he sent them to me. I was flattered and the two families were more than welcome. They brought with them their clothes and weapons and little else. Both men were bitter, not about King Cnut whom they believed behaved well, but their neighbours who had coveted their farms.

The captain had to wait for the next tide and so I told him I had a letter for him to take to Jorvik. He did not mind that as his next port of call was Jorvik. As Bersi, Gandálfr, the families and I walked back from the river, the mile or so to Norton, they told me all. Nils Nilsson was the elder of the two heads of the families. His sons were of an age with Bersi and would soon be warriors. "We could have stayed in Zealand but it would have meant death. We would have taken many of them with us but our family, our clan, would have perished."

Eidel Galmrsson nodded his agreement, "My cousin is right. My brother and uncle both died and seven warriors. We stood no chance and now we have nothing except the clothes on our backs."

I was silent for a moment and then I pointed to the blackened piece of earth that lay close to Billingham. "When the Norse came, some ten days ago, we fought a battle here and we could all have died. We did not. Regard this as a rebirth. I will give you land and my people will help you to build a home. You have weapons and we can find tools for you. I promise you that here in Norton there is justice and men can live freely. For my part, I am happy that you have come. We do not have many warriors but we have land to spare. Your numbers might not make a difference in Zealand, but here they do and they will. Welcome."

Mary, being the kindest person I know, was both gracious and welcoming and she insisted that they all stay with us until their houses were built. As it happened, we still had one burnt-out farm that could be quickly rebuilt and the next day I had men repair it. It meant that both families shared it while the new farm, adjacent to the burnt-out farm, was built.

Bersi and Haraldrsson returned from the north after their visit with the eorl. Their news was dire. Other places had suffered raids that were far worse than ours. Some were destroyed completely and their people were taken as slaves. The eorl had been forced to mount some of his men and use them as riders to patrol the rivers which the raiders used. Our preparations had been wise ones.

The Sword of Cnut

Chapter 1

Norton 1019

When the unknown rider came from Stockadeton we had already been sent a warning. Alfred, the hersir of the settlement there, had sent his son with a message that a rider was waiting at the ferry across the river. The only way across our river was either by a ferry or a long ride west to the bridge at Persebrig. Alf kept the ferry moored on the Stockadeton side. It meant he could not be surprised by raiders from the south. When the man finally arrived, I was mailed and armed. It was a precaution only. It was Tofti, one of King Cnut's oathsworn. I knew him and relaxed as he dismounted. He rubbed his backside ruefully.

"When I was ordered to bring you a message, my lord, I did not know how far I had to travel."

I smiled, "You will stay?"

He nodded, "It is a long ride from Jorvik, my lord."

"Come. Bersi, see to the horse."

Mary was always a magnificent hostess. She had spied us in conversation and when she saw Bersi leading the horse to my stables she had anticipated what was needed. By the time we entered my hall, there was ale waiting and the thralls were already preparing a bed for Tofti.

The warrior was gracious and bowed, "I am sorry for this unexpected intrusion, my lady, but I come on the king's business."

"You are most welcome. I will leave you with my husband."

Tofti smiled as she left, "You have chosen a good one there, Sven Saxon Sword. She is a real lady."

I nodded, "And this village was her home before she was taken. The three sisters spun well."

His hand went to his Hammer of Thor. King Cnut was a Christian and had demanded this kingdom was too. Tofti was like me, pragmatic. We paid lip service to the White Christ but in our hearts, we were still the pagans who believed in the three sisters, the Norns.

"This is good ale."

"The river gives us good water. So, what brings one of King Cnut's most trusted warriors all the way to Norton in this cold spring?"

"The king is at Jorvik and we are about to take ship to Denmark. Now that he is king of Denmark too, he needs to put that kingdom in

The Sword of Cnut

While most of the men worked on the new farm, I had the rest working on the drekar. We had already cleaned the hull and painted it with pine tar. Now dried out, she was ready to have ropes, sheets and timbers replaced where needed for she would go to sea again. The arrival of the two families had made me desirous to trade. It took just two weeks to complete the fitting out of the ship, for **'Falcon'** was a well-maintained ship, to ready her for sea. By then the new farm was built and I asked for volunteers to sail with me. I had more than enough offers. I chose Gandálfr and Beorn the Grim as experienced sailors but the other sixteen were all young men. I thought it was important to make sailors of them. We were a sea-faring race although now tied to the land. Bersi was unhappy to be left at home but I placated him by asking him to help Haraldr and Osgar train the men at the wapentake.

Ethelbert of Billingham had proved to be a useful man. When we were planning our voyage, he had given us valuable information. He had been born south of the river and his father had known where jet was to be found. He gave us directions and I hoped that we would be able to find it easily for none of us had mined before. I was not a fool and I had planned a seal hunt as well as the jet hunt. Both could be traded. If we traded then we could become more prosperous and encourage settlers to arrive. Not all would be like Eidel and Nils, men forced from their homes. There would be others who would choose to come to a land that was at peace. I knew that peace depended largely on the skill of the king and I wondered if running two kingdoms might prove to be too difficult. His brother had lost Norway and that, I now knew, had resulted in increased raids.

Our departure depended upon the tide. We were on the drekar at dawn and the drekar was in the channel of the beck. We watched as the water seeped in from the river and filled the bog. Folki was my helmsman. He was young but he had sailed with his father, Thorgeir, who had been my foster father's helmsman. This would be his first voyage as a captain but I was confident in his skills. That was largely because the voyage would see us simply sailing down the river, following the coast and landing at Hwitebi. We would never leave sight of land. If we sailed back to Ribe and Denmark then we would need a compass as well as more skill. This voyage was a test.

We hoisted the sail for the gods had sent us a wind from the north and west. **'Falcon'** edged her way down the beck to the river. We had the obstacle of the sunken ship to negotiate but managed it on the rising tide. The twisting river was a test of Folki's skill. I stood with him, my hand on the gunwale as he used the steering board to anticipate the wind

The Sword of Cnut

and the river. I saw the sweat on his brow and his white knuckles as he gripped the wood.

"Folki," I said quietly, "we know there are no rocks to hurt our hull and the rising tide and our ship's shallow draught means that even sand bars cannot hurt us. Trust the skill that came from your father."

"I would not wreck our ship, Lord Sven."

"And you will not."

My words seemed to give him a little more confidence. The sail was not fully filled for the meandering river would not allow it. It took some hours to reach the estuary and the basking seals on the north side of the river. I spied the women of Billingham picking eggs from the nests of sea birds as well as harvesting sea asparagus and, in the distance, to the north, I saw the fires of the handful of people of Seaton, who gathered salt from the sea. If there was no war then these people would prosper.

Gandálfr and Beorn pointed to the seals, "There is a richer bounty than seeking treasure in the earth, my lord. We do not know how much ore will lie beneath the sands but we can see the plentiful seals."

I nodded, "I know, Gandálfr, but the Norse will pay a high price for jet. They like snakes carved in the black gold we shall mine and I am hopeful we will not have to spend too long looking for it. When we return then we can spend as long as you like hunting the seals."

He nodded. Gandálfr was a warrior and liked to use his skills. Hunting the seals would be a better occupation for him than grubbing in the earth for jet. We had brought spades, pick axes and axes as well as hessian sacks for whatever treasure we found.

As we left the estuary we were able to make more sail. We headed south and east to avoid the rocks at the red scar at the mouth of the river. The ancient hill fort loomed up to the west. It was a reminder of a time and people who were older than we were and had lived here before the Romans had come. The cliffs to our right and the rocks at their base kept us well out to sea. We passed a couple of huddles of huts close to the beach as we sailed south and I knew they were fisherfolk. It seemed to me that they were trapped by the sea for the rocks rose behind the wooden houses. It was late afternoon when we neared the mouth of the Esk and the settlement that had been Hwitebi. As we reefed the sail and turned into the wind, I was able to see the skeleton of the abbey on the headland that had been destroyed more than a hundred years ago. Then Hwitebi had been a prosperous place. The abbey of St Hilda had once been a place of learning but the Norse had come and taken the treasure, enslaving the people. Now just a handful of people eked out a living in the shell that remained. Beorn pointed to the remains of a jetty. Over the

The Sword of Cnut

years storms had damaged it but it was a place we could use to tie up. I did not wish to run her up on the beach.

"Folki, take us there slowly. Erik Prow Jumper, be ready to tie us securely to the land." Erik had been tasked with standing at the prow to leap ashore and make us safe. The wind edged us closer and that, allied to the outgoing tide, enabled us to bump gently next to the quay. Gandálfr, Beorn and I were ready to go ashore. We wore no mail and carried no spears. I was not expecting trouble but we had helmets and swords. The quay was incomplete. Some of the planks had been washed away and we had to jump over two sections.

"We will repair the quay first." I pointed to two ruined buildings. "There should be timber there that we can salvage."

Gandálfr growled, "There are people here, I see movement. Why did they not repair the damage?"

I shrugged, "I do not think that the people of Hwitebi welcome ships. I do not blame them."

Once we reached the end of the quay, I saw that there was a stone path of sorts and it wound up the side of the cliff to the ruined abbey. We had no reason to risk the ghosts of the nuns and priests. We would stay in the remains of the port.

"What is it that we do, lord?" I heard the concern in Beorn's voice. There were just three of us on the drekar that one might call a warrior and we were in an unknown land. The rest of the crew were gathering kindling and finding shelter for the night.

"I want to speak to one who lives here to assure them that we come in peace. Do you fear people who hide away, Beorn? They will be more afraid of us than anything." Leaving the drekar secured to the quay, I sought a dwelling with smoke rising from it. That would tell me that it was inhabited. We passed three that were cold and derelict. The fourth had walls that felt warm to the touch. There was a door, of sorts, and I banged my hand upon it. "Ho, within. We are visitors and mean you no harm."

Silence greeted my words. Gandálfr said, "Let us break down the door, Lord Sven."

"Patience, Gandálfr, have you somewhere else you need to be?"

The door eventually creaked open and a face appeared. It was an old woman, "We have nothing here worth taking, Viking."

I smiled and took off my helmet. I saw now that it had been a mistake to wear them. "We are not Vikings. We live north of the Tees at Norton and we come here to seek jet. I am Lord Sven of Norton."

My tone seemed to reassure her as did my words and she opened the door a little wider. "You are miners?"

The Sword of Cnut

I smiled, "Not yet, but we will be. I only come here this evening to tell you that we mean no harm. I know that there are others who live close by and I ask you to tell them the same."

"We have learned to mistrust the words of those who sail in dragon ships such as yours."

"And if we meant harm do you think that this ancient door would keep us out?" Gandálfr was already tiring of the conversation.

She gave me a smile that showed more gaps than teeth, "Your warrior makes a good point. I will spread the word but do not expect a fulsome welcome, whatever you are, for there is little here now that is worth taking and we do not share with anyone." She pointed a bony finger, "You will find jet just around the headland. Dig beneath the sand and you will find the ore."

"That is kind of you."

She sniffed, "The sooner you dig it up the sooner you will leave and we can return to our lives." With that, she shut the door.

Gandálfr said, "Not a warm welcome."

As we headed back to the drekar I said, "Warmer than I expected and one that may save us time. Ethelbert just said that the jet was close to the sea and beneath the ground. The old woman has given us more accurate information." We had reached the ruined houses my men had cleared. "We will sleep ashore. Beorn, have our gear brought ashore and let Folki and Erik Prow Jumper stay aboard. We will repair the quay on the morrow."

When he left, Gandálfr and I examined the other ruined houses. We found one which had a partial roof remaining and we began to clear the floor so that we could sleep there, as well as the first house my men had cleared. The men arrived and while Gandálfr started a fire they finished off the clearing of the floor and the laying out of the blankets in the two former dwellings. Darkness fell as the flames illuminated what had been homes. In the one I had chosen, I saw the remains of tools and deduced that jet miners had lived here. That boded well. On our voyage down the river and along the coast we had kept fishing lines out. The harvest had been a good one. We used sea water to make a fish stew and by the time we were ready for sleep, we had fed well.

"I will take the middle watch. Beorn, you have the first and I will wake you, Gandálfr, for the third watch." I rolled in my blanket and covered myself with the seal skin cloak. I had not examined the partial roof closely. If it rained at night my cloak would ensure that I remained dry. Beorn woke me from a pleasant dream. I rose and made water. I had deliberately given myself the harder watch. It was what a leader did. I would have to try to get back to sleep when I woke Gandálfr. I

The Sword of Cnut

slipped my cloak about me for the proximity of the sea and river made for a chilly night. I saw no moon but there were scudding clouds. I sniffed the air. There would be rain.

I walked carefully over the wooden boards to my ship. The water flowed beneath the missing sections. As I neared the drekar and the wood creaked a face appeared over the gunwale. It was Erik. "It is you, lord."

"Is all well?"

"It is. The hot food was welcome and Folki is asleep."

"Go back to sleep. I will watch for a while." It was as I gingerly stepped over the last missing plank that I spied movement on the land side. I slipped my sword from its scabbard. Everyone in Hwitebi should have been abed. I moved carefully along the slippery quay making no sound. I was good at that. Whatever was moving had hidden and, as I neared the stone of the road, I stopped to watch. Then I saw the movement again. It was a boy, perhaps a youth and he was scouting out the dwelling we were using. He was clearly brave for we were armed warriors. His attention was on the tools we had left outside the room where my men slept. He was a thief. I sheathed my sword. I would not need it.

He was so intent upon studying that which he intended to steal that I was on him before he knew it. I wrapped my arms around him and lifted him from his feet. He squealed.

I hissed, "Silence thief! You are disturbing the sleep of my men."

Gandálfr burst from the door, sword in hand. The thief recoiled in terror. Gandálfr was a frightening-looking warrior.

"Peace, Gandálfr, it is just a thief who has come to steal our tools." I turned him around so that I could see him. He stank and was filthy. "Does your mother know what you do?"

I think he was emboldened by the fact that he still lived for he was almost cheeky as he said, "I have neither mother nor father. I answer to no one but myself."

Gandálfr was annoyed at his disturbed sleep, "Then let me slit his throat, Lord Sven, and have done with him."

The boy, I took him to be not yet a man, turned to squeeze closer to me, "No, lord. Let me live. I swear I will not steal from you again."

"If you are dead then I guarantee there will be no more thefts." There was a clear threat in Gandálfr's words.

"What is your name, boy?"

"Aed." It was a Saxon name.

"And what would you have done with the tools you sought to steal?"

He shrugged, "I know not but they are iron and, as such, valuable. I could have exchanged them for food."

I realised that the shaking I felt was not from fear but from the cold and hunger. "You are hungry?"

"As I have eaten nothing this day then, aye, my lord."

"Come within and I will feed you."

Gandálfr rolled his eyes and sheathed his sword, "You are feeding him? A mistake. As I am awake, I will take over the watch." He donned his cloak and went to take on the role of watchman.

I lowered Aed to the ground and we entered the den of sleeping men. I suspect others had woken at the shouts but hearing no call to arms they had gone back to sleep. The fire still glowed and I went to the pot with the last of the fish stew in the bottom. There was a piece of stale bread and I said, "Do you need a bowl?"

He grinned and said, "This one will do." He whipped out a spoon from beneath the folds of his clothes and began to eat the stew from the pot. I had never seen one eat as fast. He finished by wiping the pot with the bread. It would need little cleaning.

When he had finished I poured him some ale into a horn. He took it and drank. He smiled, "That is better than the water from the horse trough."

"You live here, in Hwitebi?"

He shook his head, "I exist here in Hwitebi and if I could fly then I would disappear and never see this inhospitable place ever again."

"Do the people of Hwitebi not care for you?"

He laughed, "I am regarded as little more than a human rat. They chase me when they see me. I live in the dark and deserted places where they cannot find me."

I asked the simple and obvious question, "Why?"

"My father was a Viking, like you. My mother was Saxon and it was she who named me. One night the others here decided that they did not want a pagan warrior living amongst them and they fell upon him and slew him. My mother tried to defend him. Her head was struck and she died."

"When was this?"

"A year since." I am just lucky that they did not kill me. Instead, they gave me a living death and shunned me."

"And how do you live?"

"Do you not listen, Lord Sven? I do not live. I exist. I find shelter. I eat what I find and I avoid the company of others. If I had stolen a tool then I would have had a weapon."

The Sword of Cnut

I was not a Christian but I could not understand these people who lived in the lee of an abbey and yet shunned an orphan because he was the offspring of a pagan. "If you promise not to steal from us then you may have a warm fire this night and the knowledge that none will harm you."

His little face suddenly lost the cynical look I had seen and became an innocent child once more, "Truly?"

I smiled and tossed him my blanket, "Here. Keep yourself warm."

I went outside and stood with Gandálfr. He shook his head, "I know you, Sven Saxon Sword. Your heart is too big. This boy is nothing but trouble and he stinks."

"Nothing that a good bath cannot cure. The Norns, Gandálfr, are spinning. Surely you can see that. He is the child of a Viking. I know not why the man stayed here but he did. He was slain and his wife died. We ignore this child at our peril. The threads are joined. Would you sever them?"

His hand went to his Hammer of Thor and he shook his head, "No, my lord, but I wish the Three Sisters had others that interested them."

I patted the sword, "Once this sword came to me then I was chosen. I can do nothing about it."

I returned indoors and saw that the boy was happily asleep, curled up into a little ball. I let him sleep and stared into the fire to see if I could discern the path I had to take.

The Sword of Cnut

Northumbria

The Sword of Cnut

Chapter 4

The Viking Child 1019

Aed slept long after my men had risen. They wrinkled their noses at his smell but said nothing. The fire was fuelled and water put on to boil. Some of the men went to the rocks to seek shellfish while others were designated by me to begin the repair to the quay. Slices of dried ham were added to the seawater and soon there was an appetising smell rising. We had a bubbling breakfast on the pot when Aed woke. He suddenly started when he saw the faces looking at him. "These are my men, Aed, and you are safe...so long as your fingers do not stray."

He nodded, "I steal to eat and to survive. You are safe from me."

The warriors laughed at the cheek of this boy. I said, "While we wait for the cooking of the food tell me of your father."

"He was Bergil the Black and he fell overboard from a ship that sailed close to the red rocks north of here. He was found by my mother who lived close by with her parents. They made me. When my grandparents died of the pestilence some two years since, my parents left their home and trekked here, for it was the closest place where others lived. At first, we were welcomed. This dwelling was the one we used. It was only when Eostre came and my father did not celebrate it that the trouble began. Some of the men demanded that he become a Christian. He said he was a Norseman and he would keep the old ways. It was soon after that he was killed while he slept and I was left alone."

We were all silent. Falling overboard from a drekar happened frequently. The low freeboard and the need to make water often combined with unexpected waves.

He looked over at the pot. "That smells cooked."

Beorn laughed, "Here is a bowl, help yourself." His tone and his words told me that my men had already accepted the boy.

As he ate, or rather inhaled, the food, he asked, "Why are you here? You are not raiders or the village would be burned. I wish it were."

Having heard his story I was tempted to take a brand and do as he had wished. "We are here to find jet."

His face lit up, "I know where it is to be found. My father was fascinated by it and he wanted to trade it. That was one of the reasons we sought a home here."

I looked at Gandálfr and said, "*Wyrd.*"

Aed said, "My father used that word. What does it mean?"

The Sword of Cnut

I explained, "It means that the Norns are spinning. We came here to find jet so that we could trade it. If you show us where it is to be found then we will feed you."

"Then let us go."

"First," said Gandálfr, "you take a bath and we put you in clothes that do not move with insect life."

The boy looked at me and I nodded, "Gandálfr is right. Your mother and father would not like the way you appear. Erik Prow Jumper, fetch clothes from the slop chest. I am sure there are some there from the ship's boys." Erik scurried off. He had been a ship's boy for four voyages. "Now take off your clothes and let the river cleanse you."

We went outside and he disrobed. It was a painful sight. I could see his ribs. The boy could not have survived another winter. I was angry at the sight of him and, leaving my men to help the boy, I strode down to the house we had visited the night before. "I am Sven Saxon Sword and I tell the people of Hwitebi that if I see any this day then they will suffer my anger. You call yourselves Christians and yet you have allowed a boy to almost starve to death. For shame. For the rest of our time here keep a safe distance or I swear there will be bloodshed."

I knew that Mary would not have applauded my words but, equally, she would not have approved of the way Aed and his family had been treated. By the time he was bathed and dressed, we had found some leather shoes and he donned those.

"Now, Aed, your side of the bargain. Take us to the jet."

Leaving three men to prepare food, we picked up the tools and followed him along the sand. The tide had receded and he took us across a scar of rock to a beach. I saw black beneath the sand immediately. He explained, "This is the best place but you have to be quick for the tide will return. My father called it his treasure trove."

The boy was right and we had little digging to do. We scraped away the wet sand and then looked for the cracks in the jet where we could use our chisels and hammers to take pieces. We needed the lumps of ore we took to be as big as possible. We made mistakes and some shattered. That was inevitable but, after an hour or so and when the tide turned, we had collected enough so that most of us were laden and we headed back to the ship. We had wasted nothing. Even our mistakes were gathered and placed in the sacks and baskets we had brought. Now that the quay was in better shape, we were able to load our precious cargo in the hold. Aed was now seen as a lucky charm and even Gandálfr smiled at him. Once more he ate first and none begrudged him the food for we had all seen his emaciated body.

The Sword of Cnut

We worked when the tide was out and there was light to see. We were observed by a couple of fishing boats that also used the tide to get in and out of the port. I could see why the quay and jetty had been built. It allowed ships to use the deeper channel in all but the lowest of tides. The fishing boats had been drawn up in the Esk further away from the sea and the vagaries of the weather.

By the end of the day, we were exhausted but we had made a good start collecting the jet. Aed seemed to be comfortable with the men and we, in turn, were grateful that his local knowledge had saved us time. The old woman's instructions had been too vague. We might have found some jet but I doubted it. The place she had directed us to was not under the water. The seam would have been exhausted years ago. It took another two days before the seam we were digging thinned out and our labours were no longer rewarded. That evening we discussed what to do.

"We have a veritable treasure already, Lord Sven. We could dig for the rest of the month and not be as lucky."

Beorn was right and I nodded. I did not like Hwitebi and the sooner we left the better. "Then we will leave on the morning tide." Aed was busily eating. It seemed we could never fill him. I nodded to him, "And the boy?"

Erik Prow Jumper shook his head, "We cannot leave him here. It is not right." Others, even Gandálfr, murmured their agreement.

I said, "Aed." He looked up, spoon poised before his mouth. "We are leaving tomorrow. If you wish you can come with us but it would mean leaving your home."

He shook his head, "This is not my home. It is a penance I serve. I will come with you for while you all look fierce, you have treated me with kindness." He frowned, "But what would I do?"

Gandálfr smiled. He had come to like the boy too, "Don't worry about that. You seem a bright youth and pick things up well. On the voyage north you can learn to be a ship's boy and when we reach Norton...Lady Mary will have her own ideas."

He was right. My wife would find a place for him. The first high tide was an hour after the sun had risen. As we untied ourselves I reflected that the folk of Hwitebi had done little for us but they now had a quay and jetty that was repaired. *Wyrd*. I doubted that we would return and I did not even waste a backward glance as we rowed into the open sea. The wind had been with us on the way south but now it was precocious and teased us. Sometimes it was against us and we rowed and then, almost as suddenly, it switched to try to drive us onto the rocks. It took most of the day to beat our way north and it was with

The Sword of Cnut

some relief that I heard Erik's call from the prow, "I see the estuary. It is our river."

It would be too late to land and hunt the seals on the north side of the estuary, and so we anchored out at sea but close enough to see the land. Aed looked south and pointed to a place on the south side of the estuary, "There, close to the Red Scar is where we lived. We were happy for a while. I doubt that the house still stands. It has gone along with my parents and I am all that is left."

"And we start again, Aed. This is our river. We have some way to journey yet. If we landed and walked we could be home within a day but we will hunt the seals and then have a slow and tortuous journey along the river. It will afford you the time to see the new land that you have chosen to be your home."

I learned that Aed was quite a perceptive youth, "Except I did not choose this home. I was chosen by it."

The next day we sculled to the rocks where the seals lay. They felt safe for it was hard to approach them from the land. Osgar had told me that his people had tried to hunt them but the mud and the bogs on the land side kept the animals safe, and by the time hunters reached them they were in the sea and safe. We had no such problem. We could land close to the rocks. We would have to be careful not to damage our ship but the seals would have to pass us to get to the sea or risk being trapped in the bogs and the mud that protected them. As we neared them they did not move. I had Gandálfr and Beorn at the prow. I did not intend to rip the keel from my drekar. When they both raised their hands I had the steerboard oars stop while the larboard ones edged us next to the rocks. Erik raised his arm when we were close enough. We dropped our two anchors.

The job of hunting was the task of warriors. Gandálfr and Beorn would join me with spears to hunt the seals. The ones with bows would stand ready to send arrows at any we had only wounded. I did not carry Oathsword but, instead, had a short sword from the drekar's chest. We slipped over the side, sliding down the ropes hung there. The water came to our ankles but we were protected by seal-skin boots. The seals were unafraid. They were rarely hunted here. I knew that we would have a short time to work. Once the blood flowed they would flee. We spread out and approached the ten that we saw. They had a sentry. He rose and roared a challenge. Gandálfr was the closest to him and my oathsworn headed for him. There was a fat seal close to me. It looked old and appeared to have enough blubber to fill a hundred lamps. I held two spears in my left hand and one in my right. They had sharpened heads for the skin of the seal was tough. Gandálfr struck first and his

The Sword of Cnut

throw was true. The seal roared as it raced at him, the spear's head already driven into his body. The seal I had chosen raised his head and I was able to drive the spear into his throat. Gandálfr's had been thrown. Mine had the strength of my arm behind it and the fat old seal died quickly. I transferred a second spear as the other seals began to react. They tried to get through us to the sea. The drekar acted as a barrier too and so they went north and south towards the open sea. I threw one spear and caught a cow in the side but she still moved towards the sea. If she reached it then she would still die but her death would be a meal for a shark. Wounded, she was moving slowly and I caught up with her and drove the spear into the back of her head. Like the fat seal, she died and I turned to see if any remained on the mudflats. We had managed to kill seven seals. That was a good number and I was happy.

I cupped my hands, "We have done the hard part. Take the seals and lay them on the deck." We had already put an old sail there. The deck needed to be protected from their blood and the sail would also cover them and stop the aerial predators, the gulls, from trying to feast on our kill.

By the time the women had arrived from Billingham to collect eggs, shellfish and sea asparagus, we were loaded. The tide was still high enough for us to begin our journey home. We manned the oars and began to row up the river. We had not gone far when we spied several more seals basking on a mudflat. This would not be as easy but we could use all that the seals provided; meat, oil and, of course, seal skin. It was worth the risk. This time we had to wade through knee-deep water to reach them but their sentry was not alert. We took five of them before the other three fled. This time I cut one of the seals open on the mud flat. Erik Prow Jumper lit a fire and I began to cook some of the offal. The heart, liver and kidneys were rich and the rendered blubber was as delicious as the skin of a roasted pig. Some of the younger crew and Aed sought shellfish to augment our meal. It was dark by the time the oil had been rendered from the fat. We stored it in a pot and all enjoyed the delicious roasted blubber. Few of the young men had ever eaten it and the joy on their faces made Gandálfr and Beorn smile as they remembered their first taste. The heart, liver and kidney were an acquired taste. We all ate some but they were very rich. The pieces that were left would be used as bait as we sailed down the river the next day. We anchored in the main channel.

The wind was, once again, with us. It was icily cold, coming as it did from the east, and we could not use a full sail as we had to keep to the safe channel, but it meant we reached the beck before dark and I risked the new channel. The smell of woodsmoke and the lanterns hung from our gates told us we were home and we dropped the anchor as the tide began to slip back to the sea. I knew that there would be barely two feet below our keel but we would be safe.

Bersi led the men from Norton to help us unload our cargo. The seals had begun to smell. It was not one of rottenness but of the sea. While they were taken, we lifted the deck to reveal the black gold that was the jet. The seals were carried any which way but the jet was carried carefully, almost reverently. I knew that most of it would be reloaded aboard the drekar for I had plans to take it to Ribe where my cousin Alf and his father-in-law, Aksel, were merchants. They were family and would know the best place to sell the jet and to make the most profit. I would not risk leaving it aboard the drekar, besides which we would need to keep some and make it into ornaments ourselves.

I was tired but I knew that we had to begin work immediately. Men were already skinning the seals and the preservation of the skin began. The fat was being rendered. The stink of rendering fat would pervade the air for many days. I helped Gandálfr and Beorn to store the jet safely. Daylight would allow us to sort the jet into sizes. The smallest pieces we would retain. We had men who were skilled with their hands and could turn the black nuggets into polished jewels that we could either sell or give as gifts. What we had collected was the bounty of the clan. The king taxed us heavily through heregeld and we would need some gold to pay him. The jet would do that.

By the time I reached my hall, Mary had already met Aed. She had, so Gunhilde told me, shaken her head when she had seen the clothes we had given him. She had found old clothes of Bersi and, after bathing him, trimming his hair and using a nit comb, she had provided him with better clothes and fed him.

"Where are they now?"

Gunhilde smiled, "It is as though she has borne another child. She has taken him to bed. I suspect she will sing him a lullaby as she did with us. You and she will share your sleeping chamber with the orphan, Father."

I sighed, "That is your mother's way. You will be the same when you wed for I can see your mother in you."

She suddenly adopted a guilty look, "And I have news for you, Father. While you were away Ragnar Ragnarsson from Rag's Worthy visited and spoke with my mother. He wishes my hand in marriage."

"And why did he wait until I was gone? Does he fear me?"

She shook her head, "No, for he did not know that you were gone and would have waited until you returned but…"

The Sword of Cnut

"But your mother wanted to know his purpose." She nodded. "And how do you feel about his offer?"

Her face lit up and without a word, I knew the answer, "Of all those who sought my hand he was the one who made my heart race. He is modest and I think, Father, that he is like you. He will be kind."

I was mollified but sad too. My son lived an ocean away and my daughter would be moving so that I would not see her every day. There would be just Bersi and how long before he left the nest?

The thralls brought me food and I ate alone. I had much to think about. My wife came down just as I was mopping up the last of the stew with the bread.

She came and kissed the top of my head and then sat next to me. "So, this waif and stray you have found, tell me his tale. All that I know is that the crew of our ship took to him and feared he would die if he was left in Hwitebi. You will tell me the truth."

I took a swallow of ale and then proceeded to tell her of the voyage and Hwitebi. It was important that she knew everything. When I had finished, she had refilled my horn. She played with her cross and smiled at me, "You know, husband, for all your pagan ways you are more of a Christian than many who purport to be followers of Jesus. You were meant to find him. He shall have a home with us although I fear he will need lessons in being civilised. He eats like an animal."

"And do not judge him for that. He lived like an animal eating scraps he found in the hogbogs. You saw his ribs?" She nodded and made the sign of the cross. "I care not if he snuffles and grunts like a pig. I want to see flesh covering his bones and then we can start to make him behave at the table."

She lifted my hand and kissed it, "You are kind. We have jet?"

"We do. When it is sorted and when all the fat is rendered from the seals, I thought to sail to Ribe and trade. Whatever we have as a surplus will bring us gold. There are things we need such as animals for breeding. I can also see Steana."

She smiled, "I miss him." She gestured towards the room that my daughter used as a bed chamber, "Gunhilde gave you her news?" I nodded. "I told Ragnar he had to return when you were here. Do not sail before he has returned."

I laughed, "I think that once he knows I have returned he will fly here."

The next day I tasked Bersi with showing Aed around the settlement. "You will be his guide, Bersi. He has much to learn. For one thing, he will be one of your slingers."

"Can he use a sling?"

The Sword of Cnut

"That is for you to discover."

He nodded and then said, "And the next time you sail I would come with you."

"Aye, that is as it should be."

When I examined the jet I was more than pleasantly surprised. I knew, from my time in Ribe and Agerhøne, that those who worked with stone and jewels liked large pieces. A good workman could shape and fashion fine items if he had larger pieces to work with. We had more than enough to sell. The smaller pieces, the shards and stones, I put to one side. They would be shared with the villagers. We had pot makers who used the clay from Stockadeton to make pots. I had ordered some to be larger in anticipation of the making of seal oil. Having hunted them, I knew we could get more so I planned on keeping just two large pots. The rest we would trade in Ribe. It was the same with the seal skin. One-third would be kept for our village and the rest traded. The bones and the blubber we would keep.

Ragnar arrived the second morning after my return. He brought with him a knife he had made. It had a handle made from the antler of a stag. He would have traded for the blade or perhaps he had taken it from a battle but it was clear that the handle and the scabbard were all his own work. The handle had carved upon it a horse and a sword. My symbols. I took the gift and gave him my thanks.

His voice was unnaturally high and showed his nerves as he spoke, "I come here, Lord Sven, to ask for the hand of Gunhilde in marriage. My father has given me a plot of land and I have built a house for me and my future family. I have stood in the shield wall and fought with you at the Battle of Billingham and there is no truer warrior than me."

I nodded, "And in all this, you have not spoken of Gunhilde."

His face fell, "She is the reason I am here. I would have her as my wife and the mother of my children."

I said, "And if I were not Lord of Norton, would you still wish her?"

"Of course. I expect nothing from the Lord of Norton for this. It is Gunhilde I wish to be my bride,"

I smiled, "Then as she approves you shall be married but it will be in the church and Father John shall hand fast you." I had seen the Hammer of Thor around his neck but he nodded and I liked that. He was as pragmatic and practical as I was.

Mary wanted the wedding sooner rather than later. She knew not if Steana had given her grandchildren and she was anxious for Gunhilde to begin. Despite Ragnar's words, I gave him a dowry of silver and jet. I was rich and my daughter deserved to benefit from my position and

The Sword of Cnut

treasure chest. The wedding feast was a chance for the village to celebrate. It was almost a victory feast for the battle was still in our memory. I invited Edward of Billingham, his sons and Osgar as well as Alfred and Eadric. The wedding was a symbol of the union of the old and the new. Ragnar's family and mine. My men sang songs of the past. The men of Billingham had not heard them and it was as though they were being taught the history of their new neighbours.

As Mary and I rolled into our blankets, I was content. It looked like peace was finally being granted to me. Perhaps Oathsword would lie in its scabbard, its work done. Maybe I could now rule a land at peace and one that would grow and prosper.

The Sword of Cnut

Chapter 5

Flotsam and Jetsam 1019

We left for Ribe two weeks after the wedding. This time we had a larger crew. It was one thing to sail down the coast with a hastily gathered crew and quite another to sail across the ocean. I had twenty-four crewmen as well as Aed, Bersi and Gandálfr. The land had been at peace and the last message we had received from the eorl was that the north was quiet and there was little likelihood of an attack from the Scots. The trickiest part was getting to the river. We had to row backwards down our channel. Once at the river, we could turn around and use the tide and the current to row towards the sea. I decided that when time allowed I would build a quay by the river. It would mean a walk to the village but life would be easier.

We managed to reach the sea before darkness fell. It was a good opportunity for the crew to learn to work together. Folki and I had already had one voyage and we were able to stand watch on watch. The ship's boys, however, were largely new. I was pleased that Bersi, who had been a ship's boy, had taken to Aed and, quite literally, showed him the ropes. Bersi was now needed on the oars but when he could he offered advice to the young boy. For his part, Aed had taken to Bersi who was as kind as his mother. It boded well. When I saw the dagger in Aed's belt I knew that Bersi had given it to him for it had once belonged to Bersi. It was clear that Aed would value the dagger above all things as it ensured he had protection. The memory of Hwitebi was like a scar that burned in his mind. He was alone and mistrustful, yet. I understood that.

We headed into the darkness. With no moon and clouds, we could not see the stars. It would have been all too easy to lose direction and so I reefed the sail. I had Bersi and Aed sleep close to the prow and I kept the mast in line with them. If I could see one or the other then I knew the ship was not being steered straight. It was not a totally accurate method but I had used it before. When dawn broke and I saw the sun directly ahead, I was pleased with myself and I woke Folki. It was my turn to sleep. I headed for the prow.

Bersi woke as I neared him. He shook Aed awake, "Time for the captain to sleep." He grinned, "The blankets are warm."

"And I thank you for that." I rolled into the blankets and Bersi laid my seal skin cloak over me. Spray from the sea was not what I needed.

The Sword of Cnut

From the sun directly above me, I deduced that it was noon when I awoke. The sail was full and billowing. Folki had found a wind. I rose and made water before heading to the steering board. Erik Prow Jumper handed me the compass and I could see we were still on course. The wind was to our larboard quarter and meant we did not have to row. It was not a strong wind but that did not matter. We would reach Ribe when we reached it. I was just enjoying the open sea.

When Leif, the ship's boy seated cross-legged at the top of the mast, shouted, "Sail to the north!" then I became alert.

I went to the larboard side and pulled myself up on the gunwale. I was too low to see the ship but if it came into view then I would know we would meet. "Where away?"

"Heading due west, my lord."

"Can you make her out?"

"No, Lord Sven. She could be a snekke or a knarr."

That meant she was not as long as a warship. Leif was to be excused. The two ships differed not in length, some knarrs were the same length as a snekke but broader in the beam. A snekke was like a snake and slim. A knarr was alike a waddling cow in calf.

"Let me know when she disappears." If she held her course then whatever vessel it was, she was heading for England.

He watched for a while and then shouted, "I can no longer see her."

"Good, you have done well."

The wind that picked up in the afternoon was welcome, at first, but when it grew stronger and was joined by rain then I knew the Norns had spun. I cursed myself for not making a blót. Mary would not have appreciated the sacrifice but it might have kept us safe.

"Reef the sails. Tie down what needs to be tied down."

Bersi came to my side, "It may pass."

"Aye, and it might worsen. Let us prepare for the worst and then I will happily look foolish if this is just a squall."

It did worsen. *'Falcon'* was a sound ship and the winter maintenance had been prescient. We sprang no leaks despite the ferocity of the storm. We plunged into troughs and were doused by waves that seemed like walls towering above us. The seals we had hunted had given the crew seal skin capes and we were drier than we might have been, but rest was hard to come by as we fought the storm all night. The renewed ropes and sheets all held and we survived. When a grey and murky dawn broke, the sea was no longer like a raging bull but seemed like a restless cow about to give birth. The crests and troughs were no longer dangerous, merely threatening, and as the day

The Sword of Cnut

progressed the wind eased along with the seas. We used more sail and Folki and I consulted about our course.

"I think we were pushed south, Lord Sven."

I nodded, "That means it might be Agerhøne we spy first and that is no bad thing." The Norns had spun.

The sighting of the ship and the storm had sharpened the ship's boys' attention and it was Aed, doing his first duty atop the cross piece, who shouted, "Something in the water to...," he paused. I understood he was trying to get the right word. He was not a sailor. "Steerboard."

I turned to look and saw, some six lengths from us, a piece of wreckage. It was the victim of the storm. "Folki, ease her over. We may discover the type of vessel that was taken by Ran." Had my wife been there she would have tut-tutted at the use of the name of a pagan god. She was not a sailor. Only sailors understood that there had to be a god controlling the seas. Odin or the father of the White Christ might rule the earth but the seas were a different matter.

It was Bersi who spied the arm, "Look, there is something alive that clings to the wreckage."

"Be ready to pull aboard whatever is there. It does not matter if it is dead or alive. We will fetch it aboard."

You never knew if the men who clung to wood were alive or had succumbed to the sea. It was not until we hauled him aboard and he spewed seawater onto the deck that we knew he lived. "Cover him with furs and keep him on his side."

I knew that if he lay on his back he might choke on his vomit and he needed to be warm before we even attempted to get some ale in him.

"Folki, resume our course."

We had, of course, brought aboard the wreckage. It could be used, for kindling if nothing else. Lodvir examined it and said, "It looks like the crosspiece from a drekar."

Gandálfr pointed at the man's face, it was tattooed, "And he looks Norse to me." He cocked an eyebrow as he said it. I knew why. Norse suggested raiders. Had this one ship been alone or was it a small fleet such as the one that had raided our river?

The man slept for a couple of hours. "Try ale in his mouth." Erik poured, gently, the ale into the survivor's mouth.

The warmth of the furs and the ale we poured into his throat brought colour back to his pale skin and he opened his eyes and saw the sky and the seabirds that were following us. He was Norse and I knew it as soon as he spoke. We had enough words in common so that I understood what he had said was, "Am I dead?"

"No, you are alive and aboard *'Falcon'*. We are heading to Denmark. Who are you and what was your ship?"

"I am Haldir Bjornson, and my ship was *'Storm Petrel.'*"

Gandálfr was blunt, as ever, and said, "You are a pirate."

He grinned, "I am a Viking and with my oar brothers we sailed the seas searching for riches."

Gandálfr snorted, "I thought so. Throw him overboard, Lord Sven."

The man's eyes filled with fear, "No, Lord Sven. I beg you."

I smiled and shook my head, "You could be a murderer and I would not throw you back. When a man is rescued from the sea it is his rescuer's duty to return him to the land. We are heading for Ribe. There you may leave us."

He looked relieved and stood. He still kept the fur about him. I saw that he was, perhaps twenty-odd summers old. He wore just a kyrtle but I could see that not only was he muscled but he had scars. He was a warrior.

Bersi asked, "And will you return to the sea that tried to kill you?"

He snorted with derision, "It was not the sea that was the problem but the drunken captain, Olaf the Fearless. Was ever a man misnamed? He swore that the storm was a squall and we did not reef the sail. The seas caught us broadside and took the mast. He had not bothered to have the hull kept clear of weeds and she foundered. The sea claimed him and the others but I was saved and, for that, I thank you." He shook his head, "It is just a pity that my brother was not saved all those years ago."

"Brother?" Bersi had a curious nature.

"Aye, my brother was a sailor. He sailed with Olaf the Fearless too. My brother was swept overboard in a storm. Olaf the Fearless did not go back for him."

"Then why did you sail with him?"

I was young when my brother died. We lived in a small place and *'Storm Petrel'* was the only ship. My choice was to take my brother's place or stay at home. I sailed with Olaf." He shook his head, "My oar brothers all said that my brother was the better sailor." He stopped and stared out to sea, "I wonder now if Olaf the Fearless got rid of my brother for he feared him." He shook his head, "It would be just like him."

Bersi said, "If he did then it was murder."

Haldir laughed, "He has done worse than murder but you may be right, he might have been the cause of my brother's death. Had Bergil the Black been captain then we would not have foundered."

The Sword of Cnut

It was as though time stood still. Even Gandálfr was taken aback and clutched his hammer of Thor. We all looked at Aed. For his part it was as though he had seen a ghost.

Haldir stared at us, "What is it? What have I said?"

"Aed here was fathered by a Viking who was plucked from the sea by the Red Scar, close to the estuary of the Tees. His name was Bergil the Black."

Haldir dropped the cloak and placed his hands on Aed's shoulders, "Where is he now?"

Aed's voice was quiet and filled with awe as he said, "He is dead. The men of Hwitebi killed him and my mother. Sven Saxon Sword has taken me in. Are you my uncle?"

Haldir changed his grip and hugged the youth, "If your father was Bergil the Black then I am and while I am sad that my brother is dead I am happy that he planted his seed." He turned, "The Norns have spun, my lord. I can see that this is all part of a web and," he dropped to one knee, "I have no sword but if I had then I would offer it to you. Let me join your crew." He glanced up at Gandálfr, "I know that there are some who would throw me overboard without a second glance, but I swear that if you give me the chance then I will be oathsworn. I have blood now and a purpose to life."

Every eye was on me and even Gandálfr smiled. "It is the Norns, Lord Sven. What can we do?"

I smiled, "Then, Haldir Bjornson, you are now part of the crew."

That it was the right thing to do was clear from the shouts and cheers. Uncle and nephew headed for the prow so that they could speak and I was left with Bersi. "What would mother say? She does not believe in the Three Sisters and yet, across the wide and empty ocean it is we who find Aed's blood kin."

I nodded. "It is better not to think too deeply about such things. We can do nothing."

Bersi said, "Except the right thing and you have done that again." He nodded towards Oathsword. "Perhaps the sword is even more powerful than we know."

It was evening and we had reefed the sail when Haldir and Aed rejoined us. "Aed tells me that you are Sven Saxon Sword known as Oathsword." I nodded. "I have heard of you. It is said that King Cnut owes his kingdom to you."

Shaking my head I said, "I have been of some service to him but so had others."

"And now you live in the land of Alfred the Saxon King who defeated Guthrum."

The Sword of Cnut

"I do."

"Olaf was supposed to raid that land with three other captains some many months ago but he fell out with them."

"And three Norsemen attacked my village and left a sunken ship and returned to Norway with but a handful of men, so it is good that you did not or else you might have fallen too." I saw him clutch his Hammer.

By the time Agerhøne came into view, we had equipped Haldir so that he did not look like a drowned rat. The tiny harbour was empty and that was disappointing. It meant that my son would not be at home.

As we tied up, we were recognised and folk flocked to greet us. I smiled at old friends and found myself touched by the warmth of their greeting. "Where is my son?"

"He is with the king dealing with the rebellious men of Zealand, but his wife and your grandson are in the hall."

I had a grandson! Leaving the others to replenish the water and ale, Bersi and I headed for the hall. A thrall opened the door and bowed, "I will tell Lady Gytha that she has a visitor."

As soon as my daughter-in-law arrived, I recognised her. It was Gytha Siggisdotter. My old friend and first oar brother was the finest pig farmer in Denmark. Gytha held a suckling babe in her arms. "Lord Sven, Bersi, Steana will be unhappy that he is abroad. This is your grandson, Sven Steanason." He had finished feeding and he looked around at the strange face. He had the bluest eyes I had ever seen. "Would you like to hold him?"

I wiped my hands on my breeks, "I feel dirty and dishevelled but I would be honoured to hold the first of my son's blood." She put him in my arms and the babe stared at me. I swear he was examining me as though for defects. I saw none in him. "How old is he?"

"He was born three months ago. The king sent for your uncle and your son a month after the birth." She went on to tell me all.

We spent a happy couple of hours with my new family and only left reluctantly. "We are bound for Ribe. I have a cargo but I shall return here before setting sail for home."

"Then I will entertain you and Bersi."

We set sail for the short journey up the coast to Ribe, the home of the jarl, my foster father. Bersi stood with me and nodded towards Aed and Haldir. "They are as close as any two men I have ever seen." The two had their heads together.

I knew that Bersi and Aed had begun to become friends but now he was being ignored. "Blood, Bersi, ties men together deeply."

The Sword of Cnut

"I know and I do not resent this but it has made me think about the Norns a little more deeply than I might. I can see now that we or should I say you, were meant to find both Aed and Haldir. You are being used by the Norns."

"And that is the price I pay for Oathsword."

"Sometimes I wonder if it is a curse."

My hand went to the pommel, as though to calm the weapon, "A curse?"

"It ties you to the king and men seek to wrench it from your hand. Mother and Steana told me when I was growing up, of the men who coveted the weapon."

"No, it is not cursed but you are right, men seek it. What would you have me do? Toss it in the ocean?"

"It would make your life easier."

"You forget the Norns. They spun the web and the discarding of the sword would cut a thread. That is always the most dangerous course of action. So long as my heart is true and I do not allow the sword to corrupt me then all will be well."

"Corrupt you?"

"When I fight with the sword I do not believe that I can be defeated. I have never sought a battle or a fight. If the sword consumed me then I might be corrupted and seek to fight all, knowing I would not be beaten. I use the sword when I have to and that is all."

Aed was forgotten as my son reflected on my words.

Ribe was a prosperous place. There were ships there but we were the only drekar. The other ships were the knarrs of Aksel and Alf which plied the seas. I left my men to lift the decks and have the cargo ready for inspection while Bersi and I sought my cousin, Alf. His house was the biggest in Ribe. It was even bigger than his father's, the jarl. The bodyguard who took me into the hall was an expensively equipped warrior. He wore the best of mail, his sword was well made and he had battle bands. I did not know him but I knew that my cousin was choosing well how to use his fortune.

I could not help but smile when I saw the man with ring-covered fingers, oiled hair and a growing waistline. Was this the boy jumper Swooping Hawk, my cousin Alf, who had leapt the shield wall at Svolder and helped to win the battle for King Sweyn? He had chosen his own course and it was not that of a warrior. We had always been close and he rose to embrace me.

"This, Eidel the Rus, is Lord Sven Saxon Sword and that weapon on his belt is a Dragon Sword."

The Sword of Cnut

The bodyguard's eyes widened. He had heard of both the sword and me. He bowed, "Forgive me, lord, for not giving you the respect I should."

I smiled, "Eidel, today I have just come as a merchant to speak with my cousin. There is no great deed planned this day."

He bowed his way out and a thrall brought ale and food, "Sit. You come as a merchant?"

"I have jet, seal skin and seal oil."

"Then you have come to the right place. My father-in-law is in his home in Sweden and I am the one who buys and sells here. He is unwell and my wife and daughters have gone to tend to him. I live the life of a bachelor here. It will be good to have your company. You can tell me your tales and I will tell you mine, although I fear mine will be duller. Now that King Cnut rules both kingdoms then we profit well and are untouched by war."

"The Norse have not raided?"

He shook his head, "The king fought a battle at sea and sank those who might have raided. We hear that there are warbands who prey on small communities but Denmark is safe."

"They came to my home but we sent them hence. That is why I need to trade. We have land but we need animals as well as settlers."

He nodded, "And I can find the latter. Denmark is crowded. I know that the king's wars in the east will thin the numbers, but there will be younger sons who want their own farms. I will spread the word." We drank the ale. The horns we used were inlaid with silver and the quality was beyond compare. "Your son rules well in your stead, Sven. I think he commands more men than you do. He took more than a hundred men to the king's wars."

I was unsure if Alf was teasing me or testing me. It did not matter. I had chosen to leave Steana as hersir so that Mary could return home to Norton, and I did not regret my decision. "We like Norton, do we not, Bersi?"

He grinned, "Aye, we do and Gunhilde has just married. One day so shall I but I will wait until I am a warrior."

Alf's face erupted into a smile, "And it is good that you have come, Bersi, for I have a gift for you. Wait here." He stood and left us in the huge hall. It allowed me to study the tapestries that hung from the walls. This was not a mead hall such as his father used. This was a place of business where he could impress other merchants and nobles. Alf was shrewd.

He returned with a pair of thralls that carried a pair of sheepskins. The two laid them on the table and then carefully unwrapped them.

The Sword of Cnut

Inside were a fine sword with a well-made scabbard, a full-face helmet, a shield and a byrnie that was the equal of Eidel's.

"These were mine in those far-off days when I was a warrior. I know that I am no warrior now and thought to give it to my son. Sadly, I now only have daughters and I would give this to blood kin. It is yours, Bersi, a gift from me. Your father always watched out for me and protected me. Hopefully, I can return the favour by giving you the protection of my mail."

Bersi dropped to his knees, "It is a princely gift and I thank you."

"None of that. Now, while I have rooms prepared for you, let us take this treasure to your ship so that I may become the merchant and assess the value of your cargo." He paused, "I will give you a fair price, Sven, but I did not become rich by losing money on trades."

"I understand and I know that whatever I am given for my cargo will be correct."

Eidel had two men with him as we were escorted to the drekar. The deck had been lifted and the men lounged on the quayside. While Bersi directed the thralls to the prow, Alf stepped aboard and cast his eye critically over the jet and the other goods. He picked up the skins and sniffed them. He lifted, carefully, the jet and looked along it. He smoothed it with his hand. He turned to me, "I will buy it. Seal oil and skins are, well, they are what they are and the price rarely changes but you have found the best jet I have ever seen. The size of the pieces is unusual, and it has been well mined for there are few marks." The thralls had returned, and he said, "Fetch men and take this cargo to my warehouse."

"Yes, master."

"Eidel, I will be safe enough with Sven Saxon Sword and his son. Stay and supervise the unloading of the cargo. I would not have this jet damaged in any way."

"Yes, my lord."

"Come, Sven, we will retire to my home."

I tossed a purse to Gandálfr, "When the cargo is unloaded then set the watch. This is for food. You can enjoy the pleasures of Ribe. Bersi and I will be staying with Alf this night."

Gandálfr was clearly unhappy that he would not be watching over me but he nodded, "Aye, Lord Sven."

Ribe was a big port and there were women there, slaves who were used by men. More money would be exchanged for those favours than for either food or drink.

Once back in the hall, Alf became businesslike. He took a wax tablet and calculated how much he would pay. It was far more than I

The Sword of Cnut

expected but I knew my cousin was being honest and that he would make a healthy profit himself. We would return to Hwitebi.

"You are happy with that?"

"I am more than happy."

"I will have the gold placed in a chest and tomorrow Eidel will escort you back to your ship, unless you wish to linger longer?"

"No, I promised Steana's wife I would visit."

"Then I shall have to make this a good feast so that I may recount your tales to my family when they return."

It was a huge hall and there were just three of us but we dined well. Alf kept a good table and we ate exotic foods that had come from far away. The spiced food was a revelation to Bersi. The thralls were kept busy bringing more and more delicacies. Eidel stood watch the whole time. I told our tales, of the raids and the intrigues. I had not seen him since the death of Edmund Ironside and I had much to tell. The story, however, which intrigued both Alf and, I could see, Eidel, was the tale of Aed and Haldir. Both men were like me, pagans who masqueraded as Christians. Eidel's hand went to his Hammer of Thor when I spoke of the story of Haldir.

I was not wearing my sword. It hung from my chair and Alf nodded to it, "The sword still retains its power even though England is now Danish. Perhaps its work is not yet done."

I had drunk well and while I was not drunk my tongue was looser than normal, "There is still much treachery and I do not think my service to the king is over."

Alf nodded, "You are right there. Before my father left, he was visited by the king. King Cnut spoke of you and your sword. I think he will send for you again."

Bersi said, "But we have only enough men for one drekar and if we man that well, then Norton is left undefended."

Alf leaned forward, "Bersi, I tell you this because your father knows it already. King Cnut cares for one thing only, his own security and safety. Oathsword is a guarantee that he will keep both kingdoms. The fact that my cousin was not needed to fight the rebels is not to be taken as a promise that King Cnut will not send for the sword and the talisman that is Sven Saxon Sword. I do not envy your father, but I do respect him. Even my father is in awe of his foster son. Oathsword is no longer a Saxon sword, nor even a Danish sword, now it is the sword of King Cnut, and he will use it to make his kingdom stronger than any other."

The Sword of Cnut

Chapter 6

The Hunt

Gytha had prepared beds for Bersi and me. I could tell that she missed my son and that this was, probably, the way that Mary felt when I was away. She made us feel more than welcome. She was keen to know all. She knew Gunhilde and was happy that she had wed, "And you, Bersi, it will not be long until you take a wife. Your father needs grandsons. This is his first but there will be more."

I laughed, "Are you a volva now?"

She was a Christian but she also liked to spin and I knew that I had touched a nerve when she flushed, "I believe that your blood is needed to keep our clans strong." She changed the subject. "I invited my father, but you know him. He is a farmer and does not like to leave his farm."

"No matter. I planned on visiting him in any case. If you have horses, Bersi and I will visit with my oldest friend on the morrow."

When I had first gone to sea my only friend had been Siggi the Pig. I was his only friend too and we formed a bond that had lasted through the years and had survived the frequent absences. I had protected him from those who mocked him and his desire only to be a farmer. He, in turn, had proved to be most loyal to me. Even though we had only fought alongside each other once, when we greeted it felt like I was meeting a shield brother.

When I saw him I saw he had not changed. He still had the ruddy complexion of one who spends more time out of doors than indoors. He was well fed and had the beginnings of a belly. "This must be Bersi." I nodded. "He looks like you, Sven. Your sons are warriors both. Mine look like me, pig farmers."

"And there is nothing wrong with that, Siggi."

"Come inside. I thought you might come. We have food and ale for you."

Time flew as we chatted. He was happy that his daughter had married Steana and now all his children were wed and had children. He was a farmer and saw such fecundity as a good thing. Like Alf, he was intrigued by the story of Haldir and Aed. "You know, Sven, that sword could have come to me." He shook his head, "I am glad that it did not but I now see a greater power at work. In many ways, I feel sorry for you. Your destiny is guided by others. Mine is in my own hands."

"You are wise, Siggi."

The Sword of Cnut

"I live by growing things. I read the weather and the land. Your life is subject to the whims of not only kings but…" his hand went to his hammer and he shook his head, "It is better not to speak of such things."

"No, and you are right. I am glad I came here because I need to buy animals from you. When I left you were kind enough to give me animals. I sold some jet and now I can pay you."

He smiled, "Then you have come at the perfect time. The new piglets are ready for market. I can let you have the first pick knowing that you will use them well."

"And calves?"

"I have a young bull and a cow I intended to sell. You can have them, too, if you would."

"Then let us make the trade now and if you could help me take them back to Agerhøne I can pay you."

"And as that affords me the chance to see my grandson too then all is well."

We took back fourteen piglets. There were three young boars amongst them. I intended to share them amongst my people. I would keep one sow and one boar as well as the bull and the cow. I would begin my own herd.

The animals meant that we would have to leave the next day and that would end my visit home. I was sad that it was ending but, when we reached the ship, I saw that the Norns had been spinning. Gandálfr had with him four men. They were young, just a little older than Bersi. While the animals were boarded he spoke to me.

"Lord Sven, these men would bring their families with them to Norton. They are all young but they want their own farms. I said that you would consider their request."

I smiled, "If they wish to come then I am happy for them to do so. I will give each of them a farm and a hide of land but we will be leaving on the morning tide. We now have a cargo of animals and time is not on our side."

Gandálfr nodded, "They know that." He turned to the men, "Go, you heard Lord Sven, be here before we sail or you are doomed to Agerhøne. We will not be returning soon."

I shook my head. He did not mean to sound so harsh but he had a very brusque manner.

I paid Siggi. The cost made little impression on the treasure in the chest. I used a little more of it to buy seeds for my farmers. That night I gave all my attention to Gytha and my grandson. I had retained some of the jet and I made it a gift to Gytha. She was delighted. "I know a man

The Sword of Cnut

who can work such stone, I will have something made for Sven. He will have a remembrance of his grandfather."

"And I will return here. Now that I have one grandson here then I will be drawn like a wolf to the moon."

She came with my grandson to see us off. Others came too for the men who were returning with me all came from Agerhøne. There were tears from both those on the quay and the women who were going with their husbands to a new life in a new country. I understood how hard that would be for them.

The voyage back was not an easy one. In many ways, it was fortunate that we had the four families with us for it meant we had more hands to clear away the mess the animals left and to keep them calm. We lost not an animal and I was relieved when we saw the seals on the mud flats for that meant we would be home within a day or so.

Laden as we were we had to wait until the tide was at its highest before attempting the beck passage. We could not simply slip over the side and we had to use a gangplank. It all added to the time it took to disembark the cargo and the passengers. By the time the crew and I had cleaned the decks and secured the drekar, night had fallen. Haldir and Aed fell in with me as we trudged up the track to the village.

"Lord, I have not asked this before, but do I have a home here?"

I nodded, "You do, Haldir. For the moment you shall share my hall with Gandálfr and Aed but we must give thought to building a warrior hall. That is for the future. For the present, we have animals and seeds to share."

Mary was just pleased that we had returned safely. She welcomed the newcomers even though it meant my hall was overcrowded. Food was prepared and I saw little of her until most of the people we had brought were wrapped in blankets and spread around my hall. She and I shared a bed chamber and it was only when we were in there that we could talk. It took some time to tell her all. Haldir, Aed, our grandson and King Cnut's war took time and she was silent when I had finished.

I tried to reassure her, "Our son will be safe. My foster father will watch over him."

"I know that. I was just thinking that we are detached living here in my home. I have taken you from your home."

"As I did with you. I am happy here and I see a place we can make better than the one I left."

She sighed, "And tomorrow you shall begin to work again as you give land to these new folk and share out the animals."

"But it means we shall grow and the clan is stronger."

The Sword of Cnut

I was doomed, it seemed, to make work for myself. The new animals and the settlers were more than welcome but it was my job to allocate the settlers' land and to distribute the animals. In the end, most people just gained one piglet. Those with boars were given them with the understanding that they would be used to fertilise the females. The pigs would be for breeding and not for eating. The farms were easier to allocate. There was plenty of woodland to be hewn down and the wood was used as timber for the buildings. My people were good people and they all helped. The choicest pieces of land were the ones closer to the becks but still not prone to flooding. That land was taken already. The wooded land had one problem, it did not have access to running water and so the fish pond in the village would become the source of water. We had to wait until the four families had rooves above their heads before I could give thought to building a warrior hall. Mary wondered at the wisdom of its building as there would be just four occupants at first: Bersi, Gandálfr, Haldir and Aed. I pointed out that there would be young men who, like Bersi, would be ready to be warriors and might choose to serve me. The trade had made me rich and I could afford to have my own oathsworn again. As much as I relished peace, I knew that it would not last. It had been made clear to me, by Alf, that King Cnut would need Sven Saxon Sword and the Dragon Sword again. I knew I had to prepare for that day.

There was a piece of land that lay between the palisade and my hall. The new men helped, along with the other men of the village, to dig the foundations. When we had cleared the trees there had been six mighty trunks that were too large for houses but would make sturdy supports for a warrior hall. Trimmed of their bark and cut to the same size, they were placed in a rectangle and their base was rammed with stones. It took a week to fit the six trunks and as we had to wait until they had settled, we could do nothing for another week. The erection of the timbers coincided with the Sunday wapentake. The new men we had acquired, all five of them, allied to the boys who, like Bersi, had become men, meant that we had, when all were gathered, a band of men that looked more formidable than the one that had sent the Norse hence. Most did not have mail. Bersi, in his new gift, looked splendid. He had changed the design on Alf's shield to incorporate a horse for we were the clan of the horse. Haraldr, the weaponsmith, had also made Herkumbl for the helmets. It was a rearing horse. I saw the men of Billingham looking enviously at my men. With a horse painted somewhere on each shield and the Herkumbl, we looked like one warband.

The Sword of Cnut

The shield wall had to be organised. While the slingers and the archers practised apart, Osgar, Gandálfr and I worked with the shield wall. Bersi might have new armour and look like a warrior but he was the least experienced of all my men. Accordingly, and to his great chagrin, he was placed in the second rank. Men who wore no mail were before him. I would deal with his pouting later for we had to teach the men how to move as one. We spent much time marching in time and changing from a double line to a wedge, to a triple line and then a single one. Haraldrsson had become proficient with the horn and as he now had a byrnie, made for him by his father, he could fight in the front line and be able to signal the orders more easily. As we rested at noon and enjoyed ale and cheese, I sought out Bersi.

"You were unhappy at your position in the line."

He nodded, "I have a good byrnie, helmet and sword."

"And little experience. There will come a time when you improve and you and Gandálfr will flank me. Until that time, you will stand behind me but I will give you a task."

He brightened, "What is that?"

"You shall carry my standard. It will be the rallying point in battle. It means you cannot use a spear and perhaps that is a good thing. I can make you a swordsman."

"I should like that. I just want to be of use to you, Father."

"And I would have you live longer than one battle. Let us take baby steps. When King Cnut sends for us it will not be to fight Norse raiders but to stand in a battle line where prisoners are not taken, and there will be no wall to run to for safety. I hope that it is not any time soon but when we do then you must be ready. Practise. When I am not available use Haldir and Gandálfr. I suspect Haldir is a better warrior than most of those in my band. I know he has no mail and his weapons are borrowed, but any man who can be a raider knows how to fight. Learn from him and my oathsworn."

Haldir had been given one of my old leather byrnies and I had given him my first helmet. We had enough swords so that he was able to choose one that suited him. He had made his own spear and shield. He had shown me that he was a warrior. When we had practised, I had seen him advising some of the other younger warriors who had just joined us. His manner was less abrasive than the irascible Gandálfr. He was a good addition to my clan.

It took a month to finish the hall by which time the weather had become colder and we had a decision to make about the drekar. Gandálfr still ate with us as did Bersi. Haldir and Aed fended for themselves as they grew closer together. Haldir had become the foster father that Sweyn Skull Taker had been for me and I was pleased.

"Do we have one more voyage before winter or do we move the drekar to higher ground as we did the last time?"

"We made a great deal of gold from the last time we sought the jet."

I nodded, "I know, Gandálfr, and it is tempting but we cannot eat jet. If we leave now there will be fewer people to harvest and to forage. I thought of having a hunt before winter. We have precious few animals that we can slaughter."

Mary shook her head, "We have none, husband. Those we have must be cossetted. They are the future. If anything we need more."

Gandálfr laughed, "Time was we would have taken the drekar and instead of seeking jet we would have raided across the seas and taken animals."

Mary rolled her eyes. "And now we are the ones who are raided. Times change, Gandálfr, and we must change with them."

He nodded sadly and drank some ale, "Aye, I am a relic, lord. I miss being a raider."

Mary reached out and touched the back of his hand, "And you miss Faramir. This time of year, when the leaves die and the land grows cold is the time of year when spirits are low. You should speak to Father John, Gandálfr. He will uplift your spirits."

He caught my eye. I knew what he was thinking. His words were a sort of falsehood, "If we hunt, my lady, then my spirits will be lifted. I do not need to burden the priest with my woes. He has enough to contend with." Gandálfr still wore his Hammer of Thor. It was hidden but I knew that it was there. "Then if we are not to raid and need no more jet then we should move the drekar. It is our lifeline and she is a good ship, lord. That is my view."

"And mine. We will move her in the next few days and then hunt. The woods to the north of us, south of Thorpe, look to me to be good places to hunt."

There had been farmers at Fulthorpe, but they had been killed by the Mercians. Thorpe was deserted and the land to the north of us was empty of people. The animals there would be like the seals on the mud flats. They would be complacent and not expecting to be hunted. It would be good to blood the young warriors like Bersi, Haraldrsson and Aed. Sinking a spear into an animal was not the same as killing a man but it would harden the heart and that was what was needed.

The hewing of the trees also meant we had kindling for our fires and when the roots of the odd pine tree were burned for pine tar along with the roots of oak and beech, we had the ash to spread on the ground

The Sword of Cnut

along with the seaweed and dung. We were planning for the future and we would make the ground fertile. We also took the soil that was deposited when the tide came in close to the beck. It ensured a boggy area to deter enemies and fertilised the ground. Once the drekar was securely stored close to the walls of Norton, then the only ships using the beck and river would be the fishing boats and they were so shallow that they could have floated on a puddle. Men had removed some of the timbers of the burnt Norse ship so that it was less of a danger to us. The part that remained would simply be a deterrent for enemies. We had stocked the village fishpond with tiny fish and knew that they would grow. Along with the dovecot we had built, my people were preparing for life in the harsh winter of the north country.

I chose young men for the hunt. Their fathers were farmers and they had much work to do on the land. This was the time to repair fences for winter, deepen ditches and plant winter crops. The young men could hunt. There were twelve of them including Bersi, Aed and the inevitable Haldir who was like Aed's shadow. We took hunting spears that were shorter than our war spears. Their heads were intended to drive deep into flesh. I also took a boar spear with a cross piece. I let Aed carry that. Some of the younger men were carrying bows for this was a hunt for food. I knew that King Sweyn had given a lodge north of Jorvik to a Mercian lord where he entertained other lords and hunted for sport. They could afford to show their skills. We were gathering food, and we would kill the animals any way we could.

We walked up the west side of the beck and passed the burnt-out mill. It was a visible reminder of the time when Mary had lived here as a girl. We had yet to rebuild the mill. We would need to if we were to make our own flour in large quantities. As I spotted the derelict walls and broken wheel, now covered by water from the beck, I knew it was another job for the future. We then took the ancient trail which was now somewhat overgrown. There had been a time when a Saxon called Wulfstan had farmed there but he and his family were long dead. I only knew his name because Osgar had spoken of him when telling me the history of the valley. When we found the fallen-in walls and cleared land, now being reclaimed by weeds and saplings, I knew we had found the farm. We stopped to get our bearings.

"If any becomes separated then this is where we will meet. Now make water and tighten your belts. We may have to run after our prey." As they did so I said, "Aed, stay close to me. The spear you carry will be our only protection if we come across a wild boar."

"Do we not hunt them?"

The Sword of Cnut

I shook my head, "If we find their tracks or their spoor then we will mark it and return with greybeards who have hunted them before. Hunting deer with antlers is one thing but a wild boar with vicious tusks is a man killer. We avoid such beasts." His face told me that he had understood. I carried two throwing spears and I had my sword at my belt. After testing the air, I set off with the breeze coming in our faces. Before we had left I had impressed upon them the need to step carefully and to be as silent as we could. As I watched the line of young warriors I thought back to my home in Denmark when Lodvir and Griotard had taken me to hunt. It had been the beginning of the making of a warrior. It would be the same with the young men I led. They would learn to be silent when they moved and their reactions would be sharpened. We lived in a time of peace but when King Cnut called then I would have to take young men to war.

Deer and other grazing animals make noise when they move but the sound of their eating and rustling also carries and it was that which I heard. I was listening for it and, Haldir apart, the others were not. I raised the spear in my right hand and the line stopped. I listened to locate the sound. It was coming from ahead of me to the left. I waved the spear and we moved forward. Despite their best efforts some of the hunters were not as silent as they ought to have been and we startled the herd. It was a large one and reflected the fact that they had not been hunted for some time. That resulted in a few things. They were numerous and they were unused to fleeing such predators. From what Osgar had told me the last wolf had been slain when Mary had been but a child. The animals took off in all directions. The wood had not been copsed and saplings had sprung up everywhere. It channelled the deer and many came racing towards us.

"Bersi, Aed, behind me." I was aware of Haldir stepping before his foster son as I raised my spear. The deer that ran at me was terrified and did not see the spear I hurled from a range of less than ten feet. It struck the chest of the animal. Its speed kept it moving and I stepped to the side as did Haldir. The animal would die and I transferred my other spear to my right hand. I was barely in time as three deer, an old hind and two younger ones came at me. This time Bersi struck first. He had disobeyed me and stepped to my side. He did not throw his spear but held both of the ones he had brought together and the older deer simply ran onto them. He held on and was driven back. When his back struck the tree the impetus drove the two spearheads into the deer's body. I had no time to watch as the young deer followed the hind. I did not have enough time to throw and instead drove my spear, using both hands, into its side. The broad head tore a hole. I held on so that when

The Sword of Cnut

the head was torn from the body it brought with it entrails that told me the animal was dead. Haldir had saved Aed with a fine throw and he, alone out of the three of us, had a spare spear.

"Are you hurt, Bersi?"

He grinned weakly and shook his head, "Just winded."

Haldir said, "And you have your first kill. We should name you Bersi Two Spears." The name stuck, at least for a while.

"Is anyone hurt? Call out your names."

Nine called out and I breathed a sigh of relief. We would take back the carcasses of animals not the body of a youth.

"Cut saplings, there are many, and sharpen the ends. Put them through the bodies of the deer."

We had killed four and the old hind was a fat one. Not all the youths had kills and it meant that we could carry the deer back and Aed and I would lead the way. Bersi and Haldir followed me carrying our biggest deer, the old hind. There was a buzz of excitement amongst the youths as they spoke of their throws. It had been a good hunt.

Aed was behind me and next to Bersi. I heard their conversation but when I saw movement ahead, I stopped and held up my hand. Everyone stopped immediately and there was silence along my line of hunters. I heard the growling of a dog. I rammed my spears into the ground and held out my hand for the boar spear. If it was a dangerous wild dog, then a boar spear would kill it quicker. I heard my men as they placed the deer on the ground and grabbed weapons. I moved forward with the spear held in two hands. As I emerged into a small clearing, I saw a strange sight. There was a dog, clearly injured in some way, backing against a tree and a wild boar was advancing towards it. As I emerged from the trees the leaves rustled and the boar, seeing a larger threat, charged me. I suppose Haldir could have done what I did. He had been a warrior and stood in a shield wall but any of the others would have died. I dropped to one knee and angled the head of the spear up. With the shaft of the spear against the tree behind me I watched the tusks and wild eyes of the boar as they raced at me. Like the deer we had hunted, the wild boar had been safe from hunters and, perhaps, did not know the danger that man represented. Whatever the reason he came at me. Spears flew from behind me as my youths tried to kill the beast. It was in vain for its skin was too thick and they bounced off. I raised the head just a little as it leapt at me and the spear went into its throat, making the head, teeth and tusks rise over my shoulder. The bar on the spear stopped the spear enough so that its own power killed the animal. It tried to tear itself free and in that tearing signed its own death warrant. It bled out on me.

The Sword of Cnut

I rose and my hunters cheered. Bersi, however, ran to the wounded dog. I could see that, just as Aed had been, it was emaciated and hungry. It had a wound to its hind leg and I was about to tell Bersi to give it a merciful death when the animal began to lick my son as he tended to the wound. "The animal is lame, Bersi."

"I will not leave him to die, Father. Had he not growled then we would be dead. I will take him home and care for him."

My son rarely defied me and he was right. The Norns had spun. It posed a problem for us, however, as we now had a wild boar to carry back. We were lucky that two of the deer we had killed were smaller than the others and two of the larger youths had to carry two deer back. Bersi carried the dog and only Aed had no burden. He carried the spare spears and we headed back to Norton.

Once we reached the burnt-out mill, Bersi ran ahead with the injured animal. It meant that as we neared the walls of my hall there were thralls to help us carry the dead animals. It was lucky that we had hunted so close to home for we still had some daylight to butcher the animals. Nothing would be wasted. The skins would be used and once the meat was taken from the bones, then the bones would be boiled to make a stock. We would then use the bones for tools and jewellery. Even the hooves would be boiled to make glue. The tusks from the wild boar would make small drinking horns. I decided that I would give one to Aed and keep the other for Gunhilde's first child. It was dark by the time we had the skins ready to be pegged out. The next day would see their preparation as the night water we kept in our pots was poured on them. The carcasses themselves were hung in our larder. The offal would be cooked immediately, and we would enjoy a fine hunter's feast.

Bersi was missing in all of this. I found him with Father John. The priest was able to tend to the wounds of humans but Bersi had prevailed on him to look at the dog.

The priest looked up when I entered, "Your son, Lord Sven, has a kind heart. Many would have left this dog to die."

"I advised him to do the same."

"The dog will live. It will limp but it will live. I have sewn up the wound and it endured my stitches stoically. It wants to live. St Francis would have approved of your son." He stood. "You will need to stop the animal from biting at the stitches and it will need to be fed." Bersi nodded.

I pointed to the kitchen. "There is some offal there that we will not eat. The dog will like it." Bersi hesitated, "Go, it is your dog, but I will watch it for a short time."

The Sword of Cnut

When he left, I stroked the dog's ear. It looked like the kind of dog that farmers used to round up sheep. This one had a rare colour; it was red and gold. "What is your tale, eh? I do not know of any farmers with a dog such as you. Did Odin send you? Are you as Heimdall, Odin's watchman?"

Bersi had returned and said, "Heimdall? Why do you call the dog that?"

As my son fed the dog I told him the tale of the guardian of the Bifrost Bridge into Asgard. The dog ate and Bersi listened. His mother had raised him a Christian but he had heard my tales and he smiled. "You are right, Father, and the name suits. He shall be Heimdall for he warned us of danger and he will be the guardian of our hall."

The dog did not seem to mind the name or perhaps he was too grateful at being fed. Whatever the reason the two became inseparable. Mary did not take to the dog at first but Father John made her come around. He had seen the bond between boy and beast and knew that it was not a bad thing. When I next visited Osgar and told him of the hunt, in case the men of Billingham wished to emulate us, we pieced together the story. Wulfstan, it seemed, had been a farmer with sheep. He had also kept dogs. While Heimdall could clearly not have been one of Wulfstan's animals, he was too young, he might have been an offspring or even the offspring of the last sheepdog. Osgar said that, with my permission, he would hunt in the woods that lay in my lands. It made me realise that I was the Lord of this valley.

The Sword of Cnut

The Danish Sea

Chapter 7

The call of the king and the war against the Wends 1020

The Christians amongst us, and that was an increasing number, all celebrated the Winter Solstice well. For those of us who followed the old ways, it was no bad thing. While they sang songs about the White Christ we ate well and enjoyed good ale. It was the time to eat the last of the autumn fruits mixed with the meat that was about to go bad and the ale that had been fermenting for a long time. We had brought back spices from Ribe, a gift from Alf, and the meat that might have turned was more than edible having been cooked in fermented ale and flavoured with spices. It was a time for peace to reign as we hunkered down to endure winter storms. We had been wise to draw the drekar to safety for those early storms were violent and fierce. When Gunhilde and Ragnar visited to tell us that she was with child and we would have another grandchild then our world was whole. That winter we had no deaths amongst the old and that was rare. Mary told me it was the bounty of the hunt that had ensured none starved. The fishpond and the dovecot had also given us a better diet than they might have enjoyed had I not been hersir. I liked my position. I had no demands save those imposed on me by myself and while I worked hard it was enjoyable work. A man cannot ask for more.

My peace was shattered in Spring, when Eorl Eirík himself came south with his mounted oathsworn to visit with me. We had just relaunched the drekar, for I intended to dig for more jet and I was checking the sheets and lines, when he and his men appeared on the causeway. I stopped immediately and waded ashore. The drekar was in the beck and the tide was on its way out. I greeted him at the Norton end of the causeway.

He smiled at me, "You must be prophetic, Sven. You will need your drekar and soon."

My heart sank but I merely nodded, "If you come to my hall, my lord, we can refresh you and you can tell me your news and commands."

"I would not impose on you. I have twenty riders with me."

"And I have a newly built warrior hall. There is room aplenty."

Mary was never put out by visitors. She regarded it as her Christian duty to make them comfortable. Food was sent to the warrior hall where Gandálfr and Haldir entertained them. The eorl ate with Mary, myself

The Sword of Cnut

and Bersi. Heimdall was in his usual position at Bersi's feet. The old Norseman did not speak of his mission until the platters were cleared. "The feast was delicious, Lady Mary. You dine well, Sven."

"We husband the land, eorl."

He nodded, "As does the king. He has sent word that he needs ships and men from England. He requests drekar from East Anglia, Mercia, Wessex and Northumbria. He specifically asked for Oathsword. You are to sail to Heiða-býr and be there by Eostre. The king has subdued the Danish rebels and now turns his attentions to the Wends."

I knew that having been named I had no choice in the matter. "Did the king state how many spears?"

He shook his head, "The message was for Oathsword and his drekar to join him. I will not be sailing. I am tasked with watching this land but it seems there is peace now. Your defeat of the Norse has made them wary of attacking your valley. You can leave men to defend your land."

I nodded and began to work out who I would take. I saw Mary's face and noticed that she toyed with her cross. She was praying. She was looking at Bersi. I had told her that Steana had served the king against the rebels. For all we knew he could be dead. When I went East to fight the Wends that could be my fate and, if I took him, Bersi's.

The eorl left the next day, he was travelling to Jorvik to order some of the Danes there to sail to Denmark. I had not told my men but they knew already. The oathsworn had told my men in the warrior hall and word had spread. Gandálfr knew that he would be coming. Bersi came to ask me if he was to be included in the wapentake.

"You are one of my warriors now but, as with all my warriors, I will give you the choice. There is as much honour in staying at home and guarding this land as there is in sailing to humble the Wends."

"I would come."

"Then you shall."

Haldir and Aed also asked to travel with me. I needed Folki and Erik Prow Jumper to guard the drekar when we landed but that left me with another twenty who would man the oars. The ship's boys we took would not be at risk. They would stay with the drekar. Aed would be both a slinger and a servant. For the rest, I waited for them to ask. I was unsurprised when the youths who had hunted with me asked to come as did those who had been to Hwitebi. Without ordering anyone I had twenty-four men to man the oars. If King Cnut expected me to bring more men I did not care. Only three of us had mail but each of them had a shield, helmet and spear. I had never fought the Wends but I hoped that we might, if we survived, profit from the war.

The Sword of Cnut

King Cnut had not given us long to ponder his decision. Within a week of the summons, we set sail to cross the sea, round the Skagerrak towards the Kattegat and then sail south for Heiða-býr. Heimdall howled as Bersi left him. He was twice the dog we had found. His leg had healed although he still limped and, like Aed, he had flesh on his bones. Mary had to tether him to stop him from following us. It meant she was distracted and we had no tears.

As we sailed down the river, with the current and a benign wind behind us, Bersi said, "I thought that Ragnar would have volunteered. He has a mail byrnie, or at least his father does."

I shook my head, "I did not expect it. He is to be a father soon. He has a wife and a new farm. The ones who come with us are all single men. They hope for glory and for treasure. You are lucky, Bersi, you have my cousin's gift. They all want what you have. Haldir wants a mail shirt too. That is the reason they volunteered. No one disappointed me."

We had to row once we reached the sea as we needed to head north and east. In many ways, it was no bad thing for we sang as we rowed. That helped the crew to keep good time and bonded them. Some knew the songs and the others had to concentrate on learning them. It stopped them thinking about their hands which were unused to rowing. The seawater that sprayed over the bow and sides of the ship did not help.

I let Gandálfr choose the song. He had a powerful voice and it carried the length of the drekar. He used the one about our last battle, Assundun.

King Edmund thought he had the chance
To end the threat of Danish blades
The English spears did advance
But we were unafraid.
We stood with spears and shields all locked
The English strode with spears held firm
To fight the Saxons who had flocked
To fight for the Wessex Wyrme.
Oathsword and Sven were brave and stout
They would stand and never rout
Oathsword and Sven were brave and stout
They would stand and never rout
The English came but the boys stood still
They used their slings with skill and speed
They hurled their stones the housecarl to kill
Then racing back they leapt the shields

The Sword of Cnut

As Alf had leapt on the Svolder's decks
The boys had hurt the English wall
It was Bersi the plan had wrecked
And the slingers all stood tall
Oathsword and Sven were brave and stout
They would stand and never rout
Oathsword and Sven were brave and stout
They would stand and never rout
The king now faced Saxon Slayer
The two warriors fought in the heart of the fight
Neither man gave nor did waver
With shields and spears all locked tight
The two men took their swords in hand
Oathsword and the English king
Did fight long into the day
Their fight was so great that the gods did sing
Warriors gave all and none did sway
Oathsword and Sven were brave and stout
They would stand and never rout
Oathsword and Sven were brave and stout
They would stand and never rout
Treachery ended the epic fight
The Mercians fled into the night
The English ran and the Danes held the field
Lord Sven had the victory sealed
Oathsword and Sven were brave and stout
They would stand and never rout
Oathsword and Sven were brave and stout
They would stand and never rout
Oathsword and Sven were brave and stout
They would stand and never rout
Oathsword and Sven were brave and stout
They would stand and never rout

By the time the new crew had learned the words we had turned to head due east and had the wind once more. The men were able to put salve on their hands and also to talk about the song. My last hearthweru had to answer many questions but I knew he enjoyed it for he was able to speak about those who had fallen. It was as though they were alive again. It was an act of remembrance. Sleeping aboard the drekar was something the younger crewmen had to become accustomed to. Folki and I stood watch on watch and the crew had three watches. Getting up

The Sword of Cnut

in the dark of night with a freshening wind was a new experience for them. The ship's boys became accustomed to trailing fishing lines astern to catch fresh fish that was eaten raw. The whole crew learned to harvest the rain from the showers we endured. That was Gandálfr's doing. He had them gather the rainwater in their waterskins. This was not Norton where water was just a few steps away.

As we turned into the Danish Sea the crew looked nothing like the youths who had boarded the ship back in the valley. Their beards and hair were rimed with salt. Their skins were reddened by the wind and the sun. Their hands were now calloused and they walked with the wide-legged stance of all sailors. More importantly, they were one crew. The weather had not been harsh but the couple of squalls and storms we had endured made them closer. They learned to work together. The Agerhøne chant was as familiar to them as any who had sailed with me from my home. I was pleased. I was especially pleased with Bersi who had, when he had not been rowing, sought to watch what Folki and I did. He would be a navigator. It was a hard skill to learn but Bersi took to it well.

Heading south to the muster we spied more sails as other ships obeyed the king's command. We had to sail carefully so that there were no collisions and that meant, sometimes, heading away from the coast to make sea room. It was as we turned slightly east one day that Bersi said, "Why is it called the Danish Sea, Father?"

I chuckled, "It is only Danes that call it so. Others call it things like the Big Sea, and the West Sea, while some still use the Roman name, Mare Suebicum. When we won the Battle of Svolder, King Sweyn claimed the sea as his. You will discover, son, that we all use different names for the same places."

When we reached the muster, the sea was filled with drekar of varying sizes. What was clear was that there would be no place on the land for us to tie the drekar. We would have to anchor. As luck would have it, or perhaps the Norns had spun, we arrived on the exact day we were supposed to.

A snekke with the royal standard flying from its mast approached each ship as they arrived. Some were asked to move for they were too close together, while most were just given instructions. So it was with us. The oathsworn who captained the snekke was known to me. I greeted him, "Glam the Fair, how goes it?"

He smiled for we had fought together in a shield wall and such things bind men.

"Sven Saxon Sword, it is good to see you. The king has been keenly awaiting your arrival." He shook his head, "I would rather stand in a

The Sword of Cnut

shield wall than be an aquatic sheepdog. Some of the captains complain as though the king could suddenly conjure a larger port. Tomorrow we sail south for the land of the Wends. It will just be a two-day sail. Have you food and water enough? I know you have had one of the longer voyages. Only Earl Godwin has had a longer one."

That told me the Earl of Wessex had been summoned. A Saxon was fighting for the Danes against the Wends. The world had changed.

"We can manage for two days. Is the muster complete?"

"There are one or two tardy folk but by and large it is." He waved, "I must go for I can see a couple of drekar trying to edge their way to the shore." He shook his head, "There is nowhere left for them to land."

Knowing what was intended for us, I gathered the crew around the mainmast. "You have all done well for I know that this was new for most of you. Tomorrow we will be under the eye of the king. We will have to sail better than I have a right to expect. With such a huge fleet everyone must be alert. We cannot afford any collisions. For today, prepare your weapons. Within three days we shall land in the Land of the Wends and we shall have to fight."

Aed asked, "Lord Sven, why do we fight the Wends?"

Haldir ruffled Aed's hair, "Because the king commands it."

"Aye he does, but I can guess the reason. He wishes for a peaceful border with his neighbours and this is the best way to do so. He has already subdued rebels. Part of Norway and Sweden are his. With the Wends no longer a threat he can come to England."

I said no more for I had been privy to the politics of King Cnut when I had helped him to conquer the kingdom. I knew what he had done to gain control of England. King Æthelred had been a bad king. England, thanks to King Alfred, had been a rich country but he had totally mismanaged the treasury. Part of that was due to the Danegeld he had paid to keep his land safe, but more had been wasted by a king who was truly badly advised. England would be rich again but to make it so the king needed his hands on the steering board. He would guide the kingdom to a prosperous future. To do so he needed Denmark at peace.

I set the example for the others by going to my chest and taking out the sack that held my byrnie. Sea water corroded metal and the byrnie was in a hessian sack filled with sand. This was the first time Bersi had needed his princely gift and he copied every move. As he emulated me and took out his mail shirt, he saw the sand fall to the deck, "I am sorry, Father. I will clean it up."

I shook my head, "The sand will not harm the drekar. It will help to keep it clean and it will, most certainly, make the deck less slippery."

The Sword of Cnut

To make the point I shook the shirt to empty all the sand from it. The feet of the crew would spread it around. I spread the byrnie over my chest as I examined it for damage. I knew that there would be none for Haraldr had looked it over before I had boarded. It was better to check now and discover the lost link that might prove disastrous. Once I was satisfied, I took out my whetstone and began to put an edge on Norse Splitter, Saxon Slayer and, of course, Oathsword. I was aware of the younger crewmen looking at the magical blade. I knew the power of the sword. It intrigued all. Everyone knew the story: the Dragon Sword was made on the orders of King Guthrum as a gift for the Saxon king. Dragon Swords were rare and the weapon I used had been coveted by King Sweyn. When all were sharp and my helmet checked, I replaced the byrnie and helmet in the chest. I would don them once the landing beach was in sight. Some of the other ships would have a whole crew that would need to don a mail shirt. My crew did not have that luxury.

The king sailed in a fifty-oar ship, *'Niord'*. Its name told me that it was an old ship. It was the name of a god of the sea. It did not do to change the name of a ship, it was bad luck and even Christians knew that. All the ships built since King Sweyn's conversion had Christian names. I had heard that the king was having a new ship built, even bigger than *'Niord'*. *'Trinity'* would be eighty paces long with, perhaps, seventy oarsmen and have a Christian name. King Cnut was being practical. *'Niord'* was bigger than any other ship in the fleet and she would be double or even triple-oared. They would be the king's oathsworn and his family and their oathsworn. Cnut had half-brothers, bastards, and the king was not a fool. He would have his family with him where they could fight for him and not cause mischief in his absence. What I did not see, as we slowly headed south, were the ships of my son and Sven Skull Taker. It was a waste of time to speculate and in my heart, I knew that nothing untoward had happened to them. Glam the Fair would have told me.

The voyage south was even harder than I had expected. The last time I had sailed with a fleet of this size had been at the battle of Svolder and there I had not had to steer. Here Folki and I needed eyes in the back of our heads as some captains tried to get closer to the king or to show their prowess as sailors by trying to overtake others. When two drekar in the middle became entangled then I saw the royal snekke, like a sheepdog, race to the two stricken vessels. I knew that the captains would not be offered solace but given sharp reprimands. It took two days to sail south and reach the land of the Wends.

It was with some relief that we saw *'Niord'* lower her sail and use her oars to edge towards the empty beach.

The Sword of Cnut

"Folki, take over. Those with mail don it."

The crew who only wore leather had already donned their protection and I saw each of them take their arming cap and helmet to put them on their heads as the sail was lowered. Soon they would be at the oars. The ones with mail then began the process of dressing. A padded undershirt was drawn over our kyrtles and then we helped each other to pull on the mail shirt. I had learned to do a little jiggle that made it sit more easily on my shoulders. I fastened my sword belt and scabbard around my waist and slipped Norse Splitter into my boot. My arming cap had been made by Mary. She was clearly no volva but I liked to think that the love she had put into the headgear would act as a sort of spell and afford me protection. When I donned my helmet I felt like a warrior. Our shields would remain on the side of the ship until we disembarked. Leaving Gandálfr to help Bersi, I went to the steering board. The crew were at their oars. There was no need for a chant. We were just moving with the tide towards the beach. Folki knew his business and I watched the other ships as my helmsman took us towards an empty patch of sand. Others tried to get close to the king. It was foolish and they risked his wrath by a collision.

"Pull together." We had open water and as we sped over the sea I knew we would be one of the first to land. "Folki, I leave the securing of the ship to you and the boys."

"All will be safe, Lord Sven."

I unfastened my shield and hefted it around my back before picking up my spear. Bersi and Gandálfr copied me. We would be the first three in the water and then ashore. That was as it should be. A leader, his son and his oathsworn should be the ones who took the risks. I went to the prow and climbed onto the gunwale, holding on to the forestay as I did so. It was not bravado. I could see the water and direct Folki in case he was in danger of steering us onto a rock. The beach was shingle and Folki kept a good line across the surf.

I shouted, "Raise oars." The momentum of the drekar would take us ashore. Gandálfr was on the larboard side and would jump down as soon as I did. Timing was all. It would not do for Sven Saxon Sword to fall flat on his face. It would be a bad omen. I landed well although the water splashed over the top of my boots. I hurried up the shingle to the sand and peered around. There was no immediate danger but I saw, in the distance, a horseman studying us. The Wends would know we were here. Gandálfr and Bersi joined me and the rest of my men soon followed. We had left the banner on the ship but Haraldrsson had his horn. The banner, to be carried by Bersi, would be saved for when we had the battle to fight.

The Sword of Cnut

Other drekar slipped alongside us and soon there were more than two hundred men gathered close to me. I recognised Earl Godwin and his Saxons. They tended to favour the two-handed war axe but enough of them had a spear so that we could make a shield wall if we were attacked. The earl came over to me, "The first to land, Seven Saxon Sword. A great honour."

I pointed to the drekar jostling to land next to the king's ship, "It was not for honour, my lord, but to avoid an accident." I pointed to the rider who was heading south, "The Wends will know we are here."

He nodded, "I have not been on a Danish raid before."

"This is not a raid, my lord, we go to war. We will make a fortified camp and the king will send out scouts. It will not be us for we do not know this land. When the king knows where the enemy is to be found we will march, meet them and defeat them."

"You sound confident. Have you fought them before?"

I shook my head, "No, but they are neither Norse nor Saxons. We know how to fight. Your King Edmund Ironside and Ulfcytel Snillingr were the only men who ever gave us a difficult battle. Both fought like Vikings. The Wends are a disorganised people. It will be a hard battle but we shall win. Perhaps they adorn their bodies with gold and silver and we shall profit from it." I saw him taking in my words and I boldly questioned his motives, "And you, my lord, why are you here?"

"I was summoned as were you."

"But you are English, and a Saxon noble. I am Danish and hold my land because of King Cnut."

I could tell that I had caught him off guard. He finally shrugged, "We had little honour or success when we fought for King Æthelred. I am a warrior and I would like to win for once. Besides, this is a crusade against the pagan Wends. We serve the Holy Roman Emperor and the Pope in this war."

I smiled, "An honest answer and I think that you will achieve victory, Earl Godwin."

The Sword of Cnut
Chapter 8

The battle on the beach

We sourced wood and made a palisade. The earl did not dispute my orders because it was known that I was close to the king. By the time it drew on to dark, we had a fire going and hot food was being prepared. We had been at sea and eaten cold rations for long enough. It was Glam the Fair who fetched us to the council of war. As we walked up the beach I asked, "My son and Jarl Skull Taker, are they here?"

He shook his head, "They did great service fighting the rebels and the king decided that they could rest. It is why he summoned men from his new kingdom. He thought that Danes should bring rebel Danes to heel, but these pagans need men from both kingdoms."

I smiled. It was a political answer. Glam was aware of Earl Godwin and his motives for his involvement. If Earl Godwin thought to gain power from his participation, he would have to work for it and his men would need to shed blood.

There was a tent erected and inside were senior leaders. I knew that I would be the most junior. It was my sword that granted me entry. King Sweyn had wanted the sword and his son knew the power it brought to a battle. He nodded at me as I entered and then returned to his consultation with the bishop next to him. Some warriors alongside whom I had fought before joined us. I introduced Earl Godwin and smiled at the suspicious looks my comrades gave him. I knew why the king had done what he had but they did not.

When all had arrived, the king stood. "We are here with God's blessing. Our purpose is holy and we come to make this land Christian." What was ironic was that most of the warriors standing before the king were pagans wearing a Christian cloak. "Lübeck is their capital and my spies have told me that they now have a castle there as well as a wall. I do not intend to bleed on their walls. We will seek, instead, their pagan temples and destroy them. That way they will have to come to fight us."

Most of the leaders cheered. Attacking temples meant relics and that, in turn, meant gold and silver. If we could turn a profit at the expense of our enemies then so much the better.

"My scouts report a warband heading towards us," he smiled, "it will save us a march and when they are destroyed, we shall have a free hand. Rise early and bring your men here. Let the Wends see my sacred

The Sword of Cnut

banner and my priests for it will draw them on and we shall win for we will fight for God and for Denmark."

Everyone cheered and, as the king sat, the council was over. As I prepared to leave Glam grabbed my arm, "The king would speak with you." He saw Earl Godwin turn and said, with a smile, to me, "I believe it has to do with your son and foster father."

I hated secrecy.

The tent flap closed and the bishops left us. The king glanced up and said, "Wait without, Glam, and see that we are not disturbed." He waved me to a seat. "I know that you are unhappy about leaving Norton but I need you here. Thanks to your wife, you are as English as any lord but unlike many, I know that I can trust you. Thorkell is not here, as you can see. He has proved to be an uncertain ally. Earl Godwin is. I suspect he is here to ingratiate himself in my good favours. That I do not mind and, indeed, understand. I intend for the English to fight together and you, Sven Saxon Sword, will be my ears in the English camp."

"Yes, my liege."

He smiled, "The Earl of Northumbria says you have done well and you are a rock. That is good. Your son and foster father also did well. That they profited from the war pleased me. This will not be a long war, Sven. I intend to return to my new kingdom just as soon as I can. Jarl Ulf, who is married to my sister Estrid, did well in the war and I have left him as regent in my absence. This new war should show his mettle." He nodded towards my sword. "Oathsword will be needed here. It is a symbol of the union of Denmark and England and it is seen as Christian. It may not be Tyr's sword or the sword in the Branstock, but it is now the most powerful sword in Christendom and I will use it."

I now understood why I had been summoned. I served two purposes. I was here to watch Earl Godwin and to bring my sword as the king's ally. That I was still being used did not upset me too much. So long as Cnut was king and treated me with such favour then my family in both England and Denmark would reap the rewards and my people would prosper. When I reached our camp I said nothing to anyone about my task. It concerned no one else and my expression gave nothing away.

"We may well fight on the morrow. I will speak with Folki and Erik Prow Jumper and then enjoy this stew that you have cooked for me."

I wanted Folki, Erik and the ship's boys to know that we might be leaving after we had engaged the enemy, "I know that the king will leave men to guard his ships but you may have to sail my drekar to safety. Can you do this?"

The Sword of Cnut

Folki nodded, "The boys responded well on the way east. All will be well. What we may have a problem with is food, lord. There are too many ships here for us to rely on the shellfish."

"I will ensure that we are well supplied."

As I headed back to the camp, I realised I had not even thought of that.

There was a buzz about my camp and it was clear that the young warriors were keen to be blooded. Some would be afraid, Siggi and I had been terrified, but that would not stop them from doing their best. It was in their blood. I sat with what I considered my inner circle, Bersi, Haldir, Aed, Haraldrsson and, of course, Gandálfr. Only Gandálfr was a known factor. He had stood at my side many times in a shield wall. I had fought with Bersi and Haraldrsson behind me but that was not the same as a battle such as this one.

King Cnut had no intention of leaving the safety of his fleet, not to mention the spiked palisade we had built, and so we waited in the dunes just two hundred paces from the beach. The elevation of the dunes meant our archers could loose their arrows from behind our rear rank of spearmen at any advancing soldiers. The slingers would have to be nimble for they were before our shields. The king had his oathsworn with him guarding the bishops and priests he had brought. Young Danish nobles also protected the dual king and his holy men. The Danish segment of his army was to his right and we, the English wing, were to the left. I was impressed by the men of Wessex for almost all of them were mailed. The rest of our contingent had a variety of armour. We waited for the arrival of the enemy.

The priests came down the line to hear confession and to bless our weapons. We knelt as they passed and accepted the blessing, it could not hurt, but many did not believe that a god who advocated no killing would add anything to our weapons. Bersi had my banner, now brought from the ship, and the horn hung from Haraldrsson's neck. We had hung the banner from a spear. Although my son had no shield, he would not be defenceless. Aed was not with the slingers. His skills were still inadequate in that area but we had given him a short sword and he would be Bersi's protector. We had formed up in three lines and that allowed my front rank to be stronger than it might otherwise. We waited.

When the Wends came it was like a barbarian horde. We heard their chants and horns in the distance and knew that they were coming. The priests hurriedly finished their absolution and shields were prepared. The shadow that was our enemy appeared on the horizon. They moved rapidly and from the sound they had horses. It was strange to be

The Sword of Cnut

fighting amongst largely English voices. This would be my first battle fighting alongside my new countrymen. Their gleaming mail and helmets were reassuring. The men of Wessex had interspersed their spears with some Danish axes. If the enemy charged with horses then they would be in for a rude shock. Whilst waiting for the approach I studied the ground before us. The stakes had been driven into the soil that was more sand than earth. It would slow rather than stop. The ground itself would stop them. The marram grass and sand were deadly to walk over. It would be interesting to see their formation.

I could hear the priests and bishops as they sang holy songs. I would rather have had a chant.

We spoke as we waited, "One thing is sure, Gandálfr, those holy men will be a target for the pagans."

He nodded and Bersi asked, "Why?"

"When we fought in England the priests were safe. Both armies were Christian. These are pagans. They fought Charlemagne when he tried to convert them and they will try to get at the priests."

Gandálfr said, "Aye, the centre will bear the brunt of the fighting. I wonder if that is why he has nobles close to him."

Bersi asked, "Because they are good warriors?"

He shook his head, "No, because if they die then there is less of a threat to the king."

My cynical hearthweru was right. Glam and the king's bodyguard were good warriors but the nobles would be hewn like wheat.

The Wendish line drew closer. I could not make out the men. The horsemen rode ponies and looked to be without armour. They seemed to have a mixture of thrusting and throwing spears. The rest of their army was afoot and consisted of both mailed warriors and some who appeared to be bare-chested with neither helmet nor protection. The weapons they brandished also showed a lack of uniformity. There were spears but they were of varied lengths. The shields ranged from round ones as big as ours to bucklers that protected their hands. I even saw a couple of old rectangular Roman ones. Some swords were short ones, such as the Romans had used while others had two-handed ones and there were a few that had the curved end; they were like the falchions I had once seen. Like some Norsemen, I saw tattoos on the enemy warriors. What was consistent was the noise. Every one of them seemed to be screaming or shouting. I felt my men move a little. They were afraid.

"Gandálfr, they need a song. Let us start the Agerhøne chant."

We are the bird you cannot find

The Sword of Cnut

With feathers grey and black behind
Seek us if you can my friend
Our clan will beat you in the end.
Where is the bird? In the snake.
The serpent comes your gold to take.
We are the bird you cannot find
With feathers grey and black behind
Seek us if you can my friend
Our clan will beat you in the end.
Where is the bird? In the snake.
The serpent comes your gold to take.

I felt my men straighten by the time we had sung the chant three times. The enemy had drawn closer but my men had taken heart from the familiar words. The enemy stopped and we ceased to sing. An unearthly silence fell over the battlefield. I saw a mailed rider on a larger horse than that ridden by the majority of the cavalry begin to ride along the line. He had a long sword and he touched the spears and swords of the men as he passed. They were too far away to hear but I guessed that he was speaking to them and invoking courageous deeds. It was a clever move as it allowed their horses to rest and for men to steel themselves ready for the attack. Their numbers were hard to estimate but they seemed to outnumber us. Their leader returned to the front and I saw that he led fifty or so men similarly dressed. He raised his sword and there was a massed blast from what seemed to be a hundred horns and then the attack began. I heard a strange wailing that seemed to fill the air. I quickly realised what it was. Some of the horsemen carried what looked like dragons on lances and the wind rushing through them made the noise. I had heard of them but never seen them.

I shouted, "It is air which you hear, that is all. Do not fear the noise. Lock your shields and ground your spears. Rear ranks level your spears."

I had already planted the butt of Saxon Slayer in the ground and the head was angled towards the attackers. Spears appeared over both my shoulders as the men in the second and third ranks obeyed my commands.

The men on foot, especially the bare-chested ones, were keeping pace with the horsemen. To me, it looked a strange way to fight but I could see that it would be effective. They would lose men in the initial attack but our whole line would be hit simultaneously. They would quickly find any weaknesses and exploit them with their superior numbers.

The Sword of Cnut

Our slingers sent their stones as soon as the enemy was in range. Men were hurt and some fell but the horn was soon sounded to order them to fall back and they had not dented the enemy's attack. Men in our front ranks angled their shields to enable the slinger to use them as a ramp and leap over our lines and land in the soft dunes. There they would join the archers and send stones and arrows over our heads.

"Brace!"

The command was not needed for Gandálfr and Haldir. They had fought in a shield wall but the younger warriors needed the reassurance of a command. It gave the illusion that there was some order to war. There was not. Soon it would be bloody hand to hand where luck played as big a part as skill.

I saw that the horsemen were in three groups. The ones led by the leader were heading for King Cnut while the two lighter-armed horsemen were heading for our wings. We had the fearsome sight of wild warriors intent on butchering us. The stakes were not much of a barrier but they did break up the line and that was vital. The sand and marram also made some men fall and the result was that the first men who reached us came piecemeal. The tattooed warrior wielding the two-handed sword swung at me as he clambered up the dune. I was ready and I rammed Saxon Slayer into his naked chest. I had the luxury of aiming for his heart and he fell, like a stone to roll down and impede the progress of those following. The rest of my men had equal success. In that first exchange, four Wends fell dead while we lost none. The stakes were now torn down and the other Wendish warriors were able to form a more continuous line. This time some had shields and there were even two men with what looked like fish scale armour. I saw ancient Roman helmets on the heads of some men.

I shouted as the wall of men rose up from the sand, "Thrust!"

Our spears moved as one and struck faces and chests. The enemy spears and swords clattered onto our bigger shields. The wall of wood flecked with metal gave us the protection that their weaker shields did not. I pulled back and thrust again and again. I could no longer pick out my actual target and sometimes Saxon Slayer screeched along metal or clattered against wood but the Wends had to climb over dead bodies and through treacherous sand. We merely had to stand with the reassuring presence of shields in our backs.

When the first of our men fell it came as a shock but Gandálfr, who had been next to Thorgaut, the dead man, shouted, "Gunnar, step forward."

Our slingers and archers were able to choose their targets. The bare-chested men were the easy ones to hit. Their arrows did not always slay

The Sword of Cnut

them. I saw one man lumbering at Bersi with two arrows sticking from his shoulder and arm. When the stone hit his eye, I thought he must die but he kept coming. As much as I wanted to aid my son I was duelling with a mailed man, and I could do nothing. When the half-naked giant fell, killed by a clever thrust from Bersi's sword, I felt relief. My spear was becoming less effective as the enemy closed with us and so I rammed it into the foot of the mailed man before me. He screamed in pain and that gave me the chance to draw my sword.

"Oathsword!" I could not help but call out its name as I drew it and when my men echoed it, I knew I had put heart into them. I ripped it across the throat of the mailed man whose foot I had speared and almost severed his head. Oathsword was sharp. I lifted it and swung it down at the helmeted head of the next man. He wore an ancient Roman one and Oathsword sliced through the decayed metal as though it was cloth. His brains spattered the man next to him who turned in shock. Bersi's sword ended both his shock and his life.

We had been fighting for almost an hour. The ground before us was now littered with the enemy dead. I had no idea how the battle was going, for all that I could see was the killing ground before me. I could hear the clash of arms to my left and right. The priests still sang. I suppose they had little else to do. The dead before Gandálfr and I were growing, and men had to go to the sides to fill our ranks. I think that we had slain the more courageous Wends and the ones who came at us chose not to attack the mailed men who seemed to slay all in their path. They went instead for the ones to our side. I thought about initiating an attack for there was a gap before us, but I knew that would be a mistake. I would be inviting disaster. Gandálfr, Haldir and I had just four more men to slay, brave men who ran over the dead bodies and leapt in the air to try, as Alf had done at Svolder, to break our shield wall. Oathsword swept imperiously over my head gutting one half-naked man and taking the leg from a second. It coincided with the enemy horns sounding the retreat. The enemy was defeated. We could not follow but every man cheered and we descended into the battleground to end the lives of the wounded and to take their treasure.

While my men claimed what was theirs, I walked my line. Thorgaut and the man who had stepped into his place, Gunnar, were the only dead but that was still two dead too many. There were two families who had lost a son.

Bersi had planted my banner and Haraldrsson brought us a skin of ale, "A great victory, Lord Sven."

I nodded and after drinking and wiping my mouth said, "But I would they were alive."

The Sword of Cnut

"They died well, lord, and I know that they were eager to prove themselves in battle."

"Aye, but with them died the hopes of their families and the clan. Think of the children they might have sired." He did not know what to say. "Go and find treasure."

"But I did nothing."

"You stood with Bersi and my banner flying giving hope to all. Go, I need no treasure and I slew many." My son and the blower of my horn went amongst the dead.

Haldir was already stripping the mail from the man he had slain towards the end of the battle. It was old and a little rusty but to a warrior like Haldir, it was like gold. I took off my helmet and put my arming cap inside. The air felt cool with a breeze from the sea. I retrieved Saxon Slayer and examined it to see if it was damaged. It was not. Our men were searching the bodies and by the end, I knew that there would just be naked corpses left.

"Will we burn or bury them?"

I turned and saw Earl Godwin next to me. "With the wind from the sea, we will probably burn them. The smell will drift inland and tell the people that they lost. Did you lose many men?"

He shook his head. "Less than six. They were brave but reckless. Our shield wall, like yours, held." We looked up the beach to where we could see the priests giving the last rites to those who had fallen defending them and the king. "I think that the king has suffered more than most."

I shook my head, "They were young nobles who bore the brunt of the fighting. I can see that most of his bodyguards live."

"You would know. Did you fight in his bodyguard?"

I shook my head, "With them but not in them. They wanted Oathsword to fight alongside them."

"A mythical weapon. I envy you and yet I do not. I should like to hold it and wield it but I know that it would draw enemies like bees to flowers."

"I was just lucky that the Wends had not heard of it. The pagans wanted to get at the king and that made our task easier."

It was noon when Tofti came down the beach, "Sven, Earl Godwin, the king would like to speak with you." The king's bodyguard hurried back to the king.

Gandálfr had returned and I said, "Gandálfr, take charge. Have the bodies prepared for burial. We will honour them when I return."

The Sword of Cnut

He nodded, "I have your share of the treasure. They wore little mail but they had silver in their ears and around their necks. We have five torcs."

"I will leave you to divide it up."

As we headed up the beach Earl Godwin said, "You do not take the larger share?"

I shook my head, "It is not my way. Besides, I find that men fight harder if they know that they will each have an equal share."

"Interesting."

When we reached the king, I saw that it had been the place where the fiercest fighting had taken place. More than twenty-five Danish bodies lay covered with cloaks. Glam said, "We lost two bodyguards. They are a grievous loss."

I saw the huge pile of Wendish dead, "But they paid a heavier price."

I saw the captain of the king's bodyguard, Siward, moving among the wounded and giving them a warrior's death. The king had fought for his mail was blood-spattered and I saw the cut marks on his shield. In comparison, my shield was almost pristine and the white sword had no damage. "Their king escaped." King Cnut looked disappointed.

Earl Godwin said, "Was that their king? The warrior on the horse?"

"I believe so but the Wends are a confederation. They have many kings. No matter. We have broken their spirit for we slew far more of their men than we lost. I have a task for the men of England. I want you, Earl Godwin, to head to the south and west. Raid their land, destroy their temples, burn their villages and take their food. You have almost five hundred men and that should suffice. I will take my warband and head west while the rest head north and drive those men who remain towards Denmark, Ulf Jarl waits in the borderlands to give them a warm welcome if they try to cross the border and make mischief in Denmark."

It was clear to me that we had the harder task as we would be heading away from Denmark and the fleet. I wondered if he was culling us as he had the nobles.

"And the fleet?"

"Do not worry about your ships, Sven Saxon Sword, I will leave two hundred men to guard them. You have, Earl Godwin, a month to take as much treasure as you can. When you return, I shall be here and you shall have served your new king."

As we headed back to our men I spoke with the earl, "So, you will be a raider. For a short time, you will become a Viking."

He laughed, "And having suffered for many years at the hands of the best, it will be good to see how it feels."

The Sword of Cnut

My men were happy to be raiders but I am not sure if some of the men, the ones who came from Mercia, felt the same. Their earl had not come with them and the warrior who led them, Leofwine, did not seem committed. It did not matter for the earl's men, the men of Jorvik and my men, made up four hundred of our warband. Earl Godwin and I ate together. We were clearly the leaders and we would plan the strategy. Neither of us knew the land but we worked out that any roads would lead to the best places to raid. We would simply head southwest. The earl had men who were skilled at scouting. I had brought new men. I did not know, yet, if they had the skills. I was more than happy to let his men lead. The earl sent his men to issue his orders. Earl Godwin was clearly a man who liked to give orders.

When he had gone I gathered my men and we carried the bodies of the two dead warriors. Both had crosses but I knew that their hammers were a more significant sign of their faith. We dug them graves that were deep in the soft sand. They were laid out as carefully as any king or prince. We placed, in the graves, their share of the treasure. We put their hands about their swords. They would have coins to spend in Valhalla and a sword to show their skill. Lastly, we placed their shields over their faces and their cloaks over their bodies, then covered the bodies with sand. Wind would bring more sand or perhaps there would be a deluge from the sea. Either way, none would rob our comrades.

"Odin, welcome these two warriors to Valhalla. They were true to their oath and they died well with their swords in their hands."

The followers of White Christ had many words to say at a funeral. We kept it simple. We did not need to ask Odin to take them. They had earned that right by the manner of their death. They had not needed to ask for absolution for what priests might deem a sin. They had lived their lives as we all had, by the code of a warrior. That would be enough for Odin. We placed no marker on their graves. This was neither Denmark nor England. No one would visit them but we knew where they lay and before we left the land of the Wends we would say farewell once more.

The Sword of Cnut

Chapter 9

The English Raiders

The battle had not yielded much mail. Haldir gained a byrnie, while Haraldrsson took the fish plate armour. It was old but his father would rework it when we were back in Norton. What we did gain were weapons. Many of them were most unusual in design, reflecting their origins. However, it was the treasure that made the men sing the song of Agerhøne as we marched west. The torcs had been cut up and the coins evenly distributed. We had a set of scales with us and we carefully weighed everything out so that no one gained more than another. It paid to be fair. It was Gandálfr who supervised the division. Not only was he fair but he also intimidated all the young men with his glowering glares. None would argue with him. Aed also gained a helmet. A Wendish youth, obviously the son of a noble from his helmet and sword. had died. He had not been slain by a warrior but by a stray arrow from some archer. The helmet, baldric and sword were too small for even a young warrior and Aed wore them proudly. When we marched to war, beneath the sword cross banner, we looked like warriors. He would soon outgrow the helmet but that did not matter.

Earl Godwin's scouts were good and towards the evening of the second day, they reported the finding of a small town ahead. We camped three miles from where the scouts had reported it and the earl and I planned our attack. "My scouts said that there was a palisade but it was only two or three paces high."

"Then we will use our shields to boost men over the walls. If we make a dawn attack they will be sleepy and our slingers and archers can take care of their sentries."

The earl approved and commented, as he ate, that he had heard of such Viking attacks in the past and it would be interesting to take part in one.

We left our camp in the middle of the night. Had we been in a Christian country then we would have heard the churches sounding Lauds. Here all was silent. We needed time to get there for we had to move silently. The last thing we needed was a garrison who were alert to danger and had manned the walls. The town was small but there could be up to two hundred men inside its walls. Both the earl and I wanted as few casualties as possible. We demonstrated to the Saxons the technique we would employ, and the town was soon surrounded by

The Sword of Cnut

men who all knew the plan and what they had to do. In deference to our skills, the men of Jorvik and my men were given the most difficult task, the gatehouse.

Gandálfr, Haldir, Bersi and I would be the first ones over. We had mail and good shields. I knew my wife would not approve of my putting our son in such danger but the present from Alf had left me with no choice. I could not allow a warrior without mail to be lifted up to the walls. We wore our shields on our backs and the men who lifted us would use one of their shields. We needed no spears for this would be sword work. Once the three of us and the six Jorvik men had secured the gate we would open it to allow the rest of our men through. Haraldrsson would lead them. While every other wall would be attacked as well as the secondary gates, our gate was the most important as it would be the best guarded and if those sentries were killed, then the rest would have a much easier task.

To coordinate the attacks, Earl Godwin used a young warrior who would run around the waiting men. As soon as he passed us we were to count to one hundred and then attack. It was a crude method but it would be silent and even if all the attacks did not take place at precisely the same time, the few moments' difference would not hurt.

After he passed us, we hurried to the ditch and I began to count. Our archers and slingers stood ready to send missiles at any face that appeared, but we were lucky. There were none to be seen. We negotiated the stakes at the bottom of the ditch and then clambered up the sides which were too overgrown to be an obstacle. The eight warriors who would help us had no mail and they climbed up first before pulling us up. Once at the side of the wall close to the gatehouse, Grettir and Frithiof held the shield as low as they could, I stepped onto it and nodded when I was balanced. With Oathsword safely in my scabbard, I had both hands free. They lifted me up and, when I reached the palisade, I grabbed it and pulled myself up. They saw me grab the top and gave one last push. It meant that I was able to slip my leg over the top and stand on the fighting platform. I had drawn my sword even before my foot touched the wood and it was then that there was a cry from the far side of the town. Our attack was no longer a secret. I was the first on the walkway and I ran towards the tower. As I did a face appeared at the top. An arrow from one of our watching archers slew him before he could cry out but then the door to the tower opened and a Wendish warrior stepped out. He saw my shadow, I guess, and began to draw his sword. It was too late for that as I rammed Oathsword into him and hurled his body to the ground below. I entered the tower where I saw guards, there looked to be three of them. I went on the offensive

The Sword of Cnut

immediately. I drew Norse Splitter as I swung my sword in an arc. My dagger darted out to penetrate the eye of a man to my left and it was then that one of the Wends stabbed at me with a sword. He struck mail. My sword hit flesh. The last man died when Gandálfr and Haldir entered.

Slipping my dagger back into my boot, I pointed to the ladder that led to the tower, "Gandálfr, clear the tower. Haldir," Bersi appeared, "and Bersi, follow me."

Descending the ladder was the most dangerous part of the whole thing but, thanks to the shield across my back, as I reached the bottom and a sword was swung at me, it hit the boss and not my byrnie. I whipped around slashing with Oathsword as I did so. My blade met flesh and bone. The night sentries wore no mail.

Stepping through the door at the base of the tower we were at the gate, and it was unguarded. The gatekeepers must have been the men I had slain. "Haldir and Bersi, open the gate." I swung my shield around and guarded the two of them as they lifted the heavy bar. It was as it crashed to the ground that defenders appeared. Four of them ran at me.

"Oathsword!" I used the word both as an alarm and a rallying cry. I was rewarded by a cheer as my men poured in and my son and Haldir joined me. The four warriors who attacked us died quickly. They were not warriors and we were.

We swept through the town so quickly that we lost not a man from Norton. Having buried two on the beach already that was a good thing. I met Earl Godwin in the centre of the town. They had an open square and the last of their warriors had made their final stand there. The sun was rising in the east, and we took that as a good sign. Earl Godwin thanked his Christian god, and we thanked Odin.

Earl Godwin was in a good mood, "We will do as you did, Seven Saxon Sword. I will not take the greater share, but we shall share equally."

"You command, my lord, and I am happy with any decision that you make."

The temple produced the greatest finds. There were gifts and offerings on what passed for a pagan altar. There was gold, jewels and, best of all, large quantities of silver that ensured that every one of us would be richer. Two more of my men, Grettir and Frithiof, gained mail shirts from the dead that we slew in the square. They were not as good as ours. For some reason, the Wends still clung to the fishplate mail. While it was effective enough it broke too easily and once one plate was loosened the rest soon followed. We found the buried hordes kept by the villagers. These were pagans and deserved no charity. We took

The Sword of Cnut

everything. The women and children were sent on their way out of the town. I knew that some raiders would have taken them as slaves but there was no point as, in our case, we did not have the room on the drekar and for another, we had enough slaves. Mary ensured that the ones we had were well-treated and would not run. More would merely create an imbalance. The greatest find was food. They had full granaries and they had many animals which meant that we were fed well. We shared that out too and I sent back two men, who had been slightly wounded in the fighting, with a cow we had taken. They would see the healers left with the fleet and then rejoin us.

We destroyed their temple while our scouts sought our next target. When they returned, the next day, it was with the news that there was another town just twenty miles away and this time there was neither wall nor ditch. The earl did not think it was as rich as the one we had taken but we were under orders. We had to destroy towns and temples. We left at dawn as the earl and I had decided to attack as soon as we arrived. If we scouted, they might make a defence. We moved in five warbands, to surround the town. It did not guarantee that none would escape but there would be so few that it would not cause a problem.

We raced from the cover of trees, hedgerows and fields to cover the last one hundred paces. It was frighteningly easy. Their men were slaughtered and within less than half an hour the town was ours. The temple was burned, and the women and children were set free. It was not charity. It had not been charity the first time. The women and children would spread the word of the ruthless band of raiders and that fear would help us. In addition, whichever town or village took them in would have to feed them and that meant their populace would have less food and be weaker. These ideas came from me and the men of Jorvik. They were unknown by the Saxons.

The hams and cheese we took would last a long time and being shared equally meant we could raid for longer. It was then that the local Wends decided to do something about the nuisance of the raiders. Our scouts reported an army coming to bring us to battle. Foolishly the Wends did not have as many scouts as we did, and our scouts slew theirs. Having taken horses in both towns we were now more mobile.

They reported to the earl and to me. "They are camped ten miles from here to the east, my lord. They are in a town that has no high wall but there is a gate and a ditch. They are camped outside the town. We counted fifty of their horsemen and three hundred men on foot. There are, perhaps, more than a hundred townsfolk."

The earl turned to me, "They will outnumber us."

The Sword of Cnut

"Discount their horsemen. They will be the same ones who tried to outflank us in the first battle. Their horses are too small, and their weapons cannot penetrate armour. The townsfolk? Have you seen any in their towns yet who can defeat us?" He shook his head. "We defeat the men on foot and we win."

I saw his eyes light up, "And if we attack at night then we can almost guarantee victory."

"A night battle can be confusing." I did not want the English lord to think that this would be easy.

"Not if we use two wings, your Danes from the north and my men of Wessex from the south. I will use Mercia as a reserve to attack in the west when they are committed."

Neither of us put much faith in the Mercians. The surprise that had been spoiled in the first raid had been caused by a careless Mercian. I wondered if Eadric Streona was more typical of Mercians than I had been led to believe. We knew that this would be a harder attack to coordinate, and we spent some time calculating how long it would take us to get into position. We both decided to use silent killers to slay their sentries and then fall upon their camp. The Mercians would attack when the horns sounded. When the earl clasped my arm in the warrior's grip, I knew that we two would do as we had said. We were risking all but if we succeeded then there would be no enemies for us to worry about and we would be able to do as the king had ordered and raid.

We moved more confidently now. The men with the new mail had been warned of the increased risk of noise and they heeded the advice we gave. I led with Gandálfr at my side and Bersi, Haldir and Haraldrsson ahead of a column of twos. We moved quickly along the track, and I hoped we would have the time to deploy into a shield wall when we reached the camp. The scouts had told us that the enemy camp was on the west side of the town. As we were approaching from the west our men should arrive at the same time. It would be the deployment that would be different. We smelled both the town and the camp before we heard the buzz of noise from the camp. It was late but the Wendish warriors were expecting a fight and, as with our men, that meant some men sat up later than they should to talk. The glow of their fires, even though they were dying, was also a marker. The walls of the town would have been a threat but the camp itself eliminated that threat. The townsfolk would not bother with a watch having a warband outside their walls. We heard the neigh of horses ahead. I had planned for the eventuality and I waved to Grettir and Frithiof and four slingers. They slipped off into the night. My two young warriors would slay the horse

The Sword of Cnut

guards and the slingers would remain there to calm the horses. I did not want alarmed horses to warn the camp.

The path through the woods ended just forty paces from the camp and I saw that the three sentries were not close to the woods, which is where I would have placed them, but just ten paces from the camp. As we formed lines I signalled to the archers with us to target the sentries. They would not loose until I waved my sword. Even the men of Jorvik heeded my commands. I was Sven Saxon Sword and I wielded Oathsword. This time we would use a single line. We needed as many men as we could to wreak havoc as quickly as possible. My young warriors would be at the fore of this fight. With my shield before me and Saxon Slayer in my hand, I pointed and ten bows sent their arrows. Even as the sentries died, I waved my spear and we ran.

Some of those talking close to the fires had either heard the flight of arrows or seen the men fall. They shouted the alarm at exactly the same time as a shout went up from the south. The confusion was clear. Those who had raised the alarm close to us looked to the south. There was hesitation and in that hesitation lay death. We entered the camp, filled with men sleeping beneath cloaks and, as the men rose from their sleep, we slew them. The ones who had been awake grabbed weapons but we were upon them.

"Now, Haraldrsson." My young horn bearer sounded three blasts on his horn and they were echoed a heartbeat later from the south. If the Mercians did as they had been ordered then all would be well.

My shield blocked the ineffectual odd blow that was struck and my right hand thrust and stabbed with my spear. This was not war, it was slaughter. My consolation, as I killed yet another awakened warrior, was that this would end the war sooner rather than later and I could go home. When I heard the clash of arms from the west I knew that the Mercians had arrived. I had secured the enemy horses and we were almost at the town gates. As we neared them I saw the fatal mistake made by the leader of the enemy horde. They had left the gates open. Perhaps some of their chiefs had stayed within the town. The wall was one that would have slowed down men and could have been defended. The open gate negated that. I was the first to reach the town and we poured through.

I was right. Not all of their men were camped. A chief and six bodyguards, all mailed, emerged from a large building. This was not the time for heroics. "Haraldrsson, shield wall."

As the horn sounded then the men of Norton obeyed and ran to form our shield wall. The Sunday morning training had paid off and we had a wall with twenty men before the Wends even knew we were there. The

The Sword of Cnut

Wendish chief shouted something and some villagers armed with a variety of weapons joined his mailed men. They too made a shield wall and they advanced. They were just ten paces from us when they charged. It was not enough to give them enough power to bowl us over but it was enough to allow them the first thrust. The seven mailed men struck first and they came at Gandálfr, Haldir, Haraldrsson and me for Bersi stood behind me with my banner. I was a leader and if he killed me then my men might lose heart. He had a mighty war hammer and even as I thrust Saxon Slayer at his chest he swung the weapon. My spear struck his shoulder and embedded itself in the metal links there. It was a good mail shirt and Saxon Slayer stuck. The hammer hit my shield and had I not padded the back of it then my arm might have broken. As it was my arm was numbed and my shield dropped a little. He had a triumphant look on his face as he raised his hammer. Dropping my spear I drew Oathsword and lunged, below his shield, at his unprotected knee. Many might have called it a dishonourable blow but I had witnessed little honour in war and I won any way that I could. My sharpened tip slid off his kneecap. I knew he was hurt when the hammer failed to fall. I pulled my sword back and took advantage of his scream and arched back. I drove the sword up under his chin and into his skull. He was dead. I pulled out my sword and his body fell backwards onto the townsfolk behind.

    The remaining bodyguards roared. They were oathsworn and their leader was dead. They would follow him into the Otherworld and take my men with them. The warrior who was battering Haraldrsson with his two-handed sword was almost like a berserker. The weaponsmith's son was crouching beneath his shield as the flurry of blows landed. I swept my sword backhand across the unprotected neck of the warrior and almost severed his head. Gandálfr and Haldir had the beating of their two opponents and my men outnumbered the last of the oathsworn. They died but they had kept their oaths.

    The townsfolk who had followed the leader now took to their heels. My archers and slingers had arrived at my shield wall and they cut down the fleeing men before racing forward to claim their treasure.

    "Are you hurt, Haraldrsson?"

    The horn bearer shook his head but I heard the shock in his voice, he was shaken, "No, Lord Sven, but I had no defence against the wild warrior."

    Gandálfr smiled, "Use that wildness against them, as Lord Sven did. You had a sword you could have used, or a dagger. A wild man does not think and rarely defends. A man has many vulnerable parts. Your shield was well made, and you wore mail. You had the advantage." He

The Sword of Cnut

looked at my shield, "But your shield, Lord Sven, will need to be repaired before we fight again." The crack was clearly visible.

We had time to repair the shield. We had suffered wounded men and, although the victory was complete, the earl chose to stay a week in the town while we scoured the countryside for temples and treasure. We now had spare mail shirts to take back and the captured horses not only mounted our scouts but gave us horses to carry back our booty. Our two wounded men had rejoined us and that was good for another five had wounds that meant they would not be in the fore of a fight. The town and temple were burned as we left and we headed back towards the beach. The land around the town had been devastated and we moved back, much more slowly now as we were laden with treasure, to the drekar we had left on the beach. We arrived back two days before the muster time. The king was already there and he was well pleased with both our efforts and the success of the overall campaign. The Wends had sued for peace. They gave hostages but refused to convert. King Cnut was a practical man. The Emperor and the Pope would be happy that we had humiliated the pagans and understand that conversion would have to come after a more committed crusade.

He held a feast on the beach. We were tough men and did not need a roof. We ate well and drank the barrels of captured ale. He honoured the earl and me by having us next to him. "The warriors of my new kingdom did well. You suffered fewer losses than did any other and yet you destroyed more temples." He shook his head, "Strange that I was not sent the treasure from them." Before either of us could offer an explanation, he held up his hand, "I am satisfied. I have the treasure I took and the Wends have given me Danegeld. When you return home I would have you enforce both my laws and my will. Collect my heregeld and punish all those who would transgress. I want lawlessness punished so that England can become rich once more."

We left the next day. In addition to the cow we had captured in the first week of the campaign, we had a young bull, some goats and sheep as well as fowl. Norton would benefit. The last thing we did, before we left, was to visit the graves of Gunnar and Thorgaut. There I made a blót with a cockerel. It was to ask Ran for a safe voyage home and to honour the dead. We saw the patch of bloody sand as we set the sail and headed towards the Skagerrak. We were going home.

Chapter 10

Cnut's law

The blót worked and we had a safe voyage home. It was both swift and without incident. My first task, even before I had greeted my wife, was to visit with the families of Gunnar and Thorgaut. We had treasure to share with them. It would not make up for the loss of a son but it showed them that the shield brothers of the dead men were thinking of them. That done, I greeted my wife. For once she was pleased that we had raided. This had been for a greater purpose than mere greed, for we had been on a crusade and working for God. I knew the reality was different. We had not converted anyone and the temples we had razed would be raised once more.

"And now you are home."

I nodded, "When the ship is unloaded we will take it for an autumn voyage to collect jet and harvest the seals, and then I will be lord of this land. King Cnut would have his law enforced. He is returning soon to England and from his words, I believe that he sees England as his home and that is a good thing."

The young bull and the cow would be kept at my hall but the bull would be there to service any cows. The animals we had taken were shared out equitably. On the way home Grettir and Frithiof had each requested a farm. I had asked if they had a wife in mind and both had shaken their heads. The mail they had won made them both attractive prospects for marriage, and having a farm even more so. I had, of course, agreed. We had more forest than we needed and the extra farms would produce more food to feed the clan and the valley. That evening, as I ate with Bersi and Mary, I told her of the changes and she approved.

"We are growing, husband, and the clan is becoming more Christian. It is a shame that the hersir cannot become one too."

I sighed, "I do not flaunt my Hammer of Thor and I attend Father John's services."

"Where you mumble the words."

I shrugged, "It is Latin."

"When Bersi marries it will be a Christian wedding and not a simple Danish handfast."

"As Bersi is yet to find a wife, that is a moot point."

The Sword of Cnut

Bersi was strangely silent. I knew more of him as Bersi the warrior than I did as Bersi the son of the hersir. I did not see as much of him around Norton as I did when we sailed the drekar.

Mary asked, "And Haldir and Aed, what of them?"

"Haldir would have a farm too but as he, Aed and Gandálfr are the only occupants of my warrior hall he said he would wait. That will not be long for many of the other young men who went to Denmark have decided that they wish to be warriors. I will have oathsworn once more."

"But if you are now at home then why would you need them?"

"Because, my love, we may be at peace but I need warriors to keep that peace. The king wants his land to be one ruled by law. There are too many bandits and brigands yet for me to hang up Oathsword."

At the back of my mind was the thought that the land was not yet safe from foreign intervention. The Scots had been quiet but that was because King Malcolm did not wish to risk the ire of Eorl Eirík. The old Norse Jarl was a force to be reckoned with. The Scots had defeated the Northumbrians at Carham but they had not taken one hide of land south of the Tweed.

We spent a week at home while we started work on the new farms. Four of the young men who had been with me in Denmark chose to live in the warrior hall and so we were able to mark out the land that would be given to Haldir and Aed. There was no rush but the three new farms provoked interest in the unmarried daughters of the older farmers. A maid could be married as young as eleven, sometimes even ten, it all depended on their woman's moon, and we had young women who were almost sixteen. Their fathers were loath to let them marry a landless man and so the three new farmers attracted attention.

In that week I visited with Edward of Billingham and my other leaders. I told them of the need to enforce the law of Cnut. It was a simple enough law. Any wrongdoers would be brought to me and I would punish them. The greater crimes were punishable by death, the lesser ones by fines administered by me. King Cnut's laws meant that the revenue thus collected was to be divided equally between the administrator of the law and the crown.

The one who was most relieved when I told him was Edward. My other leaders had too few people to worry about but Edward had not enjoyed the role of judge. When I visited with him I found him to be a happier man than when I had first met him. He had been able to become a farmer once more and, having Osgar and me to marshal his men, he had few worries. I was delighted for him; he was a man reborn.

The Sword of Cnut

As Osgar escorted me to the causeway, I asked, "Since I have been here there have been no crimes that I know of. Were there others before I came?"

He nodded, "Theft mainly. Lord Edward...well he is a kindly man in many ways. Remember when the Mercians came, he would not come to your aid?" I nodded. "That is typical of the man. If he can get away without doing anything then he will. Often when men brought crimes to him he would rule that they could not be proven one way or another. Men began to take the law into their own hands. If there was murder, men took their own revenge. You are right, Lord Sven, since your arrival the land has had few crimes but the threat of the Mercians and the Norse brought men together. It is in the nature of some men not to want to work too hard and if they can take from another then they will. Like Lord Edward, I am happy that you will be the judge. You have a keen eye."

"I sail to Hwitebi in a week to collect jet and to hunt seals, so if there are any crimes the hearing will have to wait until I return." I saw him react to my words. "Speak, Osgar, you fought with me against the Mercians and we are shield brothers. Do not hide your wishes and thoughts from me."

"I should like to dig for jet. My father was called Halfdan the Black." He smiled, "He was Norse and settled here when my mother carried me in her womb. He loved jet and had a jet stone embedded in the pommel of his sword. His Herkumbl was also made of jet. I know it is a fancy but I would like to honour him by using jet."

"I can give you jet, Osgar. You need not travel."

"But I want to. The thought of finding the right piece of jet and bringing it back is part of the notion. If I work and dig for the jet and then carve it and fit it myself, the act will honour my father and his memory."

"Then of course you shall come and I will be pleased to have you aboard my ship."

As I headed back to my home I could see the webs and threads of the three sisters. I had taken Mary from Norton but others, like Halfdan the Black, Bergil the Black, Pers and Ragnar had made the journey the other way and now our threads were joined. In the case of Ragnar and Gunhilde, it was through marriage and when my unborn grandchild came into the world, then there would be a baby that was evidence of their spinning.

Perhaps it was the Norns or something else for when I reached my home there was a messenger there, "Lord Sven, I come from Lord Ragnar. He told me that your daughter has given birth to a boy. He is

The Sword of Cnut

now a grandfather. There is another Ragnar. The baby and the mother are well."

I was delighted, of course, but Mary insisted on riding to our daughter. Gandálfr and Bersi came with us as we rode the mile or so to the new house of my daughter. The couple and the baby were alone when we arrived. Ragnar had no thralls yet. I realised that I could have brought a couple of Wends back from the wars. I had not needed them but my daughter did. A farm was hard to work without labourers. The baby was asleep and my daughter looked tired. Mary took charge immediately, "I shall stay here and tend to our daughter. I do not need you but I will need Seara. Return to Norton and bring her."

They were orders. Mary could act like an Empress when she chose. Seara had been the orphan we had first rescued. She had proved invaluable and now, at thirteen or more summers, helped Mary to run the house. It was not quite dark when we reached Norton. Bersi said, "I will ride with Seara. If you let me have Verðandi then we can ride double."

"Of course."

Seara seemed more than happy to endure the back of my horse.

Gandálfr and I ate with the new men in the warrior hall. Haldir and Aed were still building their home and they slept in the warrior hall. Frigga the cook brought the food intended for us into the main hall and we enjoyed a night of man talk. It began with talk about the baby and the future. We had just spoken of the time when young Ragnar might be taught to use a sword when Bersi returned, "You are late, son. Was there a problem?"

He looked flushed, "No, it was just that Mother wanted me to cut wood and I stayed longer than I should. I have stabled Verðandi."

"Good, then sit and eat."

Haldir said, "And now that your sister has given birth, perhaps you will cast your eye on a bride."

Bersi did not answer. Gandálfr sucked on a bone and then said, "You know, Bersi, there were some comely maids amongst the Wends. You could have done worse than take one as a bride. It is too far for a Wend to run home and they are hardy folk."

I saw Haldir nodding his agreement. Men often made brides of the thralls they had taken. While it was not exactly the same with me, I had married Mary whom I had taken in a raid.

Bersi shook his head and spoke more forcefully than I had expected, "No, Gandálfr, for the Wends are pagans and Mother would not approve. The bride I shall choose will come from this valley and will be free. I will not enslave a woman to marry her."

The Sword of Cnut

Haldir said, "It sounds like you have chosen already."

Bersi did not answer but merely smiled.

Their faces told me that everyone wanted to talk about it but Bersi's silence had to be respected. I changed the subject, "Osgar will come with us when we sail to Hwitebi."

"Good, an extra warrior will be handy." Gandálfr nodded. He got on well with Osgar.

I saw a cloud appear on Aed's face, "Aed, if you do not wish to come then you need not."

He shook his head, "I hate the place and the people. They treated me badly but I will face my fears and return. I am now a warrior, well almost. I have a leather byrnie studded with metal, a helmet, a short sword and my sling. They will not see a frightened mouse that they can taunt and hunt." We had given Haldir and Aed one of the deer hides and the two had made the byrnie.

I watched Haldir's fingers tighten on the knife he was using to carve meat, "Haldir, what is done is done. I know that you feel anger about the way your foster son was treated, but Cnut's law means that you cannot have retribution."

He nodded, "I know but it is hard, lord. You and your people would never have done what they did and those people should be punished."

"I know but it is not for us to punish them. There will be retribution but from a higher plane."

Gandálfr snorted, "That is Lady Mary talking, Lord Sven. It is the Christian way to think that the White Christ punishes wrongdoers at the end of time. I agree with Haldir. We should destroy Hwitebi and wipe them from the face of the earth." He smiled, "We will not, of course, but it is a comforting thought that we could."

I shook my head, "Keep such thoughts in your head, Gandálfr, for if my wife heard them…"

He held his hands up, "Lord, I would face any wyrme from Hel before I would risk the wrath of my lady."

It made us all laugh and the subject was dropped.

Seara and my wife stayed with my daughter for two days. On her return, Mary sent two thralls back to work the fields for Ragnar. It would make us short-handed for a while but Gunhilde needed the help. "It is good that Gunhilde is strong for there is little help for her there."

I sighed, knowing what lay beneath her words, "If you invited them to stay here with us you would insult both of them. Ragnar and Gunhilde are making their own life as we did. They will survive."

"They need help."

"Then let them keep the thralls. I can always take more."

The Sword of Cnut

She gave me a sharp look. The subject of slaves was a difficult one for her. She understood the need but did not like the practice.

"Bersi and I will leave in four days. We should only be away for a week and when we return we will draw the ship ashore. We can prepare for winter."

She smiled, "And the new year promises to be a fruitful one. Many of the women are carrying children. War does many things but one of them is to make men wish to leave their mark before they leave for war."

Two of the ship's boys were now big enough to take an oar. Aed had grown and he would also take an oar. It meant we needed more ship's boys. With Osgar we had another oarsman and hunter. We were waved off down the beck channel and passed the rotting ribs of the Norse raider. This time we had to use the oars. Gandálfr chose the chant. It was a new one for many of the crew. He was clever. The learning of a new chant took the mind from the chafing of the hands.

Sweyn Skull Taker was a great lord
Sailing from Agerhøne with his sons aboard
Sea Serpent sailed and ruled the waves
Taking Franks and Saxons slaves
When King Sweyn took him west
He had with him the men that were best
Griotard the Grim, Lodvir the Long
Made the crew whole and strong
From Frankia where the clan took gold
To Wessex where they were strong and bold
The clan obeyed the wishes of the king
But it was of Skull Taker that they sing
With the Dragon Sword to fight for the clan
All sailed to war, every man
We are the bird you cannot find
With feathers grey and black behind
Seek us if you can my friend
Our clan will beat you in the end.
Where is the bird? In the snake.
The serpent comes your gold to take.

The cunning king who faced our blades
Showed us he was not afraid
Trapped by the sea and by walls of stone

The Sword of Cnut

Sweyn Skull Taker fought as if alone
The clan prevailed Skull Taker hit
Saved by the sword which slashed and slit
From Frankia where the clan took gold
To Wessex where they were strong and bold
The clan obeyed the wishes of the king
But it was of Skull Taker that they sing
And when they returned to Agerhøne
The clan was stronger through the wounds they had borne
With higher walls and home much stronger
They are ready to fight for Sweyn Skull Taker
From Frankia where the clan took gold
To Wessex where they were strong and bold
The clan obeyed the wishes of the king
But it was of Skull Taker that they sing
We are the bird you cannot find
With feathers grey and black behind
Seek us if you can my friend
Our clan will beat you in the end.
Where is the bird? In the snake.
The serpent comes your gold to take.

By the time we reached the sea, the chant was known and, as the men doused their hands in buckets of seawater, we used the sail to head down the coast to Hwitebi. The saltwater helped to harden the hands.

We were forced to hove to at the estuary of the Esk. The tide was against us and I did not wish to risk the channel at night. There was no rush to reach the beach with the jet. We could sail in at dawn. We put out two sea anchors and set the watch. I had the last watch and I was woken by Folki well before dawn. I realised, half an hour into my watch, that the tide was on the rise. I looked to the east and saw the first glimmer of light. We had endured cold food for the last days and I made the decision to wake the crew so that we could have a hot meal on the beach. We did not raise the sail but silently rowed into the harbour. We were like a silent spirit or ghost as the oars took us gently towards the settlement.

Young Eidel was at the prow, looking for danger, and when he waved to point ahead, I hurried from the steering board towards the falcon prow. The drekar that was tied up at the quay was a surprise. More than that it was a sharp shock for it had the look of a Norse raider. She was two hundred paces from us but her lines were clear. The first rays from the east illuminated the drekar and her prow was a dragon

The Sword of Cnut

with a face carved to look like a woman with long flowing hair. I made an instant decision. I put the steering board over and headed for the beach that I knew lay to the southeast of the port. It was a small one and was where we had dug the jet. It was better to approach the strange ship by land than risk a sea battle. The ship could have put in for repairs but the Norse raid had made me wary of all Norwegians.

Gandálfr nodded his approval, "It looks like a raider. This is a good decision, Lord Sven."

"Arm yourselves. Folki, when we land keep the ship's boys aboard and take the drekar out to sea. I would not have her driven onto the rocks."

"If she is a raider then they do not know their business. There was no sentry." Haldir had sharp eyes and saw what I had seen. Perhaps it was not a raider but the crew of a drekar that put in for repairs or water. Such things happened.

While we donned our mail and took our shields we waited just off the shore. We knew the beach. There was a long shelf of rock. I spied it to steerboard. "Folki, edge us to the rock. The water is not deep there and we can wade ashore."

I was ready first and I leapt into the sea. The water was knee-deep. I would have to empty the water from my boots once we reached the sand but it meant we could approach silently and without being seen. The cliffs hid us from the ship and the houses. We did not take our spears. If this was innocent then they would be an encumbrance and if there was danger then this would not be a fight between shield walls but one between warriors. Swords would be best.

"Aed, stay on the ship."

"But lord, I know Hwitebi."

"That knowledge will not be needed but I need as many crewmen with Folki as I can. You can row but you are not yet a warrior." He nodded and I smiled, "Fear not, you shall come ashore when we have settled the matter of this strange ship."

As we jumped into the water Haldir, standing close to me, said, "It is not a strange ship, Lord Sven, I know her. She is *'Grid'* and her crew come from the islands to the north of the land of the Scots. She is a pirate but I did not know she raided this far south." Grid was the name of a beautiful goddess and explained the face of the dragon.

"Then we will have to fight." I shook my head, "I came here to dig for jet and not to fight a battle."

We were on the beach and emptying our boots of water. Gandálfr said, "The Norns are spinning. What we intend and they conjure are as different as night to day."

The Sword of Cnut

When all were ready I said, "These may be raiders but let us not judge them yet. I will speak with them but if they are belligerent then we fight and fight hard. We could sail away…"

Gandálfr shook his head, "Do not cut the threads, my lord."

He was right.

I drew Oathsword and pulled my shield around. Gandálfr and Osgar flanked me and Bersi followed with Haraldrsson and Haldir. The banner and the horn were in Norton. We had not thought that we would need them. We moved around the cliff. The repaired jetty lay between us and the drekar. The sun had now fully risen and I saw men on the beach rekindling a fire to cook a breakfast. They were so busy that they did not see our approach. It gave me time to study them. They were tattooed and some had pieces of bone in their hair. Haldir had been right. They were pirates.

As if confirmation was needed, as soon as we were seen one of those tending the fire picked up a spear and hurled it at us as he shouted the alarm. The spear cracked off my shield. Even as I ran to the other warriors I took in that the house which Aed had used for shelter was now a burnt-out ruin and smoke rose from the other dwellings that had been destroyed. I took comfort that I was upholding Cnut's law. These pirates had attacked Hwitebi. I did not like the people but they did not deserve to be attacked.

There were men on the drekar but half of the crew was ashore and we ploughed into them. We went into a natural wedge with Gandálfr, Osgar and me as the point. The man who had hurled the spear had picked up his sword but the sword of Gandálfr swept through him. The shout of alarm had allowed the others to pick up weapons and shields. I would not underestimate these men. They were hard men who would die hard. Aboard the drekar, I saw men rising from below the gunwale. They were armed and some wore mail but the crew who were ashore wore no armour. My men were all mailed and we were ready for the fight. By the time we reached the side of the drekar, the men who had been ashore were dead.

The warrior who stood on the deck of the drekar was clearly the leader. He had a tattooed face and, in his hand, he held a two-handed sword, "Who are you that challenges Thorir Grimblade and his crew?"

"I am Sven Saxon Sword and the keeper of Cnut's law here in the east. Surrender and you shall have a fair trial."

He laughed, "We are Norsemen from the north and we do not surrender to weak willed Danes."

"Then fight and pray that you can kill enough of us to stop us from taking your drekar." I saw then the look on Thorir Grimblade's face as

The Sword of Cnut

he took in our numbers and our mail. We outnumbered him. From the battle bands on the men we had slain, he had lost half of his veterans. He could not count on victory.

"Arrows!" He had men with bows ready and they drew. We had time to raise our shields but in that time the Norsemen had severed the lines holding them to the shore and Thorir Grimblade had shouted, "Loose the sail!" The tide had just turned and was on the way out. Another shower of arrows ensured that the drekar would escape but when just ten oars on each side of the ship were run out, I knew that they would have to return to the islands before they would be a threat again. When, however, I saw the faces of the three girls rise above the gunwale and begin to scream, I knew that they had taken slaves. We could do nothing about it. The Norns had spun.

"Haldir, take ten men and see if there are any villagers left in the houses."

I turned and saw Gandálfr give a warrior's death to the pirate he had gutted with his first blow. My hearthweru shrugged, "He fought well and deserved a good death. He wore the Hammer of Thor."

We watched the drekar head out to sea and turn to larboard to head up the coast. "Search the dead and then give their bodies to the sea, the tide will feed them to the fishes." The naked dead, all eighteen of them, were hurled into the sea and the tide took them. As the last one reached the mouth of the port, *'Falcon'* edged her way in. Folki had seen the pirate leave.

By the time she tied up, Haldir returned with a grim look on his face. "Perhaps the pirates were sent by the White Christ, lord. There are just six old people left alive, all women, and the rest have been butchered."

Their treatment of Aed was punished in this life. I knew that it was the end of Hwitebi. The first Vikings had destroyed the abbey and killed the priests. This last raid had taken the last of the people. I now saw the wrecked fishing boats. Such an act was unnecessary and showed that these were pirates. It was a vindictive and cruel act. When we had raided Wessex, it had been for treasure and slaves. Wanton destruction was a waste of energy and time.

Haldir and I, along with Bersi, studied Aed as he stepped onto the quay. He looked at the burnt-out house that had been his home. Haldir said, "Those who treated you so badly, Aed, have been punished."

He shook his head, "I would not wish this upon anyone. I am sorry that I came back."

"And this will be the last time this year that we do so. We will find a good seam and work it until it is gone."

The Sword of Cnut

Gandálfr beamed, "Well, the pirates did one good thing."

We all looked at him and I asked, "What?"

"They left us a good cooking pot and food within. We eat well."

I admired Gandálfr and his approach to life. Everything was on the simplest of levels. I could see why he had never married. A woman would never understand him.

By the time we had eaten and the tide had gone out, we were able to find another beach further around the headland. We managed to find the seam just before the tide returned to cover the jet with seawater. We would have to return the next day.

It proved to be a good seam and it took us four days to dig it out. Osgar dug harder than any and none begrudged him his share. He would have the jet he desired and his weapons made more precious. We left the harbour having watched the old women leave their homes a day after we arrived. We learned, before they left. that the pirates had arrived three days before we did. The few men were quickly slaughtered and the younger women and children were taken as slaves. They would have a hard life. As we pulled out of the village, it felt like a ghost town. The repairs we had made to the quay would not last the next wild storm. The sea, the snow, the ice and the wind would gradually turn what had been a vibrant fishing port and religious centre into a haunted place filled with the ghosts of the past.

Happily, the seal hunt took away the sour taste and haunting memory of Hwitebi. Even Aed recovered some of his smile. We took ten seals, for there were even more than the last time we had hunted, and when we reached the beck channel, a few days later than planned, it felt as though we had done enough to prepare for winter.

The Sword of Cnut
Chapter 11

Eorl 1021

Mary and I had lived in this land for long enough for us to become attuned to the rhythm of the seasons. When we returned with the seals, the whole village worked hard to render the fat and preserve the skins. The village all shared in the oil, meat and skins. We would not be trading them this time. Similarly, the jet was shared equitably. It could be used for trade in the future but some, like Osgar, wished to use the jet for ornamentation. The share of Bersi, Gandálfr and mine was stored. We would trade it but not this year. The drekar was dragged up the slope and secured beneath the trees. We did not clean the hull immediately. We had learned that the birds, small animals and insects would do much of the work for us before we had to toil and take away the weed and the worms. In the short days of Mörsugur, we would remove anything that was left and coat the hull in a mixture of pine tar and the potion made from poisonous plants to keep away the worm. The ropes and the sail were stored safely in my hall. Each winter the women of the village would work, with my wife, on the sword design on the sail. Every year it grew more elaborate as they repaired and maintained the vital part of the drekar. Their close attention ensured that the sail never weakened. I knew that we would need a new one in a year or so but we had not endured bad storms and my philosophy was that if something was unbroken then do not try to mend it.

It was a good Christmas. I was not sure why the Christians celebrated the birth of the White Christ the way that they did. However, it seemed to me that the winter solstice was as good a reason to hunker down for a few days, drink well and eat the last of the food left from the harvest. Leaner days would come. Therefore, I celebrated with the rest. We hunted and had deer that were culled. I knew that in the spring we would also need to cull the wild pigs but we would let the sows give birth so that the herds were stronger.

It was during the celebrations that romance blossomed. That was not an unusual event. Too much mead and ale allied to a full belly had an effect on both men and women. The thrall who cooked for us was a Dane called Frigga. She had been taken by the men of Wessex as a young child and we had captured her when we had raided the land of Wessex. She had lived with us in Agerhøne and, although we had never given her freedom, she seemed happy enough to live in the land that

The Sword of Cnut

now had a Danish King. She had shown great skill as a cook and she and Mary got on well. She had nurtured the young orphan we had taken in, Seara, and all had been harmonious.

Two days after Christmas, Haldir approached Mary and me as we sat before a roaring fire in my hall. He looked serious and I feared that, perhaps, Aed was ill. "What is the matter, Haldir? Did you eat too much shellfish at the feast?"

He shook his head, "No, Lord Sven, but I come to ask you, ask you both for something. I know that you have done much for me and my foster son already but I have to ask."

Mary was intrigued, "Speak, Haldir. You know that my husband and I listen and then judge."

"I would wed."

Mary beamed, "And that is good. Who is the maid?"

He shook his head, "She is no maid, but a woman grown. She belongs to you. I would marry Frigga, your thrall."

I looked at Mary. She was the one who managed the thralls. She nodded, "And Frigga, is she happy to be wed? It is her decision also."

"It is."

My wife's face creased into a smile, "Then she shall be freed and you shall wed. It is good that Aed has a mother. He may be almost a man grown but a mother gives something a father cannot."

I was the lord of the land and I could make decisions that others could not. They were wed within the week. Haldir was right, Frigga was a woman and now she had the chance for something that had been denied her as a thrall, family. That we had a second celebration in such a short space of time tested our resources. The salted seal meat proved to be the difference. We had a fine feast but a different one from the one celebrating the birth of the White Christ. Augmented by a few of the older doves, we ate well.

It was at that feast, as my folk crowded into my hall and songs were sung that Bersi approached Mary and me. I had drunk well but I was not drunk and I wondered what was happening for he had Seara, the orphan, by the hand. Haraldr the weaponsmith was singing a song of Thor and all attention was on him. Bersi had planned his assault well.

"Mother, Father, on this wedding day I would ask permission to marry, I would wed Seara."

Mary reacted first. "But she is a child."

Seara shook her head, "I have had my woman's moon already, my lady. I am a woman. I know I am slight of build but I am a woman."

Many things now made sense. When Bersi and Seara had ridden my horse, I had noticed that they took longer on the journey than was necessary. Bersi had been speaking of moving out of the hall. I had assumed he meant to move into the warrior hall but now I saw the reason behind it.

I was happy but Mary, I could tell, was not, "Haldir and Frigga had a hasty marriage and that was because of their age. Neither are young. You two have no such excuse." She looked at me, "What do you say, Lord Sven?"

When she addressed me by my title and gave me the glowering look, I knew what she wished of me. I was supposed to agree with her. "For my part, I am content that you wish to wed." My wife rolled her eyes, "But Lady Mary is right. There is no need for haste and, besides, we have no food for a third feast."

Bersi burst out, "But we have no need for a feast. We would be wed."

"And our son will, when he is ready for marriage, have a feast which is fitting for the son of Lord Sven Saxon Sword."

I smiled at my wife's use of my title once more. It was her version of the Oathsword and she chose to use it wisely. "Let us say that if you still feel the same then you can wed after the spring cull of the wild pigs." I thought I was being clever, as I would decide when we hunted the pigs.

My wife had other ideas, "I think that if you still feel the same when the New Year begins, you shall be wed on Lady Day."

I saw the disappointment on Bersi's face. It meant he would have to wait until Einmánuður. Seara, however, took it as a victory. "We can wait and I thank my lady and you, my lord. You should know that we are both sure of this decision and it has not been taken lightly. Bersi and I grew close from the first that I came to your hall. We have become closer since that time. He will be a fine warrior and I will bear him many children."

"Then I am happy." My wife said nothing.

That night as I tried to sleep, my wife would not let me. She worried at the marriage like a cat with a loose thread. "He is too young."

I sighed, "You thought that Gunhilde was too old. Steana was married when he was but a year or two older than his brother."

She said nothing and I made the mistake of saying, triumphantly, "You do not want Bersi to be married for he is the last of your chicks."

Her angry answer told me that I was right, "Nonsense! You know nothing. Stick to waving your sword around for this is my domain. I see that I have little say in this but I will ensure that nothing untoward happens and I will pray that they come to their senses before Lady Day."

The Sword of Cnut

I shook my head, "And did we change our mind?"

She said nothing and that, in itself, was a victory. I had managed that rarest of things, the last word in an argument.

Her attitude soured, somewhat, the mood of the hall. It was good that Haldir and Frigga were so happy and Seara was able to hide in the kitchen and help the new bride prepare food. Mary found tasks for Bersi. She chose to ride to visit Gunhilde on a more regular basis and Bersi would be her guardian. I took him to one side when he returned and had the angry look of one who was about to say something he would regret.

"Bersi, you know that I have taught you to fight in a shield wall as though you have a heart that is of ice."

He nodded, "We are not at war."

"You are. You are at war with your mother. The difference is that this war will be over when you and Seara are wed, and trust me you will be wed. You can either let your mother's attitude anger you or you can treat it as the calloused hands you endure at the oars. It will pass and you will be toughened by the experience."

I saw him think about my words and he nodded, "It is just a couple of moons to wait."

"And we have a hunt to prepare. We need Haraldr to make more boar spears. The hunting of wild boars is a dangerous thing. We need to think of it as a battle."

I had given him something else to think about and as we entered Gói the days became just a little longer, so we prepared for the hunt. I had chosen the hunters already. They would be the men who had sailed with me to war with the Wends. Haraldr also came with us because he wanted to see his new weapons used. The old, damaged mail we had brought back from the war was put to good use. We also made sure that every hunter had a leather byrnie. Most still had the one they had worn to war when they had no mail. Now they would have protection from the tusks and teeth of the wild boar.

Bersi, Gandálfr and I scouted out the forest three days before the hunt. I might have taken Haldir but he and Frigga spent as much time as they could together. We found the signs of the wild boar and I realised that we might have waited too long. There were more signs of pigs than deer and that meant we might have a larger herd to deal with. Gandálfr was philosophical about the whole thing, "We can hunt for two or three days if we have to, my lord. This wood is just half a day from our home. If we spend a week hunting, then that just delays the work on the drekar by a week and all that we need to do with the ship is trade. We have no war. We have the luxury of time." I hoped he was right.

The Sword of Cnut

The hunt went better than we could have hoped. I think it was because we were now a warband, a band of brothers. When the wild old boar raced from the undergrowth and surprised us, my young warriors turned and formed a hedgehog of boar spears. Had any of them panicked or fled then one of them might have been hurt, but as it was the old boar died a good death and none of my warriors suffered even a graze. We had the luxury of choosing our prey. We picked the old and the lame. We wanted a strong herd of wild pigs. We returned to the woods for three days and ensured a good supply of meat, for the young men all became better hunters. The bones and tusks would be used too. While some meat was hung for the wedding feast of Bersi and Seara and much was distributed amongst the families of the hunters, we salted and stored more. The successful hunt boded well for the marriage. Mary did not see the good fortune in it but the pagans amongst us did.

When Seara and Bersi confirmed their intention to wed, then my wife had no choice in the matter. She had expected them to falter but they had not. Father John, not me, her husband, was the one who made her see that this was a good thing. He spent some time counselling her so that when the pair were wed she shed maternal tears.

While we had waited for the wedding, my men and I had helped Bersi to make his home. It was in the grounds of my hall but there was plenty of room. He did not need a hall and so we used a simpler construction. Posts were laid at an angle to make a triangular building. It was one storied but beneath the floor was storage space which would also function as a means of keeping the home warm. There would be just one room but the apex of the roof would allow chambers to be built there for the inevitable children. Seara would still work in the kitchen. The difference would be that she would now dine with us in the hall. It was those times that made Mary and Seara as close as they had been before Bersi had given his news.

The drekar was relaunched a week after the marriage. We planned a voyage to Denmark. We did not have much to trade but we hoped to buy things in Ribe we could not buy in England.

Our plans were somewhat scuppered when a messenger arrived, Glam again, inviting me to a meeting with the king in Jorvik. I knew that it was not an invite but a command. Bersi and Gandálfr would accompany me. Haldir was now an effective lieutenant and he could command the men in my absence. It was not as though I expected trouble. The border had been quiet for some time but it was as well to be prepared.

On the ride south, Glam was unusually close-mouthed. When I pressed him for some idea about the purpose of the meeting, he shook his head, "Lord Sven, I am King Cnut's oathsworn. I will be the next captain of his guard when Siward...well when Siward no longer commands them. My life is the king and he told me that you were not to know the purpose of the meeting."

I wracked my brain to think of how I might have offended him or let him down. I could think of nothing but the closer we came to the city the more nervous I was. Kings could be petty at times and King Cnut's father had been the most vindictive of men. I wondered if King Cnut had inherited those traits.

Jorvik was still Roman. The walls were the same ones that had been built almost a thousand years earlier. The buildings that lay within the walls were made of stone as well as wood. The stone reflected the Roman influence. The king had taken over the old Roman Praetorium. Glam had told me that the heated floor and baths still functioned and the king enjoyed that luxury. He also told me that they had arrived by water. The river flowed through the city to empty into the sea and we were Danes. A ship was always preferable to a horse. There was, in addition to the Praetorium, a mead hall that had been built when the Danes had first taken the city. That was where we were taken. The king's hearthweru were within and recognising both me and Gandálfr, we were greeted with cheers. When the king smiled I was relieved. I was not to be censured.

"Hail, Sven Saxon Sword, your presence is always welcome for there is no more loyal warrior in either kingdom."

His hearthweru began to bang the table with the pommels of their daggers and chanted, "Oathsword! Oathsword! Oathsword!" until the king raised his hands for silence.

"And I summoned you to reward you as I should have done much sooner. You are now to be an eorl. Eorl Sven Saxon Sword of Norton." My jaw dropped open at the unexpected honour.

That brought an even greater cheer. Glam leaned in and said, "Now you see why I could say nothing. The king wanted to see this look on your face."

King Cnut came over and put his arm around my shoulder, "You and I need to talk...alone." He led me from the hall. Gandálfr looked as though he was going to follow me but a shake of my head sent him back to the table. The king said nothing until we were in his Praetorium. Two guards stood at the door and a servant brought us mead.

"It is right that you are rewarded but I owe it to you, of all people, to explain the timing of this announcement. I have banished Thorkell the Tall. I had word that he was planning to overthrow me." He saw my face, "I did not have enough evidence to accuse him directly and the

The Sword of Cnut

Jomsvikings are a dangerous enemy for even a king to make. Thorkell betrayed my father and me once before and the banishment is to ensure that I do not lose this kingdom as we so nearly did in the past. There is also other news. Eorl Eirík is going to be away from Northumbria. His reason is more understandable. He is making a pilgrimage to Rome and," he gave an apologetic smile, "he goes to give a message to the Pope from me. So you see, Sven, I need a leader in the north who can command in Eirík's absence. He has kept the Scots at bay through his presence and his reputation. He will return, but while he is in Rome I need you to be my rock in the north."

I emptied the horn, "I am flattered but I do not command a large army. If I used every man in the valley, I would only be able to field one hundred or so men."

He nodded, "And that is why, when you leave, I will give you a written document from me. There are many lords in the north. Some are Danish and some are English. They will obey your orders. Ealdred of Bebbanburg is Earl of Bernicia and he will be under your command. Since his uncle, Eadwulf Cudel, was defeated by the Scots, he has improved the defences in that part of my land."

I nodded. I would not be able to go to Ribe and trade. Moreover, I would have to spend longer away from Norton than I wished. I would need more hearthweru. An eorl cannot risk murder on the road.

The king smiled at my silence, "I can see your mind at work. Do not fear, Sven, you will not be alone. I have appointed another of my hearthweru, Siward, as eorl of Jorvik. He is a good warrior."

I nodded. I had fought alongside Siward when he was a young warrior. He was fearless. He had slain many Wends in our war.

"There will be coins for you to pay your men. The heregeld that is paid to me is to keep the kingdom safe. What better way to use it than to give it to Oathsword? I am not a fool, Sven, and I know that professional warriors can do more than the fyrd or bondi. It will not be a fortune but you know how to husband gold and silver. You will choose good warriors, I know that."

"And you will return to Lundenwic, King Cnut?"

He smiled and tapped his nose, "I can tell you for you are trustworthy. I intend to move around my kingdom. I want my enemies to fear my arrival and I want my friends to know that I support them. There will not be a palace where assassins can come, as they did for Edmund Ironside."

"But the Queen?"

"Understands better than most. She is Norman and Norse blood courses through her veins."

The Sword of Cnut

As the queen was his second wife, I realised that kings were different from other men. They married for political reasons. I wondered if the king's travels allowed him to enjoy a variety of women. I had served him as a warrior and I had never bothered to worry much about his life away from war.

I was feted by the king. The other new eorl, Siward, sat close to me and spent most of the feast asking me about the land he had been given to rule. He had recently been serving the king in Wessex and the north was new to him. I confess that I liked Siward. Younger than I was, he was a warrior who had the scars of battle upon him. He was, however, ambitious. I would have done the job of eorl in Eirík's absence without the title, but the title was important to Siward and I could tell, from his words, that he sought more land to rule. It was clear to me that he would never threaten the king, he was no Thorkell, but he was ruthless.

"I have the easier task, Sven, for the lands in my charge have been Danish for a long time. You have Northumbria to deal with."

I gave him what little knowledge I had of the lands he controlled, "You know that Thurbrand the Hold lives on the Hull and it was he and his family who murdered Uhtred the Bold?"

He frowned, "Bebbanburg is far to the north and Holderness is to the south of here."

"Nonetheless, there is bad blood there. I have had dealings with Thurbrand and his sons. I do not trust them. They did little to actually support the king's claim to the throne. Indeed, while I fought alongside Uhtred once, I have yet to fight alongside Thurbrand. Have him watched for he is a snake."

"Thank you. I had heard of the murder but, as the king did not punish the family, I thought it was over."

"The king had other matters on his mind at the time; not least the crown." He nodded, thoughtfully. "What I would have you do, if you would, is, when I am called north, to have men watch the river. I know it is sixty miles twixt here and my river but, if the crossing of the Tees was lost, then King Cnut would lose half of Northumbria."

He held out his arm and I clasped it, "I swear that I will be vigilant. I do not intend to languish here in Jorvik. I will travel around the land that is in my charge so that they know there is a Danish hand here."

I told him about Hwitebi, the Norse raiders and the island pirates. He shook his head, "We need a fleet of ships to patrol our waters."

"And keeping a fleet at sea is expensive. Our warriors are fewer than our farmers. Here, in the north, you will find that winter is your best defence. The short days and the cold that grips the land means that

The Sword of Cnut

the people in your charge will be safe then. Of course, here in Jorvik, you have a problem that I do not."

"And what is that?"

"Flooding. You have two rivers and the land here is flat. It is what makes it so good as farmland. You will need your ships just to ensure you can be safe when the rivers rise."

King Cnut came over, as the feast drew to a close. He put his arms around our shoulders, "It is good that my two new eorls get on so well. I can watch the rest of my land knowing that the two of you will be a wall against predators."

There was something in his tone that I picked up on. Siward did not but I had been with the king since he had been a boy. "Who is it that you fear, King Cnut?"

He frowned and I knew I had said the wrong thing for King Cnut would not admit to fearing anyone. "I fear no one, Oathsword, but I am wary of the Scots. When King Malcolm defeated Eadwulf it set a precedent. Eirík of Lade kept them at bay but with him gone..."

"Then the Scots might try to take more of their land back."

"It is not their land!"

"They think it is, King Cnut, and I think you are right. They will try to wrest it back." I saw, immediately, what he was getting at. "I need to be closer to the Scots."

"Aye, you do. Eirík will be away for at least a year. A pilgrimage to Rome is not a swift journey. You will need to give me a year. When he returns then you can go back to your life at Norton."

Eorl Siward said, "I will go with you, Sven."

"No! I need you to establish Cnut's Law here first. There will come a time when you may go north to help Oathsword, but that time is not now." He smiled, "I am confident that Cnut's Sword will be more than a match for my enemies in the north."

The next day I was ready to leave early. Siward came to see me off. "You know that I will do all that I can to help you, Sven. I will not disobey the king, but I believe I can establish his law more quickly than he thinks."

"Thank you, Siward, but I know the king well and it would not do to risk his wrath. Knowing that you have offered your help is enough. What you can do is send to me any warriors who are swords for hire. I have the coins from the king and I would have men who fight for coin rather than taking my farmers from their fields."

"And that I will do. When do you intend to leave for the border?"

The Sword of Cnut

"It will take me a month to prepare and then I will visit with Ealdred. The king has given me a task that is different to anything I have done before. I will have much to learn and learn quickly."

He smiled, "But you have one thing that no other man has, you have a dragon sword and that makes you special."

My two companions knew nothing of my task. They knew of my elevation and that pleased them both, but the king had been more than discreet when he had spoken with me. I waited until we had passed Shipton before I spoke. I told them of my task. "It goes without saying, Gandálfr, that you will be coming with me. I hope that Eorl Siward can find me warriors but, if not, then I will have to use the king's authority."

The parchments, duly sealed, were now in my saddlebags. I was not sure how useful they would be. The lords of the north were Northumbrian and were like warlords. If they chose not to help me I could do nothing. If I sent a message to the king then it would be as though I had failed. In the long run, the lords would suffer but, as I knew from my dealings with Uhtred and Thurbrand, the men I would meet were not Danish. They were a different breed.

"I will also come."

I looked at Bersi, "You need not. You are married and Seara will have need of you."

He shook his head, "Mother will care for her. If Steana was here then he would go with you, would he not?"

"He would, probably."

"I am of your blood and I will do this. The king has honoured you with a title and with that goes the responsibility. I cannot let you do it alone. I know that I have much to learn as a warrior but the border may be the place to be educated."

Gandálfr clapped him about the shoulders, "And I will give you my help. I have tricks to teach you that will keep you safe."

By the time we reached Norton, the next day, I had my plans in place. I would offer the young men who had sailed in the drekar the chance to come with me. They would be paid. I had to hope that Eorl Siward was successful and found men for me, for if I arrived at Bebbanburg with a handful of men then I would be laughed away. What I steeled myself for, as I neared my hall, was the task of telling Mary that her son and I would go away for a year or more. That would be my first battle for King Cnut and was not one I thought I could win.

The Sword of Cnut

Chapter 12

The Border 1022

Mary surprised me when I gave the news for she did not oppose me. I think that was because we talked during the time I had left at home, about the danger posed by the Scots. King Malcolm had ruled Scotland for a long time and he had gradually increased the land he ruled. He had allies amongst the Norse of the Isles and my perceptive wife thought that some of the raids we had endured were as a result of the Scottish king's encouragement. When it came to Bersi's involvement she was less happy but when Seara, after speaking with her husband, came to talk to us she was mollified. Seara knew that Bersi had to go with me. He was my son and as Steana lived in Denmark, my heir.

"One day my husband will be Lord of Norton and when he is this duty will stand him in good stead. I do not want him to be hurt or to die but I trust Oathsword and you, Lord Sven. God will watch over you for you are doing his work and protecting the people."

I knew that Bersi would learn to lead and so I decided then that I would give the banner to Haraldrsson. Bersi had shown me that he could stand in a shield wall and the best way to learn to lead was to stand at my side and not behind me.

Haldir was torn. He wanted to come but he had a wife and, unlike my son, was not young. He had been a wanderer and he needed roots. I saw his dilemma and eased his concern. "I need a warrior here, Haldir. I need someone who can defend Norton should it be attacked while I am away."

"And I swear that I will give my life to defend Norton."

"Better that you live to protect Norton."

Twenty of my crew chose to come with me, including Haraldrsson. He had trained to be a weaponsmith like his father but he had enjoyed being the bearer of the horn. His father understood. "What better way for a weaponsmith to learn about weapons than going to war? If you are right, Lord Sven, and this becomes a year of work, it will be good for him and when it is over he can resume his apprenticeship."

My task had been made much easier.

I used some of the king's coins to buy horses. I was not sure how many men Siward might find for me and I managed to buy forty horses and ponies. They were hardy animals but would not be used for war. They were to help us travel the land quickly. I also found a youth who

The Sword of Cnut

liked horses. Ivaldi would not fight. He had a dagger but he was a gentle youth who had an affinity for animals. His father, who raised horses just a mile or so from Norton, told me that he was happy that his son was not a warrior. "He has skills with all animals, Lord Sven. It is almost as though he can talk to them. I pray that you keep him safe from harm."

"I will. He comes with me as a horse master and that is all. I have warriors who can fight."

As well as men, we needed supplies. We still had salted meat and we would take that with us. Our fishermen salted as much fish as they could. The pond we had put in proved invaluable. There were not enough hours in the day for me to do all that I needed to do. I did not use Bersi but allowed him the time with Seara who was showing signs that she was with child.

I worried that Siward had been unsuccessful when no one had come from Jorvik and there was just a week before we left. I was relieved when Alfred sent word that a column of horsemen was waiting to cross the river on the ferry. We prepared the warrior hall for guests. It was Siward himself who had come with the men he had found. There were fifteen of them. Siward had his own ten hearthweru and so both my hall and the warrior hall were full.

"I thought to see the land to the north of me. It is fertile, Sven, and empty. When I think of the land we squabbled over in Denmark, while here there is so much land that a man could be given many hides and it would not be noticed. We should encourage more settlers."

"Aye, you are right. Between your river and my river is the richest land in this part of England."

Siward was a personable young man and got on well with Mary. He was polite and, for a warrior, remarkably gentle in his conversation. It confirmed my opinion that Siward knew what he wanted and how to get it.

He left the next day and that allowed me to get to know the new men. They were all warriors who had fought in England before. Some had fought alongside me when we had gained the crown from King Sweyn. There were others who had been raiders but, now that King Cnut ruled two kingdoms, sought adventure in different ways. They were all happy to be paid but none of them seemed overly concerned about the amount they would receive. They wanted war. That boded well for the future.

Two days before we left I visited with Edward of Billingham and Osgar. It was really Osgar I wished to speak to for he was the rock that

The Sword of Cnut

would secure the land to the north of Norton. He happily agreed to help Haldir. "You know, Eorl Sven, if you asked me then I would come."

"I know, but I will sleep easier knowing that you and Haldir watch my land."

All my plans made, we headed north for Dun Holm. The bishop would be there at the church begun by Uhtred. It would be the first test of the parchments given to me by the king. Thanks to the horses, we easily made the journey in one day. Bishop Edmund was newly appointed. The story was that St Cuthbert's voice had been heard in the new church asking that Edmund be the new bishop. Whatever the truth of the story, I found Edmund, who had been a monk, to be a most devout man. Aldhun, his predecessor had fathered children but Edmund was married to the church.

He smiled when I proffered the parchment, "You have no need of that, Eorl Sven. You have my support although, I confess, there is little I can offer in the way of warriors."

We were eating in the refectory and whilst most of the men were priests there were a dozen or so men who looked like warriors. I waved my wooden spoon around, "Any warriors would be useful. You know these men better than I do. Are there men here who might wish to fight?"

He looked around and said, "There may be one or two. They will be the younger men, the sons of those who farm and hold land. Often it is the young who seek adventure. I know that war is not adventure but young men think it is."

"Whatever you can do will help me in my endeavours. Tell me, if you can, where Eorl Eirík's men are to be found."

"They are at Cuneceastra. It is where the Romans built a fort and it is a defensible site. The Eorl left a captain in command of them. Geirrod is a good warrior even though he is still a pagan. I think that is why he stayed in England when the eorl went on pilgrimage."

I was relieved. I had wondered if all of the eorl's hearthweru had gone with him. If I could persuade them to accompany me then we had a chance. Cuneceastra was not far away. Most of the fort had been robbed by locals for stone but enough had been left to provide the warriors with somewhere that they could defend. Until Uhtred had moved St Cuthbert's bones, it had been the place where they had resided.

The eorl's men had sentries and as we rode up, the walls were manned by helmeted men with shields and spears. I had my helmet hanging from my saddle and I held up my hand, "I am Eorl Sven Saxon

The Sword of Cnut

Sword and I am here to protect the king's northern border. Which of you is Geirrod?"

The man who strode towards me was a grizzled old warrior. He had a good sword hanging from his waist and unlike many men, he wore his Hammer of Thor openly. The bishop had been right. Geirrod was a pagan.

He took off his own helmet. "I know you, you are the one called Oathsword."

I took out the parchment given to me by the king, "I have here a missive from the king."

He shrugged, "As I cannot read it is of little use. I know that you are a man of your word. Tell me what the king wishes."

"While Eorl Eirík is in Rome he has charged me with the defence of the border. The king is concerned that King Malcolm Mac Kenneth might choose this time to cause mischief."

"And you are sent to stop them with this handful of men?" The bishop had found me ten men who had horses. None had mail and all were young but they were warriors. He waved his hand around his men. "The eorl left just fifteen of us to guard this place. It is not enough."

I nodded, "I know and that is why we head for Bebbanburg. Ealdred has men and he will be keen to avenge the defeat at Carham."

"Perhaps, but he is more likely to wish to make war on Thurbrand the Hold." He looked at my sword and then at his men. "The eorl likes you and I would like to see the Dragon Sword. We will come with you."

I nodded, "And follow my orders." His eyes narrowed. I shook my head, "If you cannot agree to that then stay here and defend this…ruin."

"You would face a Scottish army with this handful of men and whatever Ealdred lets you have?"

"I gave my word and a warrior does not break his oath."

He sighed, "And I swore an oath to the eorl. I will obey you."

We rode to Hexham where we found accommodation at the abbey. I could not help but smile as Geirrod clutched at his Hammer of Thor when we entered the abbey. I was just grateful for the roof and the food. We had a long way to go to reach the Tweed and the border. We would have sixty miles to travel to reach the stronghold of the Northumbrians, Bebbanburg. Ivaldi proved to be invaluable. He was not only good with horses but offered sage advice to the men who were new to riding. He was a good addition to what was, in effect, my warband.

We managed to pick up another two warriors on our way north. That was purely and simply because of Oathsword. The two young men, Uller and Vidar, had been told tales of the sword and wished to

The Sword of Cnut

leave their homes to protect the land. That they were both the youngest of large families also helped. The choice was that they would work the land and never own it or go to war and hope to make enough silver to buy a farm.

We approached the home of the eorls of Bernicia from the south. We had passed the village of Sutherland and the port where I bought fish from the folk there and we were heading north along the coastal road, when we saw the rock topped by wooden stakes that was Bebbanburg rise up before us. None of my men had seen it before. Even the men whom we had recruited had never been there before and Eorl Eirík had stayed closer to the old Roman wall to protect both the east and the west. The Roman military road was still the best way to travel. We paused to both rest our horses and to examine the fortress.

Geirrod tossed away the bones of the fish he had just sucked clean and after wiping his hands on the mane of his horse, said, "Eorl Eirík never visited here because he said he had seen it from the sea when he came from Norway and knew it to be impregnable. In the days before even the Saxon kings lived here it was the home of a king and was called Din Guardi. The Scots might have triumphed at Carham but that only secured them the land north of the Tweed. If they wish the land across from the Tweed then they need to reduce Bebbanburg."

The position of the castle meant that enemies and friends could be seen from great distances. That the wooden gates to the south were opened as we approached showed that we had been identified as friends. Since leaving Dun Holm we had carried my banner. The sword upon the black background was recognised. The road up to the top twisted and turned. An attacker would be assaulted from the side the whole way to the wooden gatehouse. As we took the final turn, I realised that the designer of the first castle had built the road so that an attacker could be attacked from his right and left as the road twisted and turned. The sea to our right lapped right up against the base of rocks that faced the sea. Eorl Eirík might have been right, although I suspected an attacker who was willing to sacrifice lives could take it, but the cost would be high.

Mailed warriors greeted us. "Eorl Ealdred welcomes you, Sven Saxon Sword, to his home. I will take you to him while your men are taken, with your animals, to the warrior hall."

"This is Geirrod, the leader of Eorl Eirík's hearthweru and he shall come with me." I was keenly aware of my position. I would make the important decisions.

"Of course."

I nodded to Bersi. He would take care of my men.

The Sword of Cnut

I studied the defences as we headed to the mead hall. The interior of the castle, the part within the walls, was not solid rock but was domed and had earth and soil upon it. The palisade was embedded well and the soil was covered in grass so that the horses had some grazing. I could see that stone had been used as well as wood so that the fighting platform was a solid one. There were towers dotted along the walls and each one had a couple of men within. I spied a second gate to the north of the enclosure but a much smaller one than the one we had used to enter. The mead hall was as familiar inside as any in Denmark. As with many I had visited, the early pagan symbols had been crudely changed to reflect the White Christ, but it did not deter from its magnificence. This had been the stronghold of the kings of Bernicia.

The warrior who had escorted us in hurried to the side of Eorl Ealdred and spoke in his ear. Ealdred was about my age, and he sat on a chair that could have been the throne of the ancient kings. About his neck, he wore a torc. I had not seen one in this land for many years. I had seen many in the land of the Wends. The ancient kings had used the gold around their neck rather than a crown upon the head. They seemed to do things differently here in Northumbria.

"Sven Saxon Sword, your banner was recognised. What is the warrior who protects King Cnut doing here in the wild north?"

I flourished the parchment with the seal, "Eorl Eirík has gone on a pilgrimage to Rome and King Cnut has made me the eorl in his absence. The king was concerned that our neighbours to the north might choose to take advantage of his absence."

The eorl took the document. He could read. He studied it and nodded. "This is timely for I was about to leave to travel to Jorvik and my estate at Gilling... I have business there and I was already worried about leaving my home undefended. The document does not say how long you are to be here but a pilgrimage to Rome is not a quick one."

"You would leave your family?"

He smiled, "No, they would come with me. I have but one daughter, Ælfflaed. My brothers Eadwulf and Gospatric, who are both hunting this day, will come with us. My hearthweru would be needed to protect us and that would leave just twelve men to defend my home. Even for Bebbanburg that would be hard."

There was something about this I did not like but I could not put my finger on it, "Your business in Jorvik must be important to risk the loss of this jewel."

His eyes became hooded as he answered. I could not read them. He smiled but it was a cold one, "It is my business and my family's. Your arrival means that we can leave in the next day or so. We will be back

The Sword of Cnut

within a few months and then we can discuss your presence. For now, it suits me that you are here."

I liked nothing about this but I did not know why.

He waved to the warrior who had brought us, "Sigurd will take you to show you the castle. He is my captain of hearthweru and is charged with the defence of the castle."

As opposed to the cold Ealdred, Sigurd was both warm and informative. "I am glad that you have come, Eorl Sven. Our business is important but none of us wished to leave the castle with such a small force of men. We have families here. Your men are all mailed and the number of horses you have means that the border is close enough for you to reach quickly. Lord Gospatric and Lord Eadwulf are there now."

"I thought they were hunting?"

"Up here you hunt and scout at the same time. We often send armed men to the river to let the Scots know that we are vigilant."

We had reached the north wall and I saw there was a small gate there. A sentry unbarred it and we stepped out. To my surprise, there were steps that led down to a stone platform. The sea was below us.

Sigurd said, "At low tide the sea retreats but we can use this to be supplied by sea." He pointed out to the island of Lindisfarne, "There is the monastery where St Cuthbert's bones lay. Do you see just beyond it, the sails of two ships?" I nodded, "They are the eorl's. I will send a rider there to tell our captains that they can come here in two days, at high tide, to take us off."

"You would visit Jorvik by water."

"Aye, it is more comfortable than by land and after the murder of the eorl's father, we do not feel safe anywhere on the land but here in our fortress."

"Then this business must be important."

"It is." His enigmatic response was all that I could drag from him. We walked the walls. The land to the west fell sharply and the only way it could be assaulted would be by men climbing and that climb would be almost impossible. The fortress was impregnable and the only way to attack it was up the road we had taken.

I pointed to the handful of houses, "The people of Bebbanburg?"

"They fish. You can see their boats drawn up on the shore. There are twelve families there. In times of danger, they come into the fortress to help defend it." He smiled, "I have never witnessed this but I was told by old Aethelbert who was my predecessor, that in the time of Uhtred the Bold, when he was a young man, the Scots came down to ravage the land. The people came inside these walls and the Scots could not gain even a foothold. They burned the village and then Aethelbert

The Sword of Cnut

said you could follow their route back to Scotland with their bones." We spied horsemen and he said, "Here are my lord's brothers. Food will be ready soon.

The two brothers were clearly younger than Ealdred. Sigurd had told us that the elder of the two, Eadwulf, was a half-brother. They both had the lean and hungry looks of warriors. Ealdred was lucky to have two warriors as his right hands. All the warriors in the hall, with the exception of the eorl, seemed interested in my sword. As was usual, the bolder of them asked to touch the pommel. They might be Christian but every warrior wanted to feel the power of the sword. It was almost pagan to do so.

Eadwulf was particularly interested, "An oath sworn on this blade must be powerful."

I nodded, "It does not do to swear an oath on any sword and then break it. I have never broken an oath yet, but I know of men who have and their ends are never good ones." Some clutched their crosses while others put their hands beneath their tunics. They were the ones who had hidden their hammers.

Eadwulf said, "Like you, Eorl Sven, I have never broken an oath. When I swear it is for life… unto death."

The only woman at the feast was Ælfflaed and I could not help but notice that she looked uncomfortable, "Your niece looks unhappy."

"Aye, she is. This is a lonely place for a woman. It is part of the reason for our visit to Jorvik. We have kin there who live close to Gilling. My brother knows that if she is to marry well then she needs to be closer to other noble families." He nodded at Bersi who was busy in conversation with Gospatric. "Your son looks to be a good catch for a maid."

I shook my head, "And he is married already."

"A man may have two wives. Look at King Cnut."

"And he is a king. They do not follow the same rules as we do. No, Bersi is happy with his wife, as am I."

When the two ships arrived to take off the eorl and his party, I saw how convenient the harbour was. The gate leading to the landing stage was only accessible at high tide and, as there were two wooden towers above the platform, it could be easily defended. The eorl seemed quite happy for me to use his home and I wondered why. Bersi thought it was because of my closeness to the king and, as we walked the walls, Geirrod nodded his agreement. "When his uncle was defeated at Carham, I think it showed the eorl how parlous was his predicament. That was certainly the view of Eorl Eirík. They need King Cnut to be a threat here. You are that threat."

The Sword of Cnut

There was something in his voice that made me ask, "Was not Eorl Eirík a threat?"

He looked uncomfortable but said, after a moment or two of pause while he debated within himself, "Eorl Eirík is a practical man. Had the Scots come over the border then he would have fought them, but he was quite happy to sit in his hall, hunt and listen to his priest. I do not think that you will simply sit. Eorl Eirík became quite religious and that is why he has gone to Rome." I said nothing, as I stared towards the two ships now beating out to sea. "You do not intend to sit, do you?"

"No, Geirrod, I am charged with upholding King Cnut's law. I know from what was said to me by Sigurd that there are Scottish raiders who slip across the river and steal cattle, sheep and even people. I intend to stop that."

"And if it provokes a war?"

"Then it provokes a war."

He grinned, "I think, my lord, that life might become interesting once more."

The dozen or so men left to garrison the fortress were more than happy to have us there. The warrior hall was more crowded but unlike the men who had guarded Eorl Ealdred, we were all mailed warriors and the garrison knew we understood how to war.

The horses had had a hard ride and I left it for almost a week before beginning our patrols to the border. I divided the men into three groups. One was led by Geirrod and his men, one was made of Bersi and the newer, younger warriors, and the last group was my warband. Haraldrsson would be with my son. Geirrod and I would take it in turns to ride forth each day. On the fifth day, it would be the turn of Bersi and his men. They were younger and many had no mail but I wanted them to learn how to scout.

The first two patrols headed to the north and the road to Lindisfarne and Berwick. When I neared Lindisfarne, I saw that the monks had coracles and were fishing. Seeing us they headed for the shore. I told them of the new arrangement, and it seemed to please them. I gathered that Eorl Ealdred had been less aggressive.

In the second of my patrols, we went towards the Tweed. I had no intention of crossing the border, but I rode as close as I could get without provoking a response. The men of Carham just stared at us. I was letting them know that we were here. Their king had defeated Eorl Ealdred's uncle but I was showing them that we were unafraid and would challenge any crossing of the river. We left and headed to Ubbanford which lay a few miles along the Tweed. It was as we neared the place that we saw smoke rising from a building. We headed for it

The Sword of Cnut

and found a woman cradling a man. He was clearly dead, and she was keening. Two young children lay in each other's arms, sobbing. The fire had not yet taken hold and I did not dismount, "What has happened?"

She looked up at my strange accent, "Hamish of Cree came here to kill my husband. He said that we had taken his cattle. We had not. He took our animals."

We had not passed any on our way north and I assumed he had crossed the river at Ubbanford. "Leif and Erik Red Hair, put out the fire and tend to these people. The rest of you follow me. We have some cattle to recover."

That we were on their trail became clear when we passed cow dung on the track. The people of Ubbanford stayed indoors as we waded through the ford. I would speak with them on our return. The two cows that had been taken as well as the three sheep must have slowed the Scots down. I was aware that we had crossed the border but I did not hesitate. We heard the animals as they complained ahead of us. I could not see them as a bank rose ahead of us. I reined in and dismounted, "Galmr, stay with the horses. The rest of you follow me. We will catch them on foot."

Our horses were not war horses and we did not fight mounted. I knew that we could catch them. Even though we were mailed, our byrnies were like a second skin. We ran. They were not expecting pursuit and we could hear their laughter ahead. They had no rearguard and as we climbed up the bank that had slowed the animals down, we saw them. There were twenty raiders and that meant they outnumbered us but we were all mailed. I took in the two cows, three sheep and the sorry-looking horse pulling the cart laden with the family's possessions. I was upholding Cnut's law, and I did not hesitate. I drew Oathsword and ran at the men at the rear of the raiders who were driving the cattle and sheep with the flat of their blades.

It was not in my nature to kill a man by stabbing him in the back, no matter how much he deserved it, and I shouted, as I ran, "Put up your weapons and you shall live."

I should have realised that they might neither hear nor understand me, but at least the men at the rear had a warning. I blocked the weak sword blow with my shield and ripped Oathsword across the man's middle. My men had seen what the raiders had done and there was no mercy. The man who led them, Hamish of Cree, was mailed and had a long sword in his hand. He also had a shield which he slipped around to his front as he raced at me. I was leading my men and he came at me cursing in what I took to be Scottish. My shield was bigger than his although his sword was longer than Oathsword. His swing came a long

The Sword of Cnut

way and when it hit my shield I felt the power of both the sword and the blow. I did not use my edge when I struck his shield. There were pieces of metal on the shield and I did not want to blunt my weapon. The flat of my sword rang out as it hit his boss and I knew that he had felt it. Our fight was between we two and the rest of my men were busy killing the raiders. When Hamish of Cree tried his second blow, it came from above and I blocked it easily with my shield. His move, however, had opened him up for a thrust. I had quick hands and the tip darted out. His shield did not block it and as his mail had large links, my sword penetrated and I drew blood. I punched with my shield and it smashed into his face. He reeled and I swung my sword, this time using the edge, at his head. He was disorientated and his shield was slow to rise. I half severed his head.

He fell and I looked around. There were survivors, three of them. All bore wounds. I shouted, "You three shall live if you throw down your weapons," they did so, "but tell others who live on this side of the border that there is now law here and it is Cnut's law. I am Eorl Sven Saxon Sword and I will uphold it. You can have your lives but any others who cross the border intent on mischief shall pay for that incursion with their lives." I saw a spear and I took it and, after completely severing Hamish of Cree's head, I rammed it on the spear and stuck it in the bank we had climbed as a marker and a reminder. Turning to Gandálfr I said, "Let us drive these animals back across the border."

"You heard the eorl." The three wounded men took to their heels, leaving their weapons where they had thrown them. Raiding a farm with a small family was one thing, but quite another to take on mailed Danes.

Once we reached our horses we made better progress and we soon reached Ubbanford. We halted while the animals drank from the river and I took off my helmet and shouted, "Come forth and hear my words." It took time but eventually the twelve houses disgorged their occupants. The women and children hid behind their men. "You do not know me yet, but I am Eorl Sven Saxon Sword and I am sent here to enforce King Cnut's law. I do not know why you allowed raiders to cross the river and murder a man. Perhaps you are all cowards. It may be that you feel there is no support for you. I will be generous and assume that is the reason. Bebbanburg is close enough for you to send to me if any raiders cross the border. I have slain Hamish of Cree and most of his men. There may be reprisals." I shrugged, "If there is then send word to me and I will end them."

The Sword of Cnut

I saw that my words had shaken the men. Had I lit a spark which might engulf them in a border war? By the time we reached the house, it was late afternoon. The woman had recovered herself and I saw my men, having doused the flames, digging a grave. She came to me, knelt and kissed the back of my hand, "Thank you, my lord, for bringing back that which was ours."

"Do you intend to stay here or shall we take you to a place of safety?"

"This is my home. It was my father's before me. We will stay."

I admired her courage. "Leif and Erik, stay here and repair the house. I will send Bersi here to ensure that all is well and, if you think it is safe, then you can return to Bebbanburg with that patrol."

"We are happy to stay here, lord, and if the Scots are foolish enough to return then they will soon find out that we are warriors."

We headed back to the fortress. I had crossed the border and the Scots now knew they had a sword defending England from their raids.

The Sword of Cnut

Chapter 13

The Border and the River Tweed

Leif and Erik seemed quite happy to be left in a place that was half-ruined and where there was still the threat of a raid but I fretted as I headed back to the fortress. Had I done the right thing? I had no one, except Gandálfr, in whom I could confide and I knew that the last of my original men would just shrug and tell them it was the only thing I could have done. Seeing the rock that was Bebbanburg rise up ahead of me made me think of my rock, Mary, and I knew that she would have wanted me to pursue the Scots. She would have wanted it, not for vengeance but for justice, and that thought consoled me. It had been Hamish of Cree who had initiated the raid and he had paid the price. The fact that I might have angered other Scots could not be helped.

That evening as we ate in the mead hall, there was a buzz of conversation about the fight. I led warriors and a dull day of a patrol with no incident did not rouse their blood like the tale of a battle. I spoke with what I liked to think of as my council, Gandálfr, Geirrod, Bersi and Haraldrsson. The latter two tended to listen more than they spoke but I knew they would offer advice, if asked.

"Tomorrow, Bersi, you will ride to the farm. It is easy to find as it is on the road to Ubbanford. Help Leif and Erik but make sure that you ride to Ubbanford and show your presence."

"Why, Eorl Sven?"

I did not mind Haraldrsson's questions, they showed he was listening, "Today, they saw me on my horse along with my men. When they see Bersi, you and different horsemen they will know that we have more men. From what I was told today, Eorl Ealdred kept inside his fortress. These raids have been hurting the people of the border for some time." I looked at Geirrod, "Eorl Eirík did not visit here?"

"We came after Carham but when we saw Bebbanburg we knew that this land could be defended."

"Defended, aye, but not protected." I could see the hurt in the warrior's eyes. His men and his lord's reputation were suffering, "This land needs men mounted on horses or it needs more burghs on the border. We will do what we can. I know you rode forth yesterday, but I would have you ride again, tomorrow, Geirrod. Head west, towards the river and the crossing places. Show yourself. There may be other raiders who think to make mischief."

The Sword of Cnut

He nodded, "We will. Can we cross the river?"

"If you have to then, aye, but be careful. Had the raiders today been a little cannier then they could have ambushed us and we would have lost men. We are too few to throw men's lives away."

The next day the fortress felt deserted with two-thirds of my men away. We were not idle. Ivaldi saw to the horses and their horse furniture. I left most of my men repairing damaged equipment while Gandálfr and I walked amongst the villagers. I needed to find out what they thought of us as their new masters. I had been told that the people of Northumbria were different. The woman had certainly surprised me with her resolution. I learned that she was not unique. The ones in the village understood how dangerous it was to live here but the proximity of Lindisfarne, which had been the resting place of St Cuthbert, made them feel like guardians. They did not enjoy the raids but they were prepared to fight to hold on to their land.

The headman, Thorgaut, put it succinctly, "This is not Scotland, Eorl, and never has been. The river has always been the dividing line between those in the north and us. We farm well and we harvest the sea. They do not and it is easier for them to come and steal our cattle and animals than to work. God will protect us." He smiled, "And I can see that he sent you. Hamish of Cree was a bad man. He has raided around here since I was a boy and you have ended his reign of terror. Others will take his place but they have learned that King Cnut has teeth and he will use them. He is the first king that I have known who sent men to guard his land. Uhtred and the Lords of Bebbanburg were our defenders and murder took Uhtred. Since his death, the land has died a little. Perhaps your coming will bring it back to life."

I felt better when I returned to the fortress and I knew, from my words with Gandálfr, that he felt the same, "These are good people, lord. We are to be here but a year or so. It is our duty to make it safe."

"With the men we have?"

"With the warriors we have, lord, that is the difference. The ones we fought yesterday thought that they were warriors for they wielded swords, but they were not. They were bandits and brigands. There could have been twice their number and we would have won."

Geirrod arrived back first and he had with him an extra horse and on the horse were weapons. As he dismounted, he spoke, "We found men about to raid across the border at Etal. There is a river there, the Till and we came upon them as they approached the village. There are just four farms in the village and they had less than ten men. We surprised the raiders."

"Did they take anything?"

The Sword of Cnut

He grinned, "We arrived just as they were about to attack. We have endured more wounds when we have practised. We gave some weapons to the men in the village and brought the rest back. The leader of the brigands had a horse." He saw my face which remained without a smile. "I thought you would have been pleased, Eorl."

"I am pleased that you were there but this crossing, how far from here does it lie?"

"Twenty odd miles."

"And it is due west of here?"

He saw what I was getting at, "And that is twenty miles south of Ubbanford. We have too much land and too few men."

I nodded, "You did well and now we await Bersi. I can see that this task is even greater than I first thought."

When Bersi returned just Leif was with him. He explained as he unsaddled his horse, "Erik Red Hair wished to stay for there is work to do." He smiled, "I think that he is smitten by the widow, Father." I was distracted already by Geirrod's words and did not take it all in.

"But the crossing is safe?"

"Aye, we rode to the ford and watered our horses in plain sight. We were watched. Those across the border know of our presence."

That night I told them what I had decided. My ideas had been formulated during the day and made clearer by the two reports. "Tomorrow I will take my men and we will ride for Jedburgh. When I spoke today with Thorgaut, he told me that in times past it was part of Northumbria. The bishop of Lindisfarne set up a church there. It lies across the Jed Water."

"Father, that is across the border."

"I have learned that the border here is a flexible one. That is why there are so many raids. I will not raid but I wish the Scots to know that we will not suffer slave and cattle raids. They must know of Cnut's law. Thorgaut told me that there is a mormaer at Jedburgh. It was his family who made the place that was called Jedworth into a burgh. I have no intention of making war but I would threaten him. Haraldrsson, you will come with me and we will let them see our banner. I want the men resting. We have a sixty-mile ride ahead of us and I will need to rest our horses for two days after our return. That means there will be more work for you, Bersi and you, Geirrod."

They both nodded and Geirrod said, "We are being warriors once more. Our spears tasted blood and it felt good to be a warrior and not simply a guard with good armour."

The long ride necessitated a departure before dawn. We would have to rest the horses each hour. I took with me a wax tablet. I intended to

The Sword of Cnut

make a map as we rode. It would help us see the scale of the problems we faced. What I noticed, as we rode, was that the only hamlets we passed were at river crossings. There were few bridges and most of the places we used were fords. The largest place we passed through was Branxton, with five houses. Cessford had just four. I spoke with the villagers when we passed through. They saw themselves neither as Scottish nor English. This was truly the borderlands. They all told me of raids from both sides of the border and how raiders took anything that they could. I did not see a single cow. Any milk they had came from sheep or goats which could be brought indoors. The raiders had taken anything of value and the people eked out a living.

When we reached Jed Water it was close to noon. It was not an easy fording of the river. I suffered less than most of my men for I rode the largest horse. I could see why the village was no longer part of Northumbria for it looked different. The buildings were of a different construction. We arrived at the gates of the burgh. My men and I did not wear our helmets and our shields were across our backs but, nonetheless, we were clearly warriors. The gates were open but I did not attempt to enter. Eventually, a group of men approached. They had swords but no helmets and no mail. I dismounted and handed my reins to Gandálfr.

The leader of the men was about my height and just a little older than I was. His accent made it hard to understand him but when he saw my frown, he repeated his words more slowly. "I am Kenneth Mac Bruce, mormaer of this place. I rule here for King Malcolm."

"And I am Eorl Sven Saxon Sword. I serve King Cnut of England."

"This is not England."

"But it was." I smiled, "I do not come to fight, Kenneth Mac Bruce. I have come from Bebbanburg."

He nodded, "A prodigious ride just to tell me what I already know, that England has a new king."

"I come here for a different reason. Those who live close to my fortress have been raided. Those who did it have been punished."

"They were not from here."

"I know that but I would have the word spread that from now on any raids across the border will be dealt with severely. Hamish of Cree lost his head, and it now adorns a spear on the Tweed."

The mormaer snorted, "He was a bandit and you have rid the world of a pestilence. And what of raids from Northumbria?"

"While I am in residence there will be no raids. You have my word."

The Sword of Cnut

He studied my face and, seemingly satisfied, nodded as he said, "Good, I believe you. Then I will spread the word but there are many men who will not heed them."

"Then they will die but there will be no war, will there? King Malcolm won at Carham but if he tries to take more of Northumbria, then I have to tell you that King Cnut will bring an army to dispute the ownership of this land." I knew that I was exceeding my orders but King Cnut had put me in charge and I would do what I had to do. I looked him in the eye. "I am not your enemy. I am here to protect my people as you do with yours. We shall not raid but we will punish those who do."

"Good. Will you eat with us?"

I shook my head, "Thank you for the offer but we have a hard ride home." I clasped his arm. "Farewell. We understand each other?"

"We do."

I was not a fool. The mormaer would tell others and eventually, the king. How the king would react I did not know. As far as he was concerned, I might just be a Danish warlord exercising his power. Eorl Eirík's pilgrimage was becoming a poisoned chalice.

It was dark when we reached home two days after leaving and one horse was lamed. Ivaldi would have to use his magic to heal the animal. It was fortunate that we had taken one from the raiders but it told me that we would be restricted to a twenty-five mile ride from Bebbanburg. It was not a large area.

By the end of the week, we had enjoyed days without drawing a sword. It could have been that our two fights had been with the most belligerent of our enemies. I did not know. Erik Red Hair had not returned by the time eight days had passed and I went with my patrol to see that all was well. As we rode up to the farm I heard laughter. I am not a galdrammen but I knew that Erik Red Hair was lost to my men. His shamefaced look as he tossed one of the children in the area told me that.

"I am sorry, Eorl."

I dismounted and handed my reins to an irritated-looking Gandálfr. Putting my arm around his shoulders I led him towards the river so that we could speak quietly, "And what are you sorry about, Erik?"

"That I have tarried here," I said nothing. "Eorl, I would stay here and become the father to this family and the husband to the widow, but if you wish me to honour my oath then I will leave them and return with you to my duties."

I sighed, "Erik, before we left Norton I asked each man if they wished to serve. The oath you swore was to protect me. I absolve you of

The Sword of Cnut

that part of the oath. If this is what you wish then I grant it, but you should know that this border will never be a peaceful one. You will have to fight to cling on to this little piece of earth. You know that you can have a farm at Norton. You could go now and take your new family and their animals with you. There you would be safe."

"And that is more than a kind offer but Greta, well, this was her father's home. She was born here. She knows the problems and she is happy to live with them. As much as I might wish to return to Norton, where I could be close to my family, I think that my future lies here."

I nodded, "Then let us go back so that you can say farewell to your shield brothers. You know where I shall be, for a while at least, if you should change your mind."

Leif, especially, was sad at the loss of his friend. He understood the reason but it saddened him. Our ride back to Bebbanburg was silent. We had lost a man. He had not been killed but his heart had been taken from him. It made the men reflect.

The summer passed relatively peacefully. There were four occasions where our patrols arrived just as a party of bandits, for we had worked out that was what they were, arrived. The sight of armed Danes prevented any violence but I knew it was only a matter of time before we would have to fight. We had got to know the people who lived closest to the border and they spoke of men who lived further afield but were to be feared. When we ate in the mead hall we spoke of the problem.

"You have done the right thing, Eorl and you have established law here where there was none. We remain vigilant and ride each day." Geirrod grinned, "I am becoming used to callouses on my arse!"

It was at harvest time that the drekar arrived off the coast. I wondered if this heralded the return of Ealdred and his brothers who had been away longer than I had expected. It had to wait for a high tide and then it entered the harbour. Nine men disembarked. I knew none of them but they had with them their war gear and looked as though they were here to stay.

They offloaded some sacks and the captain hailed me, "We will sail directly, Eorl Sven. These are new men to serve you and one has a missive from the king for you."

I waved my thanks and watched as the drekar deftly turned to head out to sea. Once clear of the rocks the sail was unfurled and she flew south aided by a northeasterly.

"Come, we will go to the warrior hall and you can tell me all."

The letter from the king could wait. Gandálfr and Bersi were waiting for me. Geirrod was on patrol. They followed me into the hall

The Sword of Cnut

and my warriors showed them where to stow their gear. One said, "The sacks are food."

Uller said, "Vidar and I will take them to the kitchens."

Bersi poured ale into their horns and they sat around the table we used for dining. I waited. The one who had spoken was clearly the leader, "I am Thorir, and I lead these men. The king paid us to come and serve for six months." I waited. There had to be more to this story. "We were on a Norse ship that raided Gippeswic. Our ship struck rocks and we were given the choice by the king, serve him or be hanged." He gave a shrug, "For us, it was an easy choice but our captain, Oleg the Fierce, chose hanging. The man had more pride than was good for him. We swore an oath that we would serve for six months."

"And then?"

"If we are still alive we will build a snekke and return to Norway."

I took out Oathsword and laid it on the table, "It is good that you swore an oath to King Cnut but I would have one to me, on the Dragon Sword."

Their reaction told me that while they had known of the sword, they had not expected the demand.

I smiled, "This is called the Oathsword for a reason. None has ever broken his oath after swearing on it. King Cnut is many miles hence."

Thorir nodded, "I heard you were a careful man as well as being a good leader. I will swear."

They all swore the oath. I said, "Gandálfr, divide them so that they can join the patrols."

"We do not have enough horses, Eorl."

"Then we shall give some men a day off patrolling, eh, Gandálfr? Let us not spurn this gift from the king. Nine good warriors are not to be dismissed." He nodded and I added, "When we do not patrol we practise. Let us mould this new metal into a finely honed weapon."

I took the parchment and, after breaking the seal, began to read. It was a long letter. What it contained was a shock to me. It began by explaining the reason the men had been sent. It confirmed their story, but King Cnut added that he wanted the men away from temptation. The border was a perfect place. Unlike the mercenaries, these men were free. It was the next part that shocked me and explained Eorl Ealdred's decision to go to Jorvik. He and his brothers, after leaving his daughter in Jorvik, had gone to the River Hull and murdered Thurbrand the Hold. They had their revenge. The king had punished them. It was a financial punishment in the form of a heavy fine but he also took any rights to Northumbria from them. When they returned, if they returned, then they would be subject to the orders of King Cnut's eorl. Until Eirík returned

The Sword of Cnut

that would be me. Ealdred was at Gilling. The last piece of news was that Eorl Siward was to marry Ealdred's daughter. I had known his ambitions but this showed me that he could play politics well. I read it twice and then put it away. I would tell Gandálfr, Geirrod and Bersi later.

It was the monks from Lindisfarne who told us of the threat from the north. They had a fishing boat as well as coracles. It was like a snekke and they rowed to the harbour. Being a shallow draughted boat they could land at all but the lowest tide. It was a lay monk who climbed the weed-covered steps to speak to me. "The abbot told us to warn you that a warband is coming down the coast. They were seen crossing from Berwick by boat. They look intent on mischief."

"And they are coming here?"

The monk shook his head, "Such raiders are not so foolish as to risk Bebbanburg's walls. They will seek easier targets. There is one hamlet north of here, Beohyll. If they do not raid that then they will head to Ubbanford."

I nodded, "Thank the abbot. Will you be safe?"

He smiled, "The sea protects us, and the Scots are Christian. We will be safe."

Even as I hurried back to my men, I knew that I could not simply squat behind the walls of Bebbanburg. Bersi was on patrol and he was at Ubbanford. If they raided there, we would have a defence, of sorts. We had not visited Beohyll, but I knew it lay just eight miles away. It would take the raiders at least two or three hours to march from Berwick for they would have to cross the river and land. I had thirty men who I could mount, and we might reach the hamlet before the raiders. The monk had not given me numbers.

"Geirrod, mount the men, yours and mine. We leave the garrison here with those who are afoot. Raiders are coming."

He did not question me but obeyed and we were soon mounted.

As we passed through the village, I warned Thorgaut of the danger. He nodded, "We will send the women and children, along with our animals to the fortress. We men will sail our ships out to sea. There we will be safe."

As we hurried north Geirrod asked, "Why attack now?"

"Simple, the harvest is either in or being collected. The raiders seek to feed themselves at our expense."

"And we do not know the numbers we face?"

"No, but whatever we find we fight."

Our horses ensured that we reached Beohyll first. The villagers were blissfully unaware of their danger. We dismounted and I had the

The Sword of Cnut

menfolk gather their weapons while I sent the women and children down the road to my fortress. The men of the village added four men and three boys. They had bows and slings and I put them behind my shield wall. We formed up at the north side of the tiny row of houses. It was not a perfect place to fight for there was a small wood to the west of us, but it would have to do. We had protection on one side from the houses and we had shields on the other. We formed two ranks. Our main advantage was that we were all mailed.

The warband when they arrived, a short time after the women and children had departed, were a mixture of men with leather byrnies and a couple wearing mail. What they did have was superior numbers.

Geirrod was at one side of me and he said, "I estimate sixty or more of them."

"Aye, now the question is do they fight or will the sight of mailed men make them reconsider?"

Gandálfr said, "They may go to Ubbanford. That will be a test for Bersi."

"I know." My simple answer belied my rapidly beating heart that feared for my son. He had with him, Thorir, but I did not know the mettle of the new warrior.

The raiders paused just three hundred paces from us. A debate ensued. We had the advantage that we were already formed and knew what we planned to do. The enemy had come with a plan that now lay in tatters. They had planned on falling upon the settlement and destroying it. Ubbanford would have followed. The two places, added to the farms that lay between, would have given them plenty of food for the winter as well as slaves. They might have even raided the village near to my fortress. Now they would have to fight for their food and slaves. A roar told me what they had decided. They formed a crude wedge. I knew it would not be as effective as one we might use as they had a variety of shields, and their spears were of different lengths.

"Haraldrsson, plant my banner in the ground. Use your shield and spear."

"Aye, my lord."

Around me, I felt my men, the ones I had brought from Norton, stiffen. Planting the banner meant there would be no retreat. They would either win or die around the banner.

The mob of men weakened their own wedge by racing at us, each one trying to be the first to strike us. "Brace!" With the hafts of our spears braced against our right feet and supported by our right hand as well as our shield hand, we presented a solid line of spears. The second rank slid their spears over our shoulders. Our left feet were slightly

The Sword of Cnut

ahead of our right and we had a sound footing. The raiders did not for they had no rhythm and no song. They were a mob. The villagers sent their stones and arrows over our heads. They were more of a nuisance than a danger but one man was struck on the head and it slowed him. It made their line even more uneven.

The first three to die were simply impaled upon three of our spears. I heard the clatter and clash along our line as their spears struck our shields and ours theirs. I had been lucky and killed one of the men. As his body slid from Saxon Slayer another Scot, with a two-handed sword, stepped between two of his comrades to drive the sword at my face. Uller was behind me and, seeing that the warrior had no shield, he rammed his own spear at the man's face. The sword's tip was a handspan from my eye when Uller's spear drove into the screaming mouth of the warrior who was already proclaiming his victory. The force of the spear drove the man's body back.

Our two lines were now engaged but the enemy numbers overlapped ours. If we had not trained as well then it might have ended in disaster, but our two flanks merely folded back on themselves and maintained a wall of shields. The effect was to make their lines slightly thinner. We had slain six or seven in the centre and I could see that there were just four lines of men. I lifted my spear and used it overhand to thrust at the next man I could see. His shield came up to block it. I needed my sword for the long spear would tire me out quicker. I pulled back the spear and instead of thrusting at his body again, I rammed it towards his unprotected leg. There was no honour in the blow but then again there was little honour to be had fighting men who were trying to steal food. Saxon Slayer went through the fleshy part of his leg and into the ground. I let go of it as he fell. He and my spear became an obstacle to the enemy. The man could crawl away but he was out of the fight. I drew my sword and, as I did so, felt its power. I could not help but roar, "Oathsword!" The shouting of its name seemed to make my men not only cheer but fight harder. It was as though more men had been added to our ranks.

I brought it down to smash through the helmet and skull of the man next to the warrior I had speared. Where there had been two more ranks before me there was now just one and I shouted, "Push!" as I stepped onto my right leg. The last two men I had hit wore no mail and the ones in this last rank were both the weakest armed and armoured. The youth I swung at had an old short sword and a buckler that they called a targe. The shield was little bigger than his fist. The leather he wore about his head would do nothing to arrest the slice of my sword and the terrified youth simply turned and ran. There was no one before me and both

The Sword of Cnut

Gandálfr and Geirrod had enjoyed the same luck as me for they had similar skills and the three of us found ourselves with no enemies.

I needed to issue no command for my two warriors simply turned to attack men at the side. My sword sliced through the spine of the man who wore a simple kyrtle. As our breakthrough widened the opening, more of my men joined us. We had split the enemy who were now being attacked on two sides by mailed men. These were raiders. They had not come to fight a battle, they had come to steal food. They had expected villagers and they had found a warband of warriors. They fled. That is to say, those at the rear fled but when those engaged turned, they were simply slain.

By the time we heard Bersi and his patrol arrive, it was over and we were giving the badly wounded a warrior's death. I pointed Oathsword, "Follow them, Bersi, and make sure they cross the river. You need not close with them but show them that we rule this side of the border."

"Aye, Eorl. Ride."

Around me, men banged their shields and chanted, "Oathsword!" We had saved many lives and, as I looked around, saw that we had suffered only a few wounds that would soon heal. The enemy had lost a third of the raiders. They would not return.

The Sword of Cnut

Chapter 14

Eorl Siward 1023

Bersi, when he returned, told us that five of the raiders had succumbed to their wounds on the way to the river. He had watched the survivors as they were ferried back to Berwick and then returned. We headed back to our fortress laden with weapons, helmets and a few pieces of mail. They would be either used or we would take them home for Haraldr to work his magic upon. The next day we would not patrol. There would be no need. Instead, we tended wounds, sharpened weapons and repaired mail. Ivaldi saw to the horses. When we did resume our patrols, a week later, we found that the mood of the farmers and villagers was almost euphoric. This was the time of year, so they told us, when they often lost half of their food. We had stopped that and it meant they would not suffer death and disease from malnutrition. The people who had cowered from us when we arrived now welcomed us. We had become part of the land.

It was almost the end of Gormánuður when the mormaer and his oathsworn rode up to the fortress. Kenneth Mac Bruce came with just six men, and he was clearly not intent on war. I invited him in. "You will stay the night?"

"I would not inconvenience you, eorl, I only come with a message from King Malcolm."

"I insist that you stay. I told you I was not your enemy and I meant it."

He looked relieved, "Then I will accept your offer."

While the men were housed, he and I, along with Gandálfr and Geirrod, sat in the hall and drank mead, "The king sent me. His constable at Berwick told him of the attack on your land." He shook his head, "The constable was less than honest. He made it seem that the attack by Colm Mac Duff was the dead man's own decision. It was not true for he was aided by the constable who supplied the boats. There will be a new constable in Berwick, Robert of Dumfries. King Malcolm hopes that this will not instigate reprisals."

I shook my head, "I told you that we are here to stop raids. We have done that but if there were many of them then I might be forced to cross the river and deter others."

"There will be no need for that. You have my word and that of my king."

The Sword of Cnut

I reached over to clasp his arm, "Then that is good enough for me."

It was a good night. Men shared stories of battles and heroes and, of course, they all wanted to hear the story of Oathsword. I was no Sweyn One Eye, but I did my best. When our guests left, the next day, I felt happier with the way events were shaping.

Over the next weeks as winter gripped the land and the days became shorter, we patrolled less. Animals had been culled and food stored. The King of Scotland had meant what he had said and the land was at peace. Christmas came and went. Bersi and I missed our wives but it was a price my title meant I had to pay.

It was Þorri when the knarr arrived in the port. It was the time of year when we had storms and I was surprised to see the vessel as she beat her way towards our harbour. At first, I assumed she had suffered damage but as I watched her closely, I realised that she was whole and that her visit was intentional. Knowing that she wished to tie up I had plenty of men ready. To my great surprise, I saw that it was Eorl Siward who was aboard and he had with him a cloaked figure. The lines were thrown, and we tied the knarr to the mooring post.

The captain shouted, "Eorl, I can stay but an hour and then I must take the tide out."

Eorl Siward nodded, "We will be landed in less time than that. Look lively there." I saw that he had with him fifteen men, his hearthweru, but it was the cloaked figure whom he helped ashore first. I saw that it was his new bride, Ælfflaed.

I held out my hand to help her ashore, "Welcome home, my lady."

She smiled, "And thank you for keeping it safe for us and protecting my people."

We had to wait until the knarr had left and we were seated in the hall to discover all.

Eorl Siward was plain-spoken, after all, we were both warriors and had been elevated at the same time. We were equals. "Eorl Eirík will not be returning."

I saw Geirrod's face. To many, it might have appeared impassive but I saw the flicker in his eyes. He wanted to know his position.

"I am the new Eorl of Northumbria and I am here to take over from you, Eorl Sven. The king is pleased with what you have done," he smiled, "word has reached us from many places that the border is now safer. You are discharged and may return home."

I looked at his bride and said, "And your wife's father?"

"He will return to his home, as will his brothers…eventually." The slight shake of the head told me not to pursue the point and I did not ask more.

The Sword of Cnut

"And what of me and my men?"

Eorl Siward turned to Geirrod and said, "Your lord is in Lundenwic. He is ill. I am no doctor but I do not think he will live much longer. He made his peace in Rome but he has returned with…" he shrugged, "the doctors do not know. I am happy to take on any of your men and you."

Geirrod shook his head, "I will put it to my men, but I am Eorl Eirík's man. I will travel to Lundenwic."

Siward looked at me, "And I am happy to keep any of your men here as well, Eorl Sven."

"Like Geirrod, I will put it to them but I doubt that any will remain. One of my men, Erik, has already chosen to stay here. He has a farm close to the Twizell and he is a good warrior."

"That is good to know."

The mercenaries hired by Cnut and the ones who had been pirates remained, but those who had followed us from Dun Holm and the road north came back with us. We had more warriors to defend the valley and that was good.

The majority of Geirrod's men stayed with the eorl. He and three others rode south with us. We had done the task that was appointed to us and I was satisfied. As the fortress receded in the distance, Geirrod asked, "Are you not unhappy that you are not the Eorl of Northumbria, lord? Eorl Siward is younger. He will be richer because of this appointment."

I shook my head, "He is ambitious. He has married well, and I do not begrudge him the honour. He has gained the earldom through his deeds and a marriage. My home is in Norton. and I do not need riches. Northumbria is a poisoned chalice and I wish him good luck. The truce that has come will not last. Eventually, the Scots will wish for the whole of Northumbria and Eorl Siward will have to fight and fight hard." He nodded. "And what of you?"

"If Lord Eirík is dying then I should be there at the end. I cannot fight an illness but I swore to be his warrior unto death."

Bersi asked, "And when he does die?"

"Then I will return to Lade. The eorl was a jarl there and we left there through force. I will return and see if they need an old warrior and his sword."

"And that might mean that one day you have to fight Danes."

"I know and it would be interesting to cross swords with you, Eorl Sven. I have seen you fight and know that you are a mighty warrior with a fine sword, but who knows…"

Our journey south was the reverse of the one north and we stopped at both the abbey and Dun Holm. The difference was that we were riding in cold and wet weather. The roads were treacherous and the wind was what Gandálfr called a lazy wind. It did not go around you but through you. It took many days and on the last day we reached my home by noon, or what passed for noon with thick black clouds overhead. Geirrod was anxious to get to Lundenwic as soon as he could. He had one spare horse that he and his men could use and they did not stay in Norton but headed for the ferry. He had been a good warrior and I would miss him.

Mary watched the hearthweru as they headed for the river, "Did they not wish to stay? This weather is not the weather for travelling."

"They are on a mission to reach Eorl Eirík before he dies."

She made the sign of the cross, "Then God speed his journey. I can see you have much to tell us but we have news for you." She led Bersi and me to the hall where Seara was suckling a baby. "You have a granddaughter, Agnetha." The dog, Heimdall, had growled until we entered the hall and now leapt up to plant his paws on Bersi's chest and lick him.

Bersi's face lit up. He ruffled Heimdall's fur. He had been silent for much of the journey south and I knew why. He had put his wife and child from his mind while we had been in the north. It did not do to dwell on things over which you had no control but the closer to our home we came, the more worried he was. The relief now was palpable. Seara said, "And Heimdall has been a good watchdog. When our daughter stirs he lets me know. We are all three glad that you are home." Bersi knelt and kissed Seara's hand.

I asked, "And the birth?"

"Easier than Gunhilde's for she is younger. It bodes well for the future."

"Good."

"You are not disappointed that it is not a boy?"

"I have two grandsons already and Bersi will give me a third. I am content." I walked over and kissed the top of Seara's head, "I will leave you three alone but when she is ready, then her grandfather will hold her. First, I need to cleanse myself of horse sweat."

Mary looked pleased, "I will have the water heated and while you undress you can tell me of the north."

Mary helped to bathe me as we talked. She approved of my actions and was happy that Erik Red Hair had a wife. "His parents will be sad."

"He has two brothers and the reason he came with me was to make enough coin to become a farmer. He has that now and a family already."

"Good."

The Sword of Cnut

"And how is my land? At peace?"

"At peace and fecund, husband. We had twenty babies born while you were away and many girls had their first woman's moon. Your warriors will be in demand."

"And while we did not make the fortunes we did fighting the Wends, they all have silver in their purses and metal to sell to Haraldr. Some will be asking for land soon."

"You will cut down more trees?"

I nodded, "The ones that lie further away, the ones where we hunt deer and pig we shall leave, but those on dry ground will be used. The animals bore young?"

"The ewes and sows have young within them. If the weather does not worsen then your farmers are hopeful that they will all have good births."

As much as I wished to stay in the cosy warmth of my hall, I had a duty and that was to the valley. I rode, with just Gandálfr, to Billingham and the other settlements. They needed to know what we had done in their name and that they were safe from any Scottish raids, at least for a while. I saw vast improvements in their farms and businesses. I had kept the peace since I had arrived and that meant we all prospered. It was hard for me to leave some places as they all wanted to talk to me and thank me. If King Cnut left me alone then I might make Norton and my valley even more prosperous.

And we were left alone, at least for a while and that suited me. I could make my land stronger and by stronger I meant more fertile. The young men who returned from Northumbria were hardened by their time in the north and when I gave them land they worked just as hard as farmers as they had as warriors. The difference now was that when we trained each Sunday we had more warriors who had experienced battle. It made everyone into a better warrior. We now had, with the men from Billingham and my settlements, more than one hundred men. Whilst more than half were bondi the other half were mailed warriors. It was Osgar who noticed the difference when he joined us for our first Sunday after we returned.

"Your men have a swagger about them, Eorl. They went to war as youths and came back as men." He looked across the beck to Billingham. It is no wonder that the Saxons were defeated by the Norse and the Danes. The Saxons play at war." I said nothing, "You know that Edward is descended from the last king of Deira? That was the land around Jorvik. Aelle was killed in battle and your people took over Deira. It was over one hundred and fifty years ago. The men of Bernicia

The Sword of Cnut

fought on and their blood runs through Uhtred's line, but Deira," he shook his head, "it is a memory."

We had stopped for an ale break and I was intrigued, "So the family of Aelle fled north?"

"Lord Edward told me the tale when he had too much ale, not long after his wife died. Aelle's wife and daughter came north with the last of the king's bodyguards, Osric. They settled here for the queen became ill and the priest from the church healed her. They saw it as a sign and Osric became the leader of the village. In those days there were less than a dozen houses. The child that was born to the queen's daughter was a boy and Osric trained him to be a warrior. He still has the torc that was brought from Loidis. That was where the family lived. It is made of gold and I know not what Lord Edward will do with it. He brings it out from time to time and shows it to his sons. The tale is passed on."

"And now Edward drowns himself in ale."

"He was never a warrior, Eorl Sven, but he never needed to be. Billingham has ever been protected, not by spears but by marshes, becks and the sea. Your land at Norton is richer and that is why you were raided. I do not think that the wolves will come again for they have learned that the sheep now have a sheepdog." He patted the sword with the new black pommel, "Our men are now stronger. Lord Edward might not be able to protect his people but I can."

The story kept me thinking, for I knew that if Norton was to remain as strong as I had made it then I had to maintain our strength.

When I had time on my hands I took Ivaldi to one side, "Do you wish to return to your father and his farm?"

"I am torn, my lord, for I like my father's farm but I have also enjoyed looking after your horses."

"Then continue to do so. Take my horses to your father's farm. I just need two here for Bersi and for me. The rest can be tended to by you. Hopefully, their numbers will increase."

He was delighted and I now had a horse master.

We still had jet and, after we sailed to the mouth of the river in my drekar and hunted the seal, we had oil. Both could be traded along with the wool that we sheared from our sheep. Persson and his people had diversified from simply being fishermen. Where they lived were marshes and little islands of grass. They had bought some sheep from my people and found that they had prospered. The meat from the salt-fed lambs was prized and the animals did so well that we had a surplus from both their wool and that of the rest of my folk. I took the decision to sail to Agerhøne. I had not seen my eldest grandson nor my son for

The Sword of Cnut

some time and it would be good to see him. Bersi, of course, would stay at Norton. He had grown in every way. Mary was happy that I would see Steana, Gytha and Sven Steanason, our grandson.

It was Tvímánuður when we sailed. The young men who would be my crew had farms, some even had wives but they had planted late and their crops would not be ready until later than the rest of the valley. They had purses and the markets of Ribe would be where they spent their silver. Haldir and Aed also came with us, Frigga had given Haldir a son and Aed had grown into a young man who would soon join my shield wall. Haraldr was a good weaponsmith, but Haldir and Aed wanted a mail byrnie from Ribe. Haraldr had many demands on his skills.

I was happy with the crew I took. Every oar was manned and my warriors were keen to sail once more. We headed down the river, towards the sea. We now had ship's boys who were new. Erik Prow Jumper now took an oar as did Aed. Folki had his work cut out to train the new boys. I helped when I could but I confess I enjoyed simply being at sea again and I let Folki berate the boys. The winds meant we had to row sometimes for an hour or so and then the wind would veer. It suited my crew as the short bursts of effort were easy to manage. When we were not rowing, I sat with Haldir, Aed and Gandálfr by the mast fish where we ate the fish caught on the fish lines we trailed. Haldir and Aed were able to tell me more about life at Norton when I had been away in Northumbria.

"It was peaceful, eorl. Your reputation meant that brigands stayed away from our lands. Visitors and travellers told us of bandits to the south and north of us but we were vigilant and no one bothered us."

"King Cnut will be pleased that his law was upheld, but disappointed that there were places it was not."

Gandálfr snorted, "The king needs to choose better eorls. Eorl Siward seems like a strong leader as does Eorl Godwin, but King Cnut has rewarded some men ill-advisedly."

"You mean like Thorkell?" He nodded, "I know that King Cnut thinks you are a good warrior, Gandálfr, but I would not make the mistake of saying that in his presence."

He laughed, "One thing I have learned, Eorl, is that kings do not appreciate candid comments. I can keep my own counsel."

"Run out oars!" Folki's voice sent my men back to the oars and I rejoined my helmsman at the steering board.

"How are the new boys?"

The Sword of Cnut

"The same as the ones they have replaced. They think that climbing the mast is a game and some of them do not listen. They will learn but this is always the time that I become annoyed."

"You were a ship's boy with your father."

"I was and I remember being the same. This voyage will see them grow."

It was on the second day at sea that Diuri, one of the new boys, had to shout down from the masthead. It was his first time as the loftiest lookout but his voice was strong as he hailed down, "Sail to the northeast, Captain. She has shields."

We were not raiding and our shields were inboard. This was a raider. The wind was from the north and that meant the ship would soon be upon us.

"Aed, up the mast and use your eyes. Diuri has done well to spot her, but you can tell me how many oars she has."

Folki said, "She may be just a raider heading for Frisia, or even the land of the East Angles."

Haldir said, "And, equally, she could be a pirate. When I raided with Olaf the Fearless, we sought any ship, no matter what the size, that had no shields along their side. If I were you, Eorl, I would arm the men. It is better to be safe than sorry."

Gandálfr nodded his agreement and I said, "Arm yourselves."

Aed scrambled up the mast and he sat on the crosspiece. He shaded his eyes against the light. I donned my helmet and strapped on Oathsword. I would not use mail. Some of the men wore leather byrnies and they would afford protection. Everyone put on their helmets.

"Eorl Sven, I recognise her. She is the pirate we saw in Hwitebi, it is *'Grid'*. She has eighteen oars on each side."

Haldir said, "Thorir Grimblade; then he has a new crew. I wonder if he will recognise us?"

The Norns had been spinning. The odds of meeting here in the middle of the great sea were slim. There was little point in bemoaning the meeting. We had to deal with it. One thing was for sure. We would be outnumbered and these men would be ruthless. We either won the race or we would die.

"Ship's boys, those with bows string them. As for the rest, today you will use your slings." We had some spears that were used for throwing and I added, "Bring the throwing spears and spread them out along the deck." I picked up my shield and went back to the steering board. It was clear that they had seen us as the Norse ship changed course slightly. We both had the wind and neither of us would need oars. I peered astern. "Can we outrun her?"

The Sword of Cnut

Folki glanced astern and studied her, "When last we saw her she was in need of repair. If they have not done so then she may have weed."

I peered aft. The drekar did not have a cargo and rode slightly higher in the water. When her prow rose, I saw the distinctive green of weed.

"Can we push *'Falcon'*?"

"The sail is well maintained, and we have new sheets. Our keel is free from weed," he nodded. He shouted, "Full sail."

It was as though I was on my horse and I had kicked her on. We leapt forward. I saw a gap appear between us and the raider. Then, a few moments later, she ran out her oars. She was coming after us. It was a race. We had taken the wind and that meant we were not sailing the course we had chosen but the speediest one. We could have stayed to fight but my crew was worth more to me than the one on the Norseman. We would run with the wind and change course when we had lost her.

Haldir and Gandálfr joined me at the steering board. Haldir pointed, "She is gaining. The oars are making the difference. They will catch us."

"And when they do we will be ready and they will be tired. The speed they are maintaining cannot be doing their ship any good. If there is weed in the hull then who knows what damage lies beneath? They may have the worm."

Gandálfr rubbed his beard, "The speed at which they are closing tells me, Eorl, that they have a large crew. We will be outnumbered and our men have yet to fight a sea battle."

"Aye, I think I am the only one aboard who was at Svolder. It cannot be helped."

Haldir said, "I was a pirate too, Eorl. Do not dismiss my experience so easily."

We ploughed on through the waves. They were not huge ones but each time our prow dipped the crew were showered with seawater. It was mesmerising to watch the drekar draw closer and closer to us. Aed had joined us and I said, "Aed, fetch me your bow."

He hurried off to bring his bow. Returning with it and his bag of arrows, he strung it and handed it to me, "Why do you need the bow, Eorl?"

"When I was a ship's boy and sailed with Sweyn Skull Taker I used a bow. It is many years since I drew one in anger but I will loose an arrow when I deem we are in range. It will tell me how close they are and it will, perhaps, be a warning to those on *'Grid'*. These are your arrows, which is the best?"

The Sword of Cnut

He selected one and looked down the shaft's length, "This one is truest."

I took the arrow and smoothed the fletch. I nocked it and held the bow in my left hand. In the time it had taken me to do so, the drekar had drawn a length closer. The oars were becoming a little more ragged but they were still driving the ship towards us. "Have the men prepare themselves. They will be coming at our larboard side." Gandálfr and Haldir hurried off. "Folki, when they close, you know what to do."

"Aye, Eorl."

The wind would be against me and so I waited a few more heartbeats before I drew back and then loosed. My shoulders complained at the draw for it was some years since I had drawn a bow but you learn, when you are young, how to aim and that never leaves you. I aimed at the centre of the drekar. I handed the bow to Aed and watched the flight of the arrow as it plunged down towards the forward part of the drekar. The men rowing the Norse ship had their backs to the falling arrow and when I heard the shout and saw one oar fall out of sequence, I knew I had hit someone. My single arrow did not slow the drekar but I knew that I would have alarmed them. Thorir Grimblade would be wondering if my arrow was a test arrow and he was about to be showered with more missiles. The drekar sped up as the rowers were urged to close with us. I saw that their steering board was put over a little more and she was aimed at our mid-section. Her ship's boys were not ready with slings and bows but grappling hooks.

"You choose your moment Folki. I will be with the others." I picked up my shield and drew Oathsword. Gandálfr and Haldir had the men ready at the larboard side. A dozen of the crew held throwing spears. Gandálfr said, "Slingers, see if you can bring down some of their boys."

Haldir shouted, "Aed, you have seen what the eorl can do. Make their helmsman fill his breeks."

That elicited a cheer from our men. Our boys hurled their stones. Only one of their ship's boys was hit but the other stones, falling in the well of the ship, hit men and, whilst not life-threatening, would have been annoying as well as distracting. I heard the creak of Aed's bow as he drew back. I looked at the drekar's stern and I saw Thorir Grimblade and his helmsman. The rest of the crew were rowing. Aed's arrow flew true. Thorir Grimblade saw it coming and his shield blocked it. The arrow stuck in the shield.

"Well done, Aed."

"But I did not hit him."

The Sword of Cnut

"The arrow in the shield tells them that they are in range and that will make the helmsman nervous. Battle is not always about the clash of arms. Sometimes it is a battle of minds."

I heard the shout from Thorir Grimblade as he urged his rowers for one last effort. Folki had been awaiting his moment. As the oars bit into the water, Folki put our steering board over to head towards the side of the drekar. We lost a little of the wind and *'Grid'* slid ahead of us.

Gandálfr was ready and, as our drekar's sudden move brought us closer to the enemy, he shouted, "Spears!" As our drekar's hull sheared and shattered oars on the raider, so a dozen or so spears were hurled. Added to the stones from our slingers, a harvest was reaped. The screams from the rowers as the splinters of wood wounded and killed men at the oars were drowned out by a crash as our hulls came together. We were lower in the water than the Norseman because of our cargo and the wider part of our drekar was stronger. The mast on *'Grid'* shifted alarmingly to larboard.

Our slingers had won the battle and only one grappling hook reached us. As Ingvar sliced his sword through the rope, the pirates who were close enough leapt aboard. Gandálfr, Haldir and I were together and the first men aboard did not even make our deck. With my shield above me, I lunged with Oathsword and my blade found flesh. When I saw the shield with the arrow in it, I knew that Thorir Grimblade was above me. He used his shield as a weapon and jumped down. Gandálfr did what all hearthweru swear to do. He took the blow for me and the Norse warrior knocked Gandálfr to the ground. His falling had saved me and now I had to save him. I punched with my shield at the pirate and slashed with my sword. He reeled and Oathsword sliced across his knee.

Folki's voice came above the clamour of battle, "The enemy ship is sinking!" Even as I blocked the blow from Grimblade's sword, I could see that the enemy drekar was no longer above us.

Haldir shouted, "Men of Norton, now is the time to push these pirates into the sea."

The blow from Grimblade on my shield was so fiercely struck that the sound was like a crack of thunder and I had to step back. The pirate thought he had me but this was my drekar and I knew every plank on her deck. I moved slightly so that my back was to the mast fish and when he swung a second time I was braced by the mast fish and I did not move. The press of men meant that neither of us could use our swords and so I pulled back my head and butted him. I had a Herkumbl on my helmet, a sword put there by Haraldr, and the force of my strike broke Grimblade's nose, I dropped Oathsword and drew Norse Splitter.

The Sword of Cnut

As blood poured from Thorir Grimblade's nose I drove my dagger under his raised arm. It penetrated the mail and his armpit. When hot blood flooded over my hand and his body went limp, I knew he was dead.

It was only as he fell that I saw we were the last two fighting. The men who had pressed behind the leader of the pirates had been slaughtered by my men. Of the other drekar, there was no sign. My men cheered but I ran to Gandálfr who was trying to raise himself from the deck.

"Stay! You are hurt." He gasped for air and shook his head. "Aed, Haldir, take off his mail." As they hurried to obey me I looked around. I could not see any bodies of my crew but a few of the pirates still moved. "Give the wounded a warrior's death. Folki, resume our course."

I knelt again as Gandálfr's byrnie was removed. I saw no blood and he had not spewed forth blood from his mouth. They were good signs. I used my hands as gently as I could. It was as I touched my hearthweru's ribs that he winced. I breathed a sigh of relief. Broken ribs were painful but they would heal. "Haldir, find a bandage and bind his wounds." He hurried off, "You saved me, Gandálfr. I thank you."

He gave a weak smile, "I am the last of your oathsworn. My sword was in my hand, and I would have gone to Valhalla. He is dead?"

"He is dead."

"And their ship?"

Aed said, "She is wreckage and the last of her crew will be feeding the fishes before night falls."

Some of their crew would survive for a time and cling, as Haldir had done, to wreckage, but unless they had Haldir's fortune and a ship picked them up, then they would die and their spirits become the seabirds that followed ships, calling to sailors for help.

As Haldir bandaged Gandálfr, I retrieved Oathsword and then went around my wounded to ask after them. By the time the dead, stripped of anything of value, had been hurled overboard, it was dark and we had time to reflect. We had been saved by our ship. In the battle of the drekar, ours had more heart. All our work over the winter had paid off. When I returned to Norton I would make a blót.

The Sword of Cnut
Chapter 15

Denmark 1024

It was good to see my son again. He had a daughter too, Bertha, and she was beautiful. My grandson was now walking. He was, however, more than a little wary of me for I was a stranger. While the damage to my drekar was repaired and Gandálfr healed, I enjoyed two days with Steana and his family. I was loath to leave and when Haldir came with the suggestion that the drekar sail to Ribe without me and trade, I did not hesitate. Many would not have done so but I trusted my crew and my cousin. Whilst I might miss speaking with my foster father, the time with my family was more valuable than silver.

That evening as I ate with Steana, for the first time in years, we both unburdened ourselves of not only what we had done in those years but also the regrets we had. I learned of warriors who had fallen in the rebellion and it saddened me for many of them were men who had been ship's boys with me and then progressed, as I had, to be in the shield wall. I told him of my elevation and he was more impressed by the title than I was. I knew it had been given so that King Cnut had more power and control over me. Gytha retired and my son and I watched the flames on the fire dance around the last log we had placed on it.

"Jarl Sweyn Skull Taker will go to war no more."

"He was hurt in the rebellion?"

"No, but he is getting old. His hair is white and his reactions are not as sharp as they once were. Sweyn One Eye wishes him to stay in Ribe."

"And my foster father agreed?" My son nodded. "Then he is getting old."

"He is also more than a little unhappy with the way that Denmark is run. Jarl Ulf taxes the people heavily. Some say it is his choice and others that the orders come from King Cnut."

"It is the same in England. The difference in England is that they are used to being taxed." I shook my head, "They called it Danegeld once as it was money to pay off we Danes. Now it is called heregeld, the money to keep England safe."

"You know him better than anyone, Father, has he changed?"

It was a good question and I shrugged my answer, "Kings are not the same as ordinary men. They are a new thing here in Denmark. King Sweyn was the first and while Cnut is not as ruthless as his father, he

The Sword of Cnut

has done things which do not meet with my approval, not that he needs it but I would like to think that he heeded the advice of one who helped to form his mind when he was young."

We watched the log in the fire as it cracked open and spat sparks. Steana leant over and flicked them back with his dagger. He then poured us another ale. I had probably had enough but I was enjoying the company of my son. I would nurse it but not drink it all. I did not wish to be up all night making water.

"So, my sister and brother have children too?" I nodded and swallowed some ale. "Then your blood continues to another generation."

"And your children will have children. It is life."

"But we cannot determine the shape their lives take, can we? That future is determined by men like King Cnut, King Olaf and the Emperor. They are at the top of the tree and we scurry around at its base seeking the scraps that they throw us."

"You and I are luckier than most. Sweyn Skull Taker and I both have high rank. Only the king or his regent gives us orders. You know that my foster father will never abuse his position."

"I do and I know that I am lucky, but Jarl Ulf is not the man now who helped us put down the rebellion. It is not what he has done but…" he held up the horn of ale. "It is the ale talking and when this one is put to bed I will join it." He drank some and said, "I miss sailing with you, Father. I miss Mother too, despite her pious looks. I am glad you came for I wondered if I would ever see you again. Your stories of life in England make me wonder if it is more dangerous for you than if you were still in Denmark."

"A man cannot undo what has been done. The Norns do not like such meddling. Your mother is happier in Norton than she was here and as I snatched her from Norton I was duty-bound to return her there. They are good people who live on my land. They are not all Danes but we are one people. Does that make sense?"

"It does and it pleases me but it still does not change the fact that when you leave neither of us knows when we shall see each other again. Bertha and Sven will grow up and only know their grandfather through the stories that are told of him. You will be as fantastical a figure as Gunnlaug the Worm Tongue and Raven the Skald."

I laughed, "I might have hoped for a better comparison than Gunnlaug the Worm Tongue."

He laughed and shook his head, "It is the ale talking, but I mention him for the last time Sweyn One Eye was here he told their tales after we had eaten. They were on my mind. My point is that I want my

The Sword of Cnut

children to know the real Sven Saxon Sword and not the legend. You are a better man than the legend."

"Thank you for that and I promise that I will try to visit as often as I can. If Haldir and Folki make good trades then we can make this an annual visit. How would that be?"

He brightened, "That would suit me well and I know that Siggi, my father-in-law, would like to see you and an annual visit is easier to plan for."

"I intend to see my old oar brother tomorrow."

"Good, for Gytha would like to have him and her mother to feast with us. Your visit was unexpected and the food we had for you was less than what we would have prepared had we known you were coming. Tomorrow, we feast."

I did not rise as early as I would have done if I had been in Norton, the ale and the lateness of the night meant it was after dawn when I rose. Gytha knew how to cook and the fried salted pork was delicious with the bread made in their ovens. "Today, I will visit with Siggi."

"And I will come too."

My son and I left to walk the few miles to Siggi's farm. I was touched by the attention I received. All wanted to know about Mary. She had always been popular in the village for she was a kind woman. Some asked me about their sons who had left Denmark to follow me. I told them that when my ship returned from Ribe, they would get to see them.

Once we had left the houses and passed the odd farm, Steana and I were able to speak, "My land is more sparsely populated than this land, Steana." He gave me a questioning look. "What I mean is that I can give land away to men who wish to follow me. You have none left to give."

"It is the same all over Denmark, Father. We are a relatively small land and there is little left to give away."

"And that may be why the king lives in England and not Denmark."

"I had not thought of that."

"Aye, there are more people in King Cnut's new realm but it is a bigger country. How King Æthelred made such a mess of running it I will never know."

"That may have had something to do with our raids, Father. It was Oathsword that helped to take it from him."

We reached Siggi's farm and, as usual, my old oar brother was busy with his sons and tending to his pigs. Siggi's life was his farm, his family and, most of all, his pigs. He was the most successful farmer on

The Sword of Cnut

the whole coast and each time I visited I was amazed at the number of beasts he had raised. He was, of course, delighted to see me.

Steana said, "Gytha would have you and her mother join us at my home, Siggi, so that you can feast with my father."

"We would be honoured."

"Then I will leave you and help my wife prepare. This will be the first time she has entertained her father and father-in-law together. She will want perfection."

He left us and Siggi said, "He is a good hersir."

"And they are a good family. We are lucky, Siggi."

He shook his head, "There was no luck involved, Sven, we both brought up our families well and I am proud of that. We both did it differently but our hearts were in the same place and that is what is important."

He took me on a tour of the farm. His pigs were fecund and more of his sows had bred litters. I knew that other farmers came to buy from him. He pointed to two sows each suckling piglets. "Both of these are ready to have their young weaned. When do you leave?"

"I intend to let my crew have some time here when they return from Ribe, say a week?"

"Then by the time you leave, I shall have a gift for you: two of the boars and four of the sows."

"That is too generous of you. I will pay you."

"I would be insulted. We both know that I would not be here now but for you. It was you who protected me. Besides, your son is the best of hersirs. While others demand that every man take arms and go to war, Steana lets men choose. He inherited his father's fairness."

The feast, that evening, was everything I hoped it would be. Siggi and I enjoyed bouncing our grandchildren on our knees and then handing over Bertha to her mother when she cried. We both competed to pull the funniest of faces to make Sven laugh and we enjoyed the best of ale and food. The evening ended with Steana singing the song of Svolder. It embarrassed me but clearly pleased the others. I went to bed that night and slept well. Siggi left after a fine breakfast, and I was content. Old friends are the best of friends and none was older than Siggi.

My ship arrived in the late afternoon. She rode higher in the water and I knew that she had traded. Most of the men, when the ship was moored, went to find the families they had left. The ones like Haldir and Aed, who had come to us from other places, stayed in the warrior hall.

Before he left, I spoke with Folki, "The trade went well?"

The Sword of Cnut

"It did. Aksel died last winter and it is your cousin, Alf, who is now the master. He paid us more for the jet we traded than last time. Now that Hwitebi is desolate there are fewer men trading jet. It puts up the price." Thorir Grimblade had much to answer for but he had paid with his ship and his life. It was *wyrd*. His destruction of the port had made our profits double.

"Then we shall visit Hwitebi again." I had not been sure of mining once more but only a fool would reject the chance of a purse such as the one Folki gave to me.

The week flew by. I made the most of my time with my family but, at the end of the week, when I announced we were leaving, it felt as though my heart would break to leave them. My men all boarded the drekar with gifts from their families. I had bought other items to take back and when the piglets arrived we were ready to sail.

Siggi and Steana came to the ship to see me off, "I will return at this time next year and there will be gifts from us." I handed over two pieces of jet, one to Siggi and one to Steana. "Siggi, you would not accept silver so accept this jet. When next I come there will be other gifts, too."

"Eorl Sven, the tide."

I waved acknowledgement and clasped first Siggi's arm and then my son's. I climbed aboard and the ship left the land. Haldir stood next to me as we headed west, "I envy you, Eorl Sven. My life as a pirate is in the past and I hope that with Aed and my wife, we can build a family such as yours."

It was as fine a compliment as I had ever been given and it pleased me.

We kept a sharp eye for pirates as we headed home. I knew that when we were younger my cousins and I had been raiders but we had never been pirates. It was a minor distinction but I knew I was different from men like Thorir Grimblade. We passed the basking seals that marked the mouth of our estuary. We did not hunt them all the time and when we did we left more alive than were hunted. The herd was a large one and I saw many young. We maintained the balance. Pirates did not for they plundered and took all. The squealing of the piglets drew my eye and nose to them. Folki and his boys would have a hard job shifting the mess that the animals left but it would be worth it as our herds of pigs prospered and the new blood made future animals stronger. We were lucky with the timing of the tides and made the beck channel in one day. We anchored when the tide was still high and had the ship emptied before the drekar bottomed. I went with Folki and the boys to anchor the drekar in the river where they would clean it and then use

The Sword of Cnut

our ship's boat to row ashore. I stayed with them to take off the prow. We would not be using the ship again and it was bad luck to leave the prow on a ship. By the time I had finished, the decks had been swabbed clean of animal dung and with four anchors the drekar would be safely moored. I decided that we would build a quay here so that the ship could be moored safely.

Mary and our families were waiting for us at my hall when we reached our home. I carried the falcon prow over my shoulder. Mary always looked pleased to see me and that made me inordinately happy. Once in the warmth of my hall and with a horn of ale a thrall had brought me I was content.

"Food will be fetched soon." Mary sat next to me and put another log on the fire. "While we wait tell me all about our son and our former home. I miss both."

She had been the matriarch of Agerhøne and everyone had asked after Mary. She was missed more than I was. I told her everything down to the minutest of detail and when I said that I would return each year I saw the envy in her eyes. She would want to come but she did not enjoy the sea. She would have to live the experience through my eyes. When I told her of Siggi and his gift she beamed, "I know you value your warriors highly but I think that the best friend you have ever had, husband, is the most peaceful of them, Siggi."

Perhaps she was right. Despite the huge gaps between our meetings, our reunions were always warm and it was as though we had seen each other the previous day. That is the true measure of friendship. I did not tell her of the pirate. I did not want to spoil the mood. She would find out eventually, but it would be in daylight and she would have the whole day to rationalise the event. If I told her now then her dreams would be haunted.

Bersi and Seara, along with their daughter, dined with us. Bersi was as interested in Agerhøne as any. Poor Seara was bewildered at the names that flew across the table. She had a straight face as I told her what some character or other had said while we laughed until tears flowed. Norton was not Agerhøne. In Agerhøne there were few who were not Danish. Mary had been rare. She had been a free woman. It was the thralls in Agerhøne who were different. Here we had Danes, Saxons and Norse blood. Our language reflected that mixture. I did not know which one was better but I did not need to make that distinction. Both were my worlds.

We did not draw the drekar up. I had no plans to sail again any time soon. It was summer and there was work enough for our men without the problems of dragging the drekar to its winter home. We built the

The Sword of Cnut

quay on the river and the summer passed peacefully. I visited with Gunhilde and Ragnar as well as the farms and villages that had prospered under our peace. I also spent time with Edward and Osgar. The time after our return was regarded, certainly by me, as the golden time. Life was good and the land prospered. Eorl Siward kept the north peaceful and I ensured that Cnut's law was upheld along the Tees. My warriors fathered children. Gunhilde and Seara were also both with child once more and as we drew the drekar up to its winter bed, I wondered if the Norns had spun me a life of peace. Would Oathsword remain sheathed? Perhaps the attack by the pirate had been the last time that Oathsword would be drawn in anger.

Chapter 16

The Swedish War 1025

Sweyn was born to Seara and Sven to Gunhilde in high summer. There would be two Svens to follow me: Sven Steanason and Sven Ragnarsson. As I grew more grey hairs and my pate thinned it was a comfort. The young men who had been slingers when the Norse had raided were now men with children of their own and they stood in the shield wall. Thanks to our victories more men had mail byrnies than leather. Haraldr and Haraldrsson's workshop ensured that when we hunted or went to war we had fine weapons. Of course, the new babies who had been born had come at a cost. The old had died. Fewer of them perished than was expected and that was because of foresight. None had starved in the winter. Any bounty that we had was shared. Mary was still the angel who took our thralls to distribute food to the old when the snows came and the land froze. Life was good.

It was Glam the Fair who ended the idyll of peace. His arrival, with an escort of ten mailed men, did not suggest a courtesy visit. King Cnut's warrior's arrival told me that he was bringing a message from the king. Mary's face told me that she knew what it entailed. Her family would be going to war. I also knew that I would not be visiting Agerhøne as I had promised. We had cleaned the drekar and relaunched her but there would be no voyage to Hwitebi and we would not be hunting seals. King Cnut needed Oathsword.

He dismounted and I saw that the young warrior I had known was now growing older. He clasped my arm and shook his head, "Your peace is over, Eorl Sven Saxon Sword, and you go to war."

I nodded, "And where to this time?"

"Let us go within your hall and I will tell all."

"Gandálfr, take Lord Glam's warriors to the warrior hall."

Mary disappeared. She would be in the kitchen helping to prepare food and Glam and I were left alone in my hall.

Glam began without preamble, "Jarl Ulf, Ulf Sprakaleggson, is fermenting trouble in Denmark. He has conspired with King Arnaud Jacob of Sweden and King Olaf of Norway. It seems he wishes to put Prince Harthacnut on the throne."

"But the prince is just eight!"

He gave me a wry smile as a thrall brought in ale and two horns. "I think that acting as regent in Denmark has given Ulf delusions. He sees

The Sword of Cnut

himself as a ruler, for the prince, if Ulf succeeded, would be a figurehead. King Cnut needs you and a crew of fifty warriors. The muster is at Roskilde by the start of Sólmánuður."

"That means we would be away in the summer when the fields need to be tended."

Glam frowned, he was a warrior and not a farmer, "There are thralls and women to work the fields."

"And if I take my men away for what I assume is a war of some months, then who will guard my lands?"

"Eorl Siward. When I leave here I ride north to Bebbanburg to give him the king's orders. I will take a ship from there to sail to the muster. Eorl Siward will provide men."

"But he will stay?"

"The Scots respect him and Northumbria is safe. Earl Ealdred will also remain in Northumbria." He saw my face and added, "The king needs Oathsword. Your son and cousin will be coming to war too." He sighed, "The king has taken to referring to you as the Sword of Cnut. You and Oathsword have become as one."

That was all that I needed; another name. "And Jarl Sweyn Skull Taker?"

He shook his head, "Like Eorl Siward, he will guard Ribe with the older warriors. The young warriors will go to war."

Mary entered, "Will you and your men be staying long, Lord Glam?"

He shook his head, "We ride to Dun Holm. The king wishes for a relic of St Cuthbert to come with us. We will take the cross he wore about his neck before his death. The king hopes that it will bring with it the support of the saint."

Mary snapped, "I doubt that the saint would sanction war, Lord Glam."

The warrior was not married and I saw him recoil from the venom in my wife's words. He stood and bowed, "I am sorry, my lady, forgive a warrior. Eorl Sven, I will see you at the muster."

After he had gone, I said, "He was a messenger only, Mary. The king is the one who makes the decisions."

She nodded, "You go to war?"

"Aye, and I have to take fifty men."

She was clever and her eyes widened as she made the calculation in her head, "Bersi?" I nodded. "Ragnar?"

"Aye, both are warriors and I cannot leave them at home and take those who have no mail. This is war and I need men who can stand in a

The Sword of Cnut

shield wall. Our drekar will be double-oared. We fight the Swedes and that sea is far from here. We may not be back before Gormánuður."

"And if you are not back by then it means that you will never return." I nodded. "I curse that sword."

I could not help but clutch the Hammer of Thor. I knew why she said what she did but the Norns had spun their webs and it did not do to anger them. What price would be paid for her words?

I did not wait until the next day but after telling Bersi, Haldir and Gandálfr, I mounted Verðandi and rode to give the news to my mailed warriors that their king called them. None of them had been called before, I had just used my young men and none could object but I saw that some of them looked disappointed. Others, like my son-in-law Ragnar, seemed happy to be going to war. It took most of the day for I was not sure when I would visit again and I wanted the ones who remained to be alert and vigilant. I did not have time to visit with Edward and Osgar. I would be taking warriors from Billingham, but not the best, Osgar would stay. I needed his eye watching the beck and my hall. Bersi dined with us as did Haldir. Our departure was not imminent but they wished to know why we went to war. For all of them, it would be new. Even Haldir had never raided or fought in the sea to the east of Denmark. We would be on land that the Swedish claimed.

"Will we fight at sea?" Aed was eating with us and he had been in the battle with the pirate. It was still fresh in his memory.

I nodded, "The Norse and the Swede both have mighty fleets. Aye, they will use their ships."

"And we will fight in mail?"

"Yes, Bersi." I glanced at Seara. I knew what Bersi meant. Fighting at sea in mail meant you either won or you died. There was no in-between. There was no retreat and mail meant death by drowning even if you were unwounded.

Mary shook her head, "I thought this Jarl Ulf was a friend of the king's. Why has he turned against his monarch?"

"The war with the Wends was almost five years ago. Since then King Cnut has stayed in England. Perhaps Ulf changed. Power can do that to a man. Remember Thorkell the Tall? He betrayed the king twice."

Bersi took his wife's hand and kissed it, "I shall make the most of my time before we leave."

Haldir nodded, "When I was a raider, I could not wait to get to sea but now that I have a wife and my own child it is different. When we are at war I shall be the warrior, but until then I will be the husband and father."

The Sword of Cnut

Aed said, "For my part, I look forward to this. I now have mail and while I will be the youngest in the shield wall, I hope to do my duty and to earn honour."

Shaking my head I said, "There is little honour in a shield wall. You fight for your life and your shield brothers but death, when it comes, can be brutal."

"Enough of this talk!" Mary's commanding voice silenced us all, "I accept that you have to go to war but there will be no more talk at the table." I nodded. She was right and the talk changed to more mundane matters such as the planting of crops and the clearing of trees.

Osgar understood why I would not be taking him but he was disappointed. "I would have liked to fight in such a battle. The Norse raid was my biggest one and looking back I can see that was just a raid. You will need our mailed men?"

There were just four of them but they were young men and two had sailed with me before. All four had done well in the battle against the Norse and I was confident they would fit in. "Aye, and that means that the majority of the men left to defend Norton will be from Billingham."

"And that is why I stay. Aye." He nodded, "Then when you come home, Eorl Sven, either your hall will be safe or my head will be atop a spear."

"And I pray that it will be the former."

The time passed far more quickly than any of us wished. It would take a week to reach Roskilde and there were not enough hours in the day for us to do that which we wished. Haraldr and his sons had their forge going all day to make arrowheads and spearheads. We were going to be fighting across the sea and we could not guarantee finding spare weapons. The ship had to be provisioned with salted fish and meat. We would augment our supplies when we were at sea by fishing but we had to be self-sufficient. Our water barrels could be replenished at Roskilde but we would have to take ale to last us until we returned. We had the spare sail examined and repaired. Some time soon we would need a new one but it would be bad luck to use one now while our other remained undamaged.

The night before we left Mary snuggled in my arms, "I thought, when we returned here, that your days of leaving were gone."

"As did I but," I was about to say the Norns had spun but thought better of it, "the king commands and we obey."

"He may be a Christian king, Husband, but I am not sure he is a good one. I can understand quelling dissent in Denmark, but why try to take more land in Sweden?"

The Sword of Cnut

I had no answer for that and I agreed with my wife. Perhaps King Cnut had more in common with his father than I had thought.

"Come home safe and bring back Bersi and Ragnar. I would not have their wives made widows and their children left fatherless."

"And I swear that so long as I am alive so shall they be." I was not sure how I would manage it and perhaps I was tempting the Norns, but it was all that I could do to ease my wife's worries. She knew that when I swore an oath I kept it.

With so many men aboard our leaving brought crowds to the river to see us off. We had built a quay on the river. It had been to enable us to unload the drekar when we came back from our trades. It now proved its value as it was easier to load the ship from the river rather than using the beck channel. The people who came to see us off would have a walk back and that walk would be a sad one. Women would wonder if sons, brothers, husbands and fathers would return. My grandchildren were there and it pained me to bid them farewell. Would I see them grow?

The oars were manned, for the wind was not the one we had requested, I waved a farewell to the land and my men sang as they rowed.

The king did call and his men they came
Each one a warrior and a Dane
The mighty fleet left our home in the west
To sail to Svolder with the best of the best
Swedes and Norse were gathered as one
To fight King Olaf Tryggvasson
Mighty ships and brave warriors' blades
The memory of Svolder never fades
The Norse abandoned their faithless king
Aboard Long Serpent their swords did bring
The Norse made a bridge of all their ships
Determined that King Sweyn they would eclipse
Brave Jarl Harald and all his crew
Felt the full force of a ship that was new
Mighty ships and brave warriors' blades
The memory of Svolder never fades
None could get close to the Norwegian King
To his perilous crown he did cling
Until Skull Taker and his hearthweru
Attacked the side of the ship that was new
Swooping Hawk leapt through the sky
To land like a warrior born to fly

The Sword of Cnut

Mighty ships and brave warriors' blades
The memory of Svolder never fades
With such great deeds the clan would sing
They cleared the drekar next to the king
Facing Olaf were the jarl and Sven
Agerhøne and Oathsword joined again
Mighty ships and brave warriors' blades
The memory of Svolder never fades
The bodyguards of the King of Norway
Fought like wolves in a savage way
It mattered not for the Dragon Sword won
Stabbing and slaying everyone
The king chose the sea as his way of death
And Long Serpent was his funeral wreath
Mighty ships and brave warriors' blades
The memory of Svolder never fades
Mighty ships and brave warriors' blades
The memory of Svolder never fades

    It seemed appropriate to sing the song of Svolder for that had been fought in the waters between Denmark and Norway. This time the Swedes would be added to the mixture as well as Danish rebels.

    Once we reached the sea we were able to use the wind. Men used salve to ease the irritation caused by the oars. By the time we reached Roskilde the hands of the rowers would be hardened. Salt water helped to harden them. Our faces would be caked in salt and our skin darkened by the sun and wind. We would look and feel different. I knew that the time at the oars and the songs we would sing would bind and bond the crew. Those bonds would be tested when we fought in a shield wall.

    It took just six days to pass through the straits and reach the port that lay close to Roskilde. Our slightly early arrival ensured a good anchorage. We were not able to tie to the quay but we had but a short way to ferry the crew ashore. Unlike other captains, I was happy for my men to go ashore, stretch their legs and spend their coppers on ale. I trusted them. The ones who were kept aboard their ships showed that their captains feared what they might do when ashore.

    I went with Bersi and Ragnar Ragnarsson to the king's hall. Ragnar Ragnarsson was my son-in-law and he might have responsibilities in the future. I would prepare him. We had yet to don our mail but I was recognised by the guards at the doors to the mead hall. They both banged the hafts of the spears on the ground and said, in unison, "Hail, Eorl Sven and Oathsword."

The Sword of Cnut

Their greeting alerted those who were within and all faces turned to us as we entered. I recognised many of the men who were there. Some had been, like me, young men at Svolder. Now, like me, they were the advisors to the young king.

King Cnut had filled out since last I had seen him. Since the war with the Wends he had lived in England and I could see that he had lived the good life and eaten well. "Welcome, my most loyal of lieutenants. I have not had the chance to thank you for the defence of my border. I do so now." He clasped my forearm and the others all cheered and banged the pommels of their daggers on the table. "You have come early and that bodes well for us. Sit, for we were talking about our plans." He spied my sword and beamed, "And, with Oathsword, wielded by the Sword of Cnut at our side we cannot do anything but win!"

I saw then what the king was trying to do. He was making the association with the sword and with me almost a symbol. The sword had never lost and by including his name he was claiming that invincibility.

I drank the ale and said little. I was listening for they all clearly knew more about the king's intentions than I did. I learned that he planned on a strategy combining both land and sea forces. We would land in Sweden and the fleet would follow us so that we had both support and, if necessary, a longphort that could be used as a seaborne fortress.

One of the other jarls, Ork, asked, "But if the enemy fleets combine and catch our ships at sea then they will be destroyed. The enemy has more ships than we do."

That began a debate which interested me for Ork was right. If I was the King of Sweden then I would relish the thought of the landing of an army and defenceless drekar waiting to be destroyed. Our army would be trapped with no way home. The king seemed confident that would not happen. Perhaps he had spies and knew the Swedes' intentions but the seed planted in my head worried me. The king had us fed but I did not get to speak to him. Roskilde was too small to accommodate all the warriors and so we would sleep on the ship. All my men had enjoyed hot food and it would not be a hardship.

The ships led by my son and cousin arrived the next day. They had six ships with them. Arriving when they did meant that they had to anchor further in the bay. I had my men row me ashore and awaited their arrival. I had seen Steana, of course, when I had last visited Denmark but I had not seen Sweyn One Eye and his son Sweyn since I had left for England. My son and cousin, along with his son, landed

The Sword of Cnut

together. Sweyn One Eye had aged. I suppose I had too but without a mirror a man did not know. His son looked, the eye apart, to be just as his father was when he was young.

I clasped Sweyn One Eye's hand. We had been oar brothers and as close as real brothers when we were young. Alf, Swooping Hawk, could never be as close to me as Sweyn. We had faced death together and survived.

"Good to see you, Sven. This is my son Sweyn Golden Hair." It was only then that I saw that his son's hair was longer than his father's, and while my cousin's was flecked with grey, his son's was lustrous and golden.

"It is good to meet you." I pointed to the road that led to Roskilde, "We have a short walk ahead of us. The king is at the mead hall."

We began to walk. I walked next to One Eye who asked, "And do we know his plans?"

I told him and he shook his head, "When we fought last time it was the advice of my father and Jarl Ulf that was heeded. He has neither now and it seems to me that his plans are flawed."

I nodded, "Yet he will not be gainsaid. After he told us yesterday of his plans, there were others who tried to offer other plans but he would have none of it."

We were alone on the road and said, quietly. "And will he do as his father did at Svolder and let others do his dying?"

"If he is ashore with us then it is hard to see how he will manage that, but we shall see."

The hall was rammed to the rafters with all the leaders who had come. I saw no sign of Earl Godwin or any other English eorl. It seemed my sword was the only one that was needed. I knew that there were English warriors of Danish extraction with the army but none were eorls. It was an army led by Danes.

The king greeted his leaders warmly and, after he had toasted them, went through a refined version of the plans he had told us the previous day. I do not think he was pleased with the muted response. There were some who cheered and banged the table with their pommels but most were silent. I knew his face and his tone. When he spoke and glared I knew that he was not happy.

"We sail at dawn. I will lead the fleet with my ship, *'The Trinity'*." That it was a Christian name was not unexpected but we preferred names that reflected our past. It was not a good sign. It was the largest ship I had ever seen and would be a target for our enemies. "We sail east and land on the southern coast of the land claimed by King Arnaud Jacob. You will all need to leave some warriors aboard your ships to

The Sword of Cnut

help sail them and then fight should they be attacked. The fleet will sail to the harbour that is nearby and they can blockade the port."

Steana whispered, "And if they are attacked then they will be lost for a handful of men cannot defend drekar."

My son was right and already I had a bad feeling about the plan. I saw, as we left to rejoin our ships, Thorstein Hammer Hand. He and I had served the king when we were younger and I liked the man. He was big and bluff but he never lied and I always liked that in a man. Moreover, he was also a modest warrior, "Hail Thorstein. We go to war once more."

He shook his head, "And I would be happier with a different plan."

"This one might work." I was trying to be both loyal and confident.

He shook his head, "The king devised this plan months ago. The Swedes know where we will land for that has not changed. We are likely to face an army waiting for us on the beach."

My heart sank. Surprise was the only chance this plan had to work. If the Swedes knew that we were coming…

The king allowed the fleet to follow his ship in whatever groups suited them. He would be at the fore and would not risk a wreck. The ones behind would have no such guarantee. This time I chose to sail with my cousin and son's ships. I trusted their crews. It meant that when we landed I would fight alongside them and I was always more comfortable fighting with men that I knew and could rely on. Inevitably, as our fleet headed east to sail the one hundred and twenty miles to Sweden, there were collisions. None were close to us but we heard the crashes as ships came together. I do not hear of any that sank but there would be damage and there would be wounds. Worse, there could be violence when we landed as crews clashed to settle the matter. It was not a good beginning. Sweyn One Eye deferred to me. I think it was because of my title. It was his father who was the jarl. It meant I was the tip of our arrow with his ship on my steerboard side and Steana's on my larboard. With freshly painted shields along the side, we made a colourful sight, The Oathsword on my sail seemed to act as a pointer and our voyage to war was a happy one. The winds helped but they were not strong enough to fly us across the sea. It was a steady progress and as we sailed around the coast of Sweden, we all knew that the Swedes would know we were coming. Their watch towers on the west coast of Sweden would send riders to Kristiansand where we guessed the Swedes were mustering. They would have confirmation of the time of our arrival.

The king's ship stood offshore at the landing site. I was surprised for there were no massed ranks of Swedish and Norse warriors ready to

The Sword of Cnut

dispute our landing. The beach was empty. King Cnut allowed ten other ships to disembark their men before he stepped ashore. By the time we landed more than half the warriors we had brought were landed ashore. The six men I left aboard were unhappy that they were not coming with us but I knew that they would be needed, not to fight but to save our ships and therefore our lives. Sometimes being a warrior meant doing things other than fighting.

We formed up. I slung my shield upon my back. Aed had begged to carry the banner and, as Haraldrsson had the horn and was happy to relinquish the honour, all was well and we followed the king in a rough and rather unruly snake as we headed for Kristiansand. Gandálfr, Bersi and Ragnar Ragnarsson flanked me as we marched with Sweyn One Eye, Steana and the men from Ribe. Haldir, Aed and Haraldrsson had become close and walked behind us. We would be wary and if there was any sign of an ambush then we could form a shield wall that I was confident would hold an enemy's attack.

Gandálfr waved his spear in an arc, "This land looks like the land between Norton and Billingham. It is soft and spongy underfoot and it is not farmed."

I knew what he was getting at. The land was vulnerable to flooding and yet I saw no sign of a river or a beck. There were places where men became stuck. I saw a warband from Zealand who found a boggy part and had to pull men whose legs had been sucked into the mud by its sticky grasp. I now understood why our enemies had not contested our landing. The ground did not suit them. It was getting dark when we saw the wooden wall around Kristiansand and the army arrayed before it. King Cnut wisely halted and we were ordered to make a camp. Steana spied a shrubby area to our left and he sent men to hack down saplings and gather brambles to make a defensive camp. Not everyone did the same but that was their choice. I would manage some sleep, knowing that an enemy creeping towards us to slit our throats would have to navigate stakes and brambles.

We lit fires both to keep insects away and to cook food. I ate with my sons and cousin. "They were ready for us."

I nodded, "Aye, Steana, but they have allowed us to camp and not attacked. Why?"

He frowned and Sweyn One Eye explained, "We have marched from the sea and are tired. They have the advantage of a town that is raised above this boggy ground and their men will be well rested. What your father means is, what have they got planned?"

We kept a good watch, and a quarter of our men were on sentry duty at any one time. We rose before dawn, but the enemy had not

The Sword of Cnut

moved. Their shield wall was in the same position before the walls of their town. The king had brought priests and bishops. They moved amongst us and those who were Christian asked for absolution. Our weapons were blessed. To my mind, it could do no harm and was almost a blót. It would not be as effective as a blót for there was no sacrifice made, but it was better than nothing. The Swedes, Norse and the traitors led by Jarl Ulf needed to do nothing. They could simply wait for us to attack, and so it was King Cnut who ordered us forward. His horn sounded and a triple line of spearmen moved over the tussocky, boggy ground to the waiting spears of our enemy. We appeared to be evenly matched in numbers and, as we fought in the same way as our enemies, it would be a bloody encounter. For my part, I was happy to be fighting alongside the men of Ribe. My men were the centre of the line and with my banner behind me, it marked the man who carried the Dragon Sword. The men we fought would have heard of it. My legend had spread far and wide. If nothing else, the traitors would have told the tale. It would both intimidate and attract spears and swords in equal measure. Gandálfr was on one side of me and Bersi stood next to Ragnar Ragnarsson on the other. This time I had Norse Splitter in my left hand, behind my shield. When I could no longer use my spear then it might be that my shorter weapon would be more effective.

We banged our shields with our spears as we marched. It helped to keep us in step and, we hoped, would frighten the enemy. The Swedes and Norse sang songs to give themselves heart but the songs were not all the same ones and somehow dissipated the effect. As we drew closer, so the front rank ceased banging and lowered their spears. This was when the weight of the long spear would begin to sap energy. I saw that we were heading for a warband that looked to be Swedish. I took comfort from the fact that only their front rank appeared to be mailed. All of my men now wore metal. After the initial clash, we would have the chance to fight men without mail. I was confident in the skill of the men of Norton. These were not the same men who had fought the Mercians all those years ago. They had been tempered by the Norse and were made of sturdier metal now.

Those who were before our king saw their chance for glory, and they broke the line as they raced to get at the Swedes facing them. It was a mistake for the enemy was on ground that was higher and drier than we were. I ignored their folly and concentrated on striking with Saxon Slayer at the warrior who had a blue shield with a yellow cross upon it. He was a Christian. The banging behind us stopped and spears slid over our shoulders. I felt the reassuring presence of the shields of Uller and Vidar in my back. Our Sundays had honed us into one

The Sword of Cnut

weapon. It would, I hoped, give us an edge. I heard the clash to my right as the first of King Cnut's army clashed with the enemy. We would be slower to engage and I wondered if after the battle there would be censure. It could look as though we were afraid to fight when that was not true. We were ensuring that our long line would strike hard.

I pulled back my spear and then thrust as we stepped towards the Swedes. My son and hearthweru were as one with me. Our spears drove towards the Swedes who were, of course, doing the same. The difference was that they were on higher ground and their spears came at our heads. We were thrusting up. My shield flicked up as the Swedish spear came at my head. I had to trust my instincts and I drove Saxon Slayer upwards. Uller's spear from behind had made the Swede lift his shield and my spear drove into the mail and then the flesh of the warrior with the blue shield. The man behind him had used his spear too but that had also hit my shield. I kept on pushing as the shields behind me gave strength to my feet. Our faces were close enough for me to see the blood as it spewed from the Swedish warrior's mouth. My spear had made a mortal wound. He was dead on his feet and could not stand against me. Behind him the warriors were not mailed and our weight, despite their elevation, did not help them. I pulled back Saxon Slayer and the body slipped from it as we clambered over their leader. Others must have fallen too for I found myself with Bersi, Ragnar Ragnarsson and Gandálfr facing their second line.

I thrust hard at the man who was above me. He was not as tall as I was, and my spear smashed into his shield. My momentum brought my shield to hit him, too, and his spear scraped along my helmet. He reeled into the man behind. Uller's spear darted out and caught the man in the eye; he screamed. He reacted by pulling up his shield. I rammed Saxon Slayer into his middle and he fell. Even as he slipped from my spear I punched with my shield at the last man in their line. A few moments earlier he had been safe behind mailed men and now he was facing the Oathsword banner. I saw the terror in his eyes. He was no coward and blocked the thrust from my spear as he stabbed at me with his slightly shorter weapon. I swept my shield to waft away his spear and then stabbed at him with Norse Splitter. He had no mail and I gutted him. As he tried to hold in his entrails, he fell.

This was the moment for composure. I looked to my left and right. We had penetrated the enemy line but the three of us risked isolation. It would have been easy for me to seek glory and race towards the gates of Kristiansand but they were closed and this was the time to consolidate what we had won. We were now on level ground with the enemy and we would win, in this part of the battle at any rate.

The Sword of Cnut

"Norton, hold the line."

I rammed my spear into the soft soil and drew Oathsword. I turned to my left and Bersi and I fell upon the men who, like the last two I had killed, wore no mail. Bersi used his spear and it made the men raise their shields. I slashed with Oathsword. I hit one man in the side and another in the leg. My son and I punched with our shields and the men fell. I gave them a warrior's death. As more men joined me so the enemy began to fall back to the gates. I knew that once we closed with the walls we would have to endure arrows and stones. With no enemies before me, I was able to look down the line. We had a bulge in our line but it was not towards the enemy. The rash attack by the men before King Cnut meant that the left and right of our lines had advanced but those in the centre had retreated. It was then that those on our right surged forward. The boiling blood of victory made them foolish and they raced at the enemy before them. A horn sounded and the Norse on the left of their line fell back. The arrows and stones which fell, thinned the ranks of the attackers and I saw piles of bodies. The attack failed and our right fell back, leaving many warriors on the ground before the wooden walls. It gave the Swedes in the centre hope and our whole line became skewed as our right and centre fell back. We were in danger of becoming isolated and when, after a short time King Cnut sounded the retreat, I was relieved. We marched back to our camp. We had wounded men, but I had lost none and I put that down to our mail and our training.

As wounded were tended and fires lit, Sweyn One Eye came over. "I do not like this, Sven. We did not lose, but if they had their wits about them then they could have fallen on us as we retreated."

I nodded, "There is a plan to all of this. We will be vigilant this night."

I was on guard with Bersi, Ragnar Ragnarsson and my men when we heard the noise in the distance. I could not make it out at first but it did not bode well and I roused the men of Ribe and Norton. By the time the wall of water surged towards us, we were all on our feet and our choice of a camp that was slightly higher than the others saved us. Water gushed and splashed up to our waists, but none drowned and only a few were swept from their feet. I knew that others who were on lower ground would have drowned. The Swedes had been clever. They had used the waters of their land to defeat us. Perhaps they had hoped that they could win a force of arms but the man-made flood guaranteed it.

As dawn broke it was clear that our army was in no condition to fight. There were bodies lying on the ground and tents had been swept away. We headed back to the fleet. The Swedes had won.

Chapter 17

Battle of Helgeå

The story of the dam and the flooding of our camp became twisted and changed over the years. It was said that the waters hurt our fleet. They did not. The waters drowned many men at our camp but not enough to hurt us and our fleet was intact and that was what saved us. The dam and the flood had been supposed to destroy our ships. The water that had flooded our camp was on the periphery of the flood. The wall of logs and peat that had cascaded down the river was designed to sink our ships. As Folki told us, the captains had decided to anchor further out from the harbour as they feared that the enemy might send their ships out to take them at night. Two smaller ships were damaged but that was all. We boarded our ships and sailed out to meet the enemy ships. King Cnut was forced into a sea battle.

We boarded our ships and we had more men at the oars than some of the other ships. King Cnut had the largest of our ships, it was eighty paces long, and he had not lost any oarsmen. It was he who led us towards the Swedish and Norse ships that had gathered to fight us. It took us half a day to row east and find them waiting close to an island, Helgeå. The Swedes had manned the island and the others that lay close by with archers, and they were their secret weapon as they could rain arrows on ships and be immune from our missiles. King Cnut headed for the harbour where the enemy fleet had gathered. We did not intend it but our ships had suffered fewer losses and so, as we headed towards the natural harbour, it was our small group of ships that found ourselves close to the king's. The Norse ships were the keenest to get to grips with the mighty ship that was King Cnut's. The smaller threttenessa swarmed around him like dogs attacking a bear. The height of the king's ship meant that it was hard for the Norse to get aboard *'The Trinity'*. The steerboard side was protected by six more of the king's ships but the larboard side had no defences and I led our handful of ships to the aid of the king.

I watched as the Norse warriors hurled grappling hooks and began to clamber up the side of the flagship.

"Folki, lower the sail, in steerboard oars." My captain bellowed out his orders.

I stood on the gunwale with Oathsword in hand and my shield over my back. I held the backstay with my left hand. We would be the same

The Sword of Cnut

height as the Norseman I intended to engage. As the sail came down and half of the oars were withdrawn, Folki put the steering board over and we slewed around to bump into the outermost Norse ship. It was like a longphort. There was one ship tied to the king's ship and the ship we boarded tied to it. The attention of the Norse warriors was on the king's ship and when I led my men aboard, we had no opposition. We hacked into unprotected backs as we crossed the Norwegian drekar. Haldir killed the helmsman and he, Aed and Haraldrsson cut the steering withies. We had disabled one enemy vessel. It had been easy thus far for most of the crew of the ship we had taken were aboard the other one, however when we boarded it we were seen, and instead of unprotected backs, we had a wall of shields.

I pulled my shield around and shouting, "Oathsword!" led my men and those of Ribe who had followed us to stem the flood of men trying to climb aboard the flagship. These were hardy warriors and like us, they were mailed. I always found that when I used the Dragon Sword, I seemed to find power, strength and skill I did not know I possessed. My body appeared to work without me making decisions. I raised my shield to block the blow from an axe without even thinking. I instinctively knew when to stab and when to slice. None came close to wounding me.

"Kill Sven Saxon Sword!"

The voice that roared out the order told me that someone knew me and my sword. Men stopped trying to get to King Cnut and, instead, came at me. A wall of men came at me and my reactions, fast though they were, could not cope with the sheer number of men. Gandálfr launched himself at the men coming at my left side, my shield side. It was almost a berserker-like attack. He hacked and chopped with his sword and the respite enabled me to eliminate some of my enemies. When my sons, Ragnar Ragnarsson and Sweyn One Eye arrived at my right side, I had more protection there. As we locked shields and pushed as one, so the Norsemen were pushed back. It was then that a Norse berserker launched himself at us. He had thrown off his byrnie and held his axe in two hands. The other Norsemen recognised his action for what it was and moved away. A berserker could kill friend as well as foe. It was then that Gandálfr sacrificed himself. He stepped between the half-naked warrior and me. He took the blow from the axe with his shield. As he did so he hacked into the side of the Norseman. The axe shattered Gandálfr's shield and broke his arm. It hung limply from his side. Gandálfr was a hard man and he bravely swung his sword a second time. It ripped through the middle of the berserker but such men seem immune to wounds. My hearthweru had wounded him twice and

The Sword of Cnut

yet the Norseman appeared to be unaffected. When his axe came down a second time, Gandálfr had no defence and the axe split my hearthweru's helmet and skull. He died. The axe stuck a little and as the berserker tried to pull it out I stepped from the shield wall and hacked across the neck of the Norseman. Even a berserker cannot fight without a head.

I was angry for I had lost the last of my oathsworn. I went a little wild, too, and with my shield before me, I ran at the wall of Norsemen who had just seen their berserker die. When I heard the shout from behind me I knew that I was not alone. I cared not if I was wounded and I sliced, hacked and stabbed for all that I was worth. I punched with the boss of my shield, I headbutted and I stamped on men who had fallen to the deck. Swords and spears cut me. I felt blood dripping from my cheek and knew that I had a wound to my leg but I cared not. This was no longer about saving the king, this was about seeking revenge for the death of Gandálfr.

When we reached the side of *'The Trinity'* there were no Norsemen left alive on the two ships we had crossed. The stern of the flagship was safe and our victory enabled Glam the Fair to lead the king's oathsworn to drive them from their ship.

King Cnut peered over the side and raised his sword in salute, "You have saved us again, Sven Saxon Sword. You shall be rewarded. The Sword of Cnut has been put to good use." He disappeared as he went to organise the fightback.

I cared not about a reward. I had lost Gandálfr. "Take our dead and wounded back aboard our ship."

Bersi nodded and said, "The mail and treasure?"

"Take it as weregeld for Gandálfr." I pointed to the ropes securing the ship to *'The Trinity.'* Cut those ropes." As we boarded our drekar I said, "And burn these ships." My men used their flints to light brands and hurl them on to the deck of the Norse ship. When Haldir threw a pot of oil, the flames licked up the mast and the ship was engulfed by fire.

By the time we had returned to our ships, the battle was over. The king and the ships that were on the far side of the flagship had defeated the enemy whose ships had been forced to return to the harbour. Only a fool attacks a harbour. The king signalled for us to leave and head west but, before he did he ordered the captured Norse ships to be burned. The burning vessels filled the horizon as we headed west. They would pay a heavy price for attacking the King of Denmark.

We followed the king's ship back to Denmark. Gandálfr's body lay next to me covered by his cloak as I peered back to see if I could see the

The Sword of Cnut

traitor's ships. I had only seen Norse and Swedish ships in the battle. I hoped that Jarl Ulf was dead.

"Did we win, Father?"

I sighed and took off my helmet, "We live and so that is a kind of victory. I did not call together men to fight this war. King Cnut did. If you want to know if we won or not, ask him. We are alive but I have lost the last of my oathsworn and so it feels like a defeat. You can never bring back the dead. We shall honour Gandálfr as we honoured Faramir when he fell, but his grumbling face will not be at my side, and I will never hear his complaints again. I would that I could." I knelt and put my hand on his face. "I will miss you, old friend. Wait for me in Valhalla."

The winds that had carried us east now slowed us as we headed west and already tired and weary warriors had to row. It took three days to get back. Whilst we buried most of our men at sea I wanted Gandálfr to have a proper funeral. He would be buried in the old-fashioned way.

Following the king meant we reached the harbour first and we tied up at the end of the quay. I left the best positions for the king and his leaders. I went ashore and sought the shipwright, Bolli. "Yes, Eorl Sven, what can I do for you?"

I pointed to a snekke that lay in his shed. It looked to be brand new. "How much for that one?"

"You have a good eye. She is as fast as a greyhound and can turn as sharply as a fleeing stag. She is one of my best ships and I could not take less than ten gold pieces."

He was overcharging me and expecting me to haggle but I simply nodded and took the gold pieces from my purse. "I will buy her."

"But she has no name and there are no oars yet."

Smiling I said, "She will not need them for she will have but one voyage. She is a funeral ship for my oathsworn."

"You would burn her, but she is a good ship!" He was incredulous.

"My oathsworn deserves nothing but the best. Have your men take her to the larboard side of my drekar." Leaving the dumfounded shipwright, I went back aboard my drekar. "Dress Gandálfr in his mail and put his helmet on his head. We bury him this night."

No one objected for the whole crew had respected the warrior who had trained them. Bersi and I went down into the snekke and laid kindling on the bottom. Then we reverently laid his body on his shield. We put his sword in his stiff fingers and made sure that his hammer of Thor lay on his chest. Finally, I covered his body with his cloak. I shouted, "Aed, fetch a lighted brand." Kneeling, I moved his cloak so that I could see his face once more, "Gandálfr, some men called you

The Sword of Cnut

The Grim, but I call you Gandálfr the Great. The day you died will become a saga that men sing often and you will always be remembered. There are warriors unborn who will sing the song of Gandálfr the Great. Farewell until I cross the bridge." I covered his face and said, as Aed climbed down with the lighted brand, "Raise the sail and then climb back aboard the drekar. This task is appointed to me, Gandálfr served me in life and now I shall serve him in death." I went to the steering board and fastened it so that it was centred.

They obeyed me and as the tide and the wind tried to push the snekke out to sea, Bersi and Aed climbed up the ropes. The side of my drekar was lined with faces. I saw Steana, Sweyn One Eye and my nephew among them. Haraldrsson held my banner and it fluttered in the dying rays of the sun. Haldir stood as still as a statue. The snekke wanted to be free and so I cut all the ropes holding her to the drekar but one. Her bow faced the east and the dark. I laid the brand under the corpse and the kindling took. I cut the last rope and my men hauled me aboard as the snekke headed out to sea. I saw faces from other ships watching and those that were just arriving in the port had to move out of the way of the burning snekke which was taking my oathsworn to the Otherworld. We watched until the flames caught the sail and then the burning boat was slowly consumed by the sea. Gandálfr the Great was in Valhalla.

Sweyn One Eye knew the pain that I was feeling and he put his arm around me, "That was well done, cuz. If you would allow me, I would be honoured to write the saga of Gandálfr the Grim."

"It is the saga of Gandálfr the Great and I know that he would like that."

I just wanted to go home but I knew I could not. King Cnut would be offended. As I had said to Bersi, only the king knew if we had a victory or not. If he thought it was a victory then we would celebrate and I would have to attend even though I did not feel like celebrating.

There was a feast and I was given a place of honour at his side. Sweyn One Eye had written a saga and King Cnut, who had fought alongside Gandálfr, allowed him to give its first rendition at the feast.

The Oathsword is the dragon blade
That fought for Denmark's king
A blade of legend so men sing,
Eorl Sven wields the blade Guthrum made
He fights with honour and with fire
Surrounded by men in mail
And a sword upon a sail

The Sword of Cnut

He serves and fights for what is right
Gandálfr was the last one to die
He raced to stand when he heard the cry
Kill Sven Saxon Sword fill the night
Surrounded by men in mail
And a sword upon a sail

He stood between the axe and Sven
When the Norsemen bit the shield
He faced the axe and never thought to yield
Blows were struck again and again
Surrounded by men in mail
And a sword upon a sail

He died that day on the Norseman's deck
His oath fulfilled and his honour kept
For his loss tears will be wept
As his body died on a Norwegian wreck
Surrounded by men in mail
And a sword upon a sail

His name will live beyond the grave
For what he did, the sword to save
In Valhalla with warriors brave
Surrounded by men in mail
And a sword upon a sail
His name will live beyond the grave
For what he did, the sword to save
In Valhalla with warriors brave
Surrounded by men in mail
And a sword upon a sail

As usual, Sweyn One Eye was not happy with his work. "I need to change some of the words but at least the king and the others know what he did."

"He will be happy, Sweyn. In many ways he was a simple man and the world will be a worse place for his loss."

The king nodded his approval, "Your reward, Eorl Sven, is that when you die your sons will not need to pay a heriot and you can make Bersi here a hersir too. You may choose the place. He will wield Oathsword for King Cnut and his heirs. We shall never lose."

The Sword of Cnut

I caught Sweyn's eye and shook my head slightly. He thought that the king should make a reward that actually cost him something. I did not care. The sooner I returned home the better.

The king seemed to read my mind. "Until I am sure that we have won this war I will keep the fleet here. I want to know that there is no threat to Denmark from the east before I return to England. We will wait until Tvímánuður until you are relieved of your obligations." The lack of a cheer should have told the king that men wanted to leave immediately, but he was a man who did not listen as well as he should.

The time we spent in the port allowed the wounded to recover. Roskilde had a good market and men spent the coins they had taken from the Norse and Swedish dead. I rarely visited and, instead, I looked often to the east, for I had marked the place where the snekke had sunk. It was one day, as I stood watching to the east, that I saw Jarl Ulf and his handful of ships enter the anchorage. There were no shields along the sides of his ships. Was this a peaceful mission? In preparation, I donned my mail and headed for the king.

I reached the hall just before Jarl Ulf. King Cnut was taking no chances and he had his bodyguards close by, I saw that Glam had an unsheathed sword in his hand. The king waved at me, "Eorl Sven, bring Oathsword here. I would have the Sword of Cnut next to me."

I had had enough of the change of name and as I stood there I said, quietly, "King Cnut, it is bad luck to rename a blade. Oathsword has a name."

Cnut was a clever man, "You misunderstand me, Eorl. I know it is bad luck to rename a sword. It is you who are the Sword of Cnut. Draw your sword now so that Jarl Ulf may see it."

I nodded and drew the sword. With Glam and myself flanking the king with unsheathed swords, there would be no mistaking the message of the king.

Jarl Ulf abased himself before the king and lay prostrate on the floor, "Forgive my foolishness, my king, I was duped." He raised his head.

King Cnut said, "Stay where you are. That is how a snake should lie, on its belly." Jarl Ulf did as he was commanded. "You say you were duped, how?"

"Men said that you had abandoned Denmark, King Cnut. It has been many years since you lived here. There was a rumour that the queen had drawn your eye from Denmark."

"Do not impugn the queen, snake, or you shall die here and now."

"I meant no disrespect, my liege."

The Sword of Cnut

"And now you wish to return as though nothing has happened between us? The men I lost did not leave my side."

"King Cnut, neither I nor my men drew a sword against you or our countrymen. Neither Dane nor Englishman was hurt by us."

"You would swear?"

"I would swear."

"Fetch a Bible." A Bible was brought within moments by one of the priests who constantly surrounded the king. "Rise." Jarl Ulf rose and the king nodded to the priest who held the Bible before Jarl Cnut. "Swear."

"I swear that neither I nor my men took arms against my king. My crime is that I was guilty of desertion."

The king waved an arm and the priest moved away. There was a look of relief on the face of Jarl Ulf. The king smiled a cruel smile and said, "Sven Saxon Sword, hold out Oathsword." I knew what was coming and did as I was ordered. I stepped forward with the blade to Ulf's face and the king said, "And now take a warrior's oath that you will never take arms against me."

It was one thing to swear on a Bible, especially for a pragmatic man like Ulf Sprakaleggson. I knew that he still wore a Hammer of Thor. He was also a warrior and knew the power of my sword. This time his hand came more slowly than it had towards the Bible. His eyes caught mine and I saw fear. His hand hovered briefly and then he grasped the blade. The look on his face was as though he had plunged it into a pail of ice. His eyes closed and his teeth clenched. The sword had power. The edge was still sharp and his fingers were cut. Blood dripped to the ground and the oath became even stronger. It was sworn in blood.

"I swear on Oathsword, that I will never take arms against my king."

"And you will be a loyal servant to me."

"And I will be a loyal servant to you."

"Then you may enter my court. I will consider your actions and decide what punishment is needed. This is not the time for a feast but you shall dine with me this night. Eorl Sven, you and Sweyn One Eye will join me, too. I would hear the song of Gandálfr once more."

I sheathed my sword. "I will tell my cuz."

Sweyn did not like the summons. "My crew and I would like to go home. Waiting here while our crops are ripening does not sit well, Sven. We obeyed his commands. We fought his war and now we wait on a whim."

"Then this night I will ask him again if we can return home. It seems he still needs me and perhaps my presence here alone might allow the rest of you to return to your families."

The Sword of Cnut

"But not you."

"You heard how he called me."

"And I do not like it. A man should have one name. You are Sven Saxon Sword and that name strikes fear into the hearts of our enemies. The Sword of Cnut is a vanity. He is trying to make himself and Oathsword one and the same."

"But you and I know that the sword has no master. It controls its own destiny. A man may covet the weapon but he can never own it. I do not own it. I am its guardian. The king is right in one respect. When I die it shall not be buried with me. Either Steana or Bersi shall carry it."

"But which one?"

I shrugged, "I know not for when it is passed on then I shall be dead. The sword will choose just as it chose me all those years ago when Siggi and I were but boys."

We dressed in our finery and went to the hall where just the king, Jarl Ulf and the king's oathsworn sat. We ate a modest meal and after it, Sweyn One Eye sang the song of Gandálfr. Glam then brought out the pieces for Skáktafl. The king sat and he waved for me to face him.

"Come, Eorl Sven, let us match our minds."

I knew how to play the game and I was a good player. When he had been younger it had been I who had taught him the game. My mind was distracted and I lost. I confess that the distraction might have been because I was trying to work out how to lose without making it too obvious. As it was, it pleased the king when I was defeated.

"You play a good game, Sven, and that is a rare victory for me. Jarl Ulf, let us test your wits, eh?"

I knew that this would be more than a game of Skáktafl. This would be a battle of wits. That became clear as, unlike when I had played him, the king interrogated Ulf. It clearly upset the jarl.

"So, what of my enemies? You may not have been in the battle, but you were privy to their plans."

"The battle cost the Norse dear, King Cnut, and their king sailed home, but that left most of his men to walk back to Norway."

"And the King of Sweden?"

"Is building his defences should you come again."

The king's hand hung over one of the pieces, "Then the threat is over." He picked up the piece and looked Ulf in the eye, "Remember the oath you took. Answer me." The threat in his voice was clear.

I saw that Jarl Ulf was torn. Had his intention been to come back and assassinate the king? The presence of the king's bodyguards, not to mention my own position, meant that could not happen. As the king placed the piece on the board the jarl snapped, "There is no threat from

The Sword of Cnut

the east." His eyes burned with hatred. Only the king and I saw it, but it was clear. The jarl then knocked the most important piece over and said, "You are too good for me. I resign." He stood and bowed, "With your permission, I will retire. I wish to rise early, King Cnut, and attend church. I have much to confess."

"That you have. You have my permission."

The jarl rose and left. King Cnut smiled at me, "A bad loser and I wonder at this change. Eorl Sven, you are loyal and, best of all, honest, what do you make of Jarl Ulf?"

I sighed, "My lord, I would not allow him back into my bosom so easily. There are some men you can trust and others…"

"Like Thorkell the Tall, you mean?" I nodded. He smiled, "Sometimes Sven, you are like a mirror into which I can speak and know that what I see is a true reflection. Tomorrow I will disband the army and the fleet. You may all return home."

As we walked back to the quay, Sweyn was in an ebullient mood, "I know not how you did it, but it is thanks to you that we can return home."

I was happy to be going back but something in the king's manner disturbed me.

When I got back to the ship I told the crew that we would be leaving the next day. Folki said, "We will need to provision the ship. The water barrels are almost empty and we need ale."

"Then on the morrow, you and I will rise early. Once the fleet hears that we can leave then every captain will seek provisions. Perhaps being close to the king has its advantages."

We rose before dawn and I went with the men to fill the barrels. That was the easy part. As the markets opened, we were the first there. Bersi went with Haldir to buy ale while I went with Folki to buy bread. It was as we neared the church that I saw Jarl Ulf heading for it. He was alone and he stopped as I approached him.

"You seek shrift, my lord?"

"I have much to confess. A man should not be forced to swear." His eyes flickered to my sword. "You are a good man, Eorl Sven, and honest too." He held out his arm and I clasped it. He turned and entered the church.

Folki called, "We have all that we need, Eorl."

"Then let us go back to the ship and take the tide."

It was as I turned that I saw Glam and four of the king's bodyguards approach. One of them was Ivar White. He was the biggest and toughest of the king's men. I did not like him. I frowned, "Church, Glam?"

The Sword of Cnut

His eyes narrowed and he nodded to Ivar and the other three, "Orders from the king."

I looked to the church door and I knew what was intended. "This is not good, Glam."

He sighed, "Sven, you were there last night. Can Jarl Ulf be trusted?"

I shook my head, "But a church? You know my views on the White Christ but it is a sacrilege."

"He will be absolved of his sins and they are legion. He will go to heaven."

"But not Valhalla."

There was a shout from within the church and the sounds of a scuffle. Glam said, "And the deed is done. What is in the past is done and cannot be changed." Glam believed in the Norns too. He was right.

Ivar came out with his three fellows, and he wiped the blood from his sword. "The traitor is dead."

I shook my head, "I will return to Norton where life is simpler. There you know your enemies." My eyes were fixed on Ivar for he was a murderer. He merely smiled back at me.

I hurried to my ship. Sweyn, his son and my sons were chatting. They too had revictualled their vessels and were happy. Sweyn saw my face and said, "What is amiss?"

"Jarl Ulf has been murdered, in church. It was on the king's orders."

Sweyn One Eye shook his head, "Then that was not in hot blood but was a cold and calculated act. This is not the same king we trained as a prince, Sven."

"Yet we made him. I do not understand this but then again the Norns always confuse me. We shall return home." I embraced Steana, "I will visit next year. If you would, explain to Siggi why this year's visit was not to be."

"Aye, Father. My children will be sad as will Gytha."

I took Sweyn's arm, "Tell your father all and let him know that I am well and think of him."

"I will."

Bersi and I climbed aboard my ship and I said, "Folki, let us go home."

The Sword of Cnut

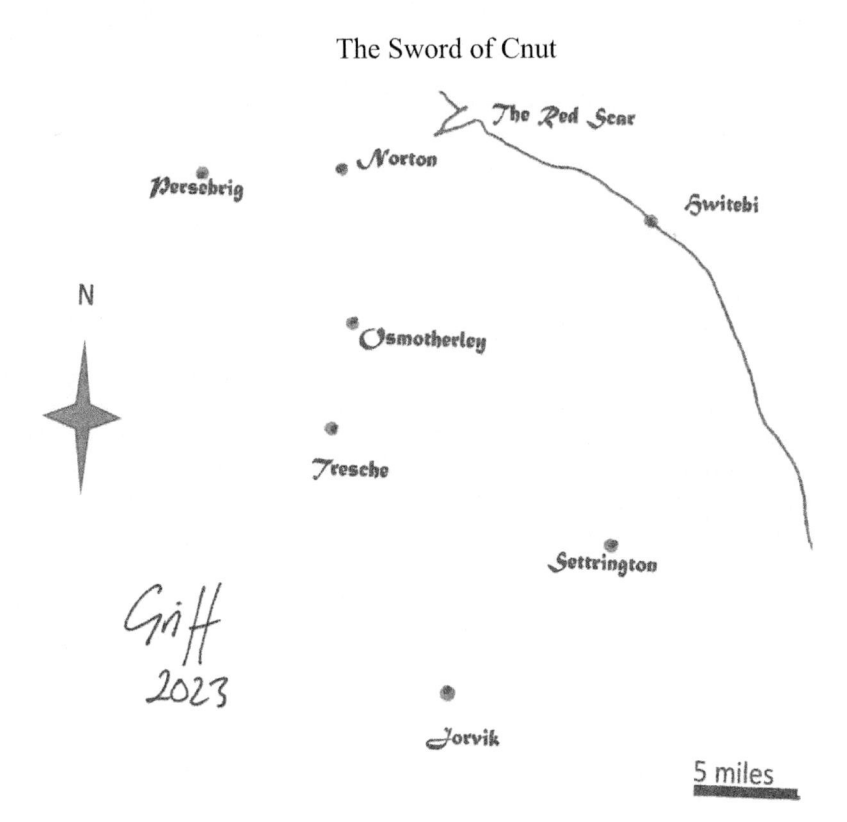

The road to Tresche

The Sword of Cnut

Chapter 18

Aelle's Torc

The voyage back was a quiet and sad one. It was not just the death of Gandálfr that affected everyone but the murder. The Christians were appalled at the place chosen for the assassination, while the pagans were at the manner. The pagans did not mind that he had been killed or that it had been in a church. What they objected to was that he had not died with a sword in his hand. King Cnut had lost some of the loyalty and trust of my men. They would still follow me into the den of a dragon but it put weight on my shoulders. They trusted me but not the king and when I next led them to war it would be on the orders of a king they did not trust.

We had not lost a warrior, my single oathsworn apart, and, by the time we tied up to the new quay, all the wounds had been healed. The men bore scars but they were borne proudly by warriors. We sailed up the river and secured ourselves to the land just as the sun set. Our late arrival meant we were unannounced. The fishing boats had long since returned from their harvest of the waters and no one shouted a warning. We were forced to tie at the quay rather than risk the beck channel as the tide was turning. It meant a longer walk along the winding path to our homes and all of us were laden. Our chests were heavy and our bodies were already weary. The walk seemed like a punishment. We had just one gate but some of the men had homes outside the walls and on the river side of the wooden palisade. The greetings they received alerted those who lived closer to my hall and as we were spotted, others came to help us.

I turned to Ragnar Ragnarsson, as we neared the welcoming sight of the open gates, "Will you travel home or stay here this night?"

"I confess, Eorl, that as much as I would travel home to see my family, I am weary beyond words and to speak truthfully, Bersi and I have become brothers in this war and I would have one last night with him. Who knows if we will have to war again?"

He meant well but he was tempting the Norns. I nodded, "Gunhilde will understand. You and Bersi are now shield brothers. You stood with me and did not flinch when the Swedes tried to slay us. Such things are not easily understood by women but we men have a bond that is as deep and dark as blood."

The Sword of Cnut

Word had reached Mary and even as we entered the hall and thralls took our chests, I could hear her as she shouted her commands. "Frigga, your husband is home. Have more food prepared. Our men will be hungry. Skadi, tell Seara that my son has returned."

I stood with Ragnar Ragnarsson and Bersi, our hands now empty, when she entered the hall. I saw her face take in that we three were whole and she rushed, first to Bersi and then to Ragnar to embrace them. Finally, she enfolded me in her arms and kissed me, "God has listened to my prayers and you are all brought back whole." She stepped back, the better to see us. I knew why. She was looking for new scars. She nodded her satisfaction and then said, "Gandálfr, is he without?"

I stepped forward and put my arm around her. Gandálfr had been my hearthweru and had lived with us since before we were married. He had been a fixture and now he was gone, "Gandálfr died, my love, at the Battle of Helgeå. He was buried at sea. My hearthweru are now all dead."

Gandálfr would have been surprised at the tears my wife shed for he always thought she disliked him. She did not but he almost flaunted his pagan beliefs and that she did not like. Her attempts to convert him all failed and he never did as I did and affected compliance.

When she recovered her composure she said, "I will say a prayer for him and we will light a candle to burn in the church."

"He is in Valhalla, my love."

She snorted her answer and shaking her head said, "Food will take time to prepare. Wash and change for you all stink of sweat and the sea. You will stay here this night, Ragnar?"

"Yes, my lady."

"I will have a bed made up for you in the warrior hall."

As we went outside to wash, Ragnar said, "She frightens me sometimes, Eorl."

"It is her manner, Ragnar. Inside she is soft as the fur on a seal cub and as gentle as a lamb. Did you not see how she reacted to the news of Gandálfr's death? This night there will be more tears."

She was right, of course, and we did smell. It was not just the sweat and the dirt that she could smell but blood. While most of the blood of our enemies had showered our mail, which we had cleaned off, some had gone through to our padded kyrtles. All that we had worn in the war would need to be washed. Bersi gave Ragnar a spare tunic to wear so that when we re-entered my hall, hair and beard combed with clean tunics, my wife smiled. "Now you look ready to eat. Sit, Anya, fetch ale. Frigga will serve the food soon and while we wait you can tell me

The Sword of Cnut

of this war which, hopefully, will signal the end of your time as a warrior."

As Anya poured me some freshly brewed ale, I sighed. I drank some and then said, "King Cnut calls me Cnut's Sword. I cannot see him letting me lie here in the sheath that is Norton."

"That sword is a curse."

I put my hand to my Hammer of Thor. It lay beneath my tunic and the cross my wife had given me was visible. My wife thought I was holding the cross. I was not. I was asking for Thor to intervene and stop the Norns from punishing us.

I told her of the war. As I always did, I avoided the description of the deaths but gave the details of the places and the events. I could not avoid telling her of the murder of the jarl. It was better that she heard it from me rather than as gossip. My warriors would have no qualms in telling their families of the infamous murder.

"The king calls himself a Christian and God will punish him for the murder."

Bersi said, "The king did not do it, Mother. It was Ivar White."

She shook her head, "Bersi, he was, from what your father said, one of the king's bodyguards. He was with Glam the Fair. The king ordered it but kept his hands clean. It was the same with Uhtred the Bold and that murder was in a holy place, Dun Holm, where the saint's bones lie. He will be punished as will all murderers."

The food had arrived and, as Seara sat, we began to eat. The voyage back from Denmark had been a good one but this was the first hot food we had enjoyed since Roskilde. We devoured it in silence. Mary was clearly upset at our news of both Gandálfr and Jarl Ulf. She had not known the jarl but he was murdered. She picked at her food.

When we were done I wiped my mouth and said, "And what of Norton? Is there aught that should worry me?"

She shook her head, "Gunhilde is well and your grandchildren are happy. The crops were harvested and the new animals you brought back from Siggi prosper. All is well."

Seara said, "There was news from Billingham, though."

I looked at Mary who nodded, "I had forgotten. Two days since we had visitors who were on their way to see Edward of Billingham."

"Visitors?"

"Relatives, so they said, from the south. It was one of Thurbrand the Hold's sons and his sons. He said he was Thurbrand of Settrington and he had discovered that Edward was distantly related. He travelled to speak with him."

The Sword of Cnut

I did not like this. "You do not think that he intended to travel north and do harm to Ealdred of Northumbria, do you? This might have been a ploy of some kind."

She laughed, "You men think all is to do with violence. I know his father was murdered by Ealdred and his sons but Thurbrand seemed more concerned with Edward. He was keen to know about his family. I think that the murder of his father just made him curious about his past."

Her arguments seemed sound. "I will visit on the morrow and meet this Thurbrand. I am Cnut's Law in this land and I need to find out if this is a vengeance raid. If I was planning to kill my father's murderer then I would try to deceive men about my intentions." The Norns were spinning and I might have to ride north to Bebbanburg once more and prevent another murder.

That night there were tears and Mary showed the emotion she had kept inside her at the table. I knew why she cried. It was not just that Gandálfr had died. He was my hearthweru and never left my side in battle. I had only described his death but she would have known that my death could have been a sword swipe away. She said nothing but fell asleep holding me tightly.

It was my right arm, on which Mary lay, that woke me. I slid it out and then went to make water. The days were still long and, as I used the pot, outside the back door of my hall, I saw the first hint of light in the east. The thralls were already up and the bread oven had been lit.

"Good morning, my lord. You have risen early."

"Aye, Skadi. I think I will have an early breakfast."

I went to wash and, at the same time, to visit with Verðandi. I stroked his head and gave him an apple. There were windfalls in a basket. "This morning you shall exercise. You are getting too fat. Eorl Sven is back and that means your work begins." He snorted and stamped his foot. He seemed to understand me. As I passed Bersi's house I saw him emerge and with him, his dog Heimdall. I smiled, "You need to make water too?"

He nodded, "Sweyn woke when he cried for food and when he wakes he thinks that everyone should rise. Heimdall and I made a tactical retreat."

I smiled, "And like me, once you are awake you cannot simply go back to bed. When I have eaten I will ride to visit Edward and Osgar. Do you wish to come?"

"A ride might be just what I need. Aye." Just then there came another wail from Bersi's home and he said, "Seara can handle the children. Heimdall and I will ride forth with you."

The Sword of Cnut

The early rising meant that we reached the causeway when the sun finally rose over the eastern horizon. It bathed the beck in light showing that the tide was out. We headed across the causeway and were halfway across when we heard a wail. Osgar had persuaded Edward to enclose the village with a wall and I saw that the gate gaped wide. We urged our horses up the slope and, at the gate, were met by Karl. He was a warrior and he had his sword in his hand.

"Treachery, Eorl. Murder has been committed."

I saw that the door to the hall was open and I dismounted and ran towards it. Inside was a savage and bloody scene. Edward of Billingham, his sons Edgar and Ethelred along with three thralls lay dead. There were two bodies close to that of Osgar and I did not recognise them. Heimdall went to lick Osgar's face and, as he did, Osgar moved. I moved to his side and knelt. I gently lifted his head.

"You live!"

He opened his eyes, and I saw the pain, "But not for long. It is a stomach wound." I saw that his hands were holding in his entrails. How he had survived I knew not. He spoke quickly knowing that his life was measured in moments. "It was Thurbrand of Settrington. They attacked us while we slept. I woke and I fought but…" His eyes closed and I wondered if he had died. His voice was barely a whisper as he spoke and I had to put my ear to his mouth to discern what he said, "They came for Aelle's torc. I would have vengeance, my lord."

I gripped his hand, "And you shall have it."

"A sword." He moved his hand and the eel-like entrails poured forth. I took Oathsword and pressed it into his palm. He opened his eyes and mouthed, "Thank you," before life left them. Osgar was dead and in Valhalla. He and Gandálfr would be together.

I did not take Oathsword away, instead, I waved over to Karl, "Tell me all. Osgar said this was done by Thurbrand of Settrington."

Karl nodded, "I found the bodies when I woke and saw the gates were open. I went and found the two men of the night watch slain. The horses they brought were gone, along with Osgar's and Lord Edward's. I found these here and you must have heard my cry. When I heard your horses, I thought that they had returned."

I shook my head, "And we did not pass them. You were not at the feast?"

"Thurbrand said he wanted a quiet feast so that he and his sons could get to know Lord Edward. I think that his lordship was flattered by the attention. Osgar stood watch and they ate. I set the sentries and went to bed. All was well when I did so."

"And the torc? Osgar said that was the reason for their visit."

The Sword of Cnut

"Thurbrand was desperate to see it. The first night of the visit his lordship kept it hidden, but my lord was persuaded to take it from its resting place, so persuasive was Thurbrand."

I nodded for all was now clear. "How many were there with Thurbrand?"

"He had two sons. There were four men with them, bodyguards. Two lie dead with Osgar."

"Then I must rouse my own men. Settrington is far to the south of the river. I can only hope that they were slowed by the ferry."

"I would come with you, Eorl."

I was loath to bring such a reliable warrior but I knew that I needed someone who would recognise the killers. I nodded and turned to Bersi, "I need you to stay here and take charge. Can you do that?"

"Of course, but do you not need me?"

"I need you, but you are needed here more. These people have lost their leader. You are the one man that I can trust to give them comfort."

He nodded. "I will send help."

"All will be well, I swear."

I retrieved Oathsword and said, "Karl, arm yourself and take Bersi's horse." I mounted Verðandi and we rode back across the causeway to Norton. My village had woken, and I was greeted by smiles. I reined in at Haraldr's workshop. His boy was fanning the coals in preparation for the day's work. "Osgar, Lord Edward and his sons are dead, murdered. I have left Bersi to manage but he will need help."

Father John was just coming passed and he heard my words, "Murder?" I nodded. "Then I am needed too."

Word spreads quickly in a small village and by the time I reached my hall people were outside their homes and there was a buzz of conversation. The joy of our return would be marred by the murder. Mary came out of the hall as I said, "Karl, find Haldir, Aed and Ragnar Ragnarsson. I need them."

He left us and Mary asked, "Where is Bersi, what is amiss?" I told her all and left nothing out. Her hand went to her mouth. "What will you do?"

"That which is right. Uphold Cnut's Law and avenge the deaths. I slept while they were murdered. If I want to sleep again then I must act and act quickly."

She made the sign of the cross, "I pray God that you are kept safe. Frigga, fetch my cloak and come with me. We are needed."

Karl appeared with my men. It was clear that he had told them everything for Haldir said, "You wish us to hunt down these killers, lord?"

The Sword of Cnut

"I am here to ask you three to do so. If you say no then I will not hold it against you. We will have to ride and ride hard."

The three nodded. Haldir said, "We need more than five men, my lord."

I shook my head, "Don your mail and arm yourself. We five will have to be enough."

The truth was we only had five good horses. I could have taken more but they would have slowed me down. Better to take fewer and catch them before they reached his stronghold. It took longer than I would have liked but when we were ready, we galloped down the road to Stockadeton. I hoped that Alf had not facilitated their crossing.

When we reached the town and the ferry Alf rushed over. We were armed and ready for war, "What is amiss, my lord? Are enemies coming?"

I frowned, "Did not five men with spare horses ride through here before dawn to take the ferry?"

Shaking his head he said, "The ferry is secured at night and our gates barred. None crossed the river this morning."

"Then they have gone to the bridge at Persebrig. We have the chance to catch them. Alf, we need to cross the ferry now." As we crossed the river I explained to the others my reasoning, "They are heading for Persebrig which lies many miles west of here. By taking the ferry we can get ahead of them and take them before they reach their stronghold."

None of the others knew the land and Ragnar asked, "Where can we catch them, Eorl?"

"There is a village with just eight houses, Tresche, and it is on the road south of here. The one that leads to Jorvik. It is also on the road to Settrington. By going to Persebrig, they have added eighteen miles to their journey. Even if they flog their animals to death, they cannot reach Tresche ahead of us. We have a straighter and shorter road to ride. We will catch them there."

Once we crossed the river and found the old Roman Road that headed south, we made good time. The hills to the east rose above us and sheltered us from the wind. The road was flat and the land was fertile. I did not wish to kill our horses and we stopped at each and every village, hamlet and farm that we passed, to water our horses and ask for news of the murderers. No news was good news and none had seen them. When they heard my name, they all offered us food. We ate whilst in the saddle. Osmotherley, Thimbleby and Knayton were the last three settlements we passed before Tresche. The farmers all confirmed that we were the first riders they had seen going in either

The Sword of Cnut

direction that day. I was saddle sore and weary when we reined in at the hamlet of Tresche. There were just a few dwellings and none of them was particularly large. A young man saw us approach and I saw that he had, with him, two boys. There were others but they were working in their fields.

I reined in, "I am Eorl Sven Saxon Sword of Norton. Have you seen five men with spare horses riding through here?"

He frowned, "Not today but a party of horsemen rode through almost a week ago."

We were in time. "What is your name?"

"I am Thord, headman of Tresche and these are my sons, Orm and Thor."

"Then here is my tale."

I told him the story and his eyes narrowed, "Murder is unheard of. My father, Thorstein, came from Denmark and we settled this land. It is peaceful and we have no murderers." He glared at his sons, "We have some who are cruel and will be punished for that when I can cut a stout piece of blackthorn." His sons recoiled and I knew that they were guilty of some wrongdoing. "There are five men who are warriors. We can help you."

"I would not have you injured for I am the one charged with upholding Cnut's Law. Have any of your men, mail?"

"I have my father's byrnie but it is old."

I had been planning all the time he had been speaking, "This is what you will do." I looked around and saw a small piece of higher ground two hundred paces from the hamlet. It had trees covering it. "We will tether our horses there and we will hide in the village. If you and your men secrete your weapons where you can get them, then when my men apprehend the killers, you can help by stopping them from fleeing back whence they came."

"Are you sure that they will come through here, Eorl Sven?"

"When the riders left here a week ago, did they ride due north or northwest?"

"Northwest to the bridge at Persebrig."

"Then they will come that way back. They will be tired and have ridden forty miles. They may not get here until the morning, but they will come."

"Orm and Thor, make up for your wildness by fetching all the men." They ran off, eager to atone for whatever crime they had committed. "Maeve." A pregnant woman emerged, "We have guests."

She bowed and said, "Food will be ready ere long, my lord."

The Sword of Cnut

After tethering our horses we sat on the blocks of timber which were used to chop wood and waited. The two boys, Orm and Thor, had clearly done something wrong for they went out of their way to ingratiate themselves into their father's good books. They brought us ale and asked if they could groom the horses. Thord was not impressed but, like all good fathers, he did not tell others of his sons' misdemeanours. I liked him. We went inside the dwelling to eat. Thord's house was the largest one in the village but it was tiny by comparison with even Haldir's. It was of triangular construction and held the five of us, just. Food was cooked outside, and I saw that inside was just for eating and sleeping. Tresche showed the most basic of lives that people led. Closer to Jorvik there would be bigger settlements and houses, but this was almost the frontier.

We finished and when the platters were taken away by Maeve, I placed a silver coin on the table. She shook her head, "You are guests, my lord."

"And we came unannounced. Take it." She was a practical woman. She nodded and took it. The next time she went to market she would be able to enrich the lives of her family. We left the house and went outside into the dusk. Thord and his men were gathered and were talking.

"The Thurbrand of Settrington who comes, is he related to Thurbrand the Hold who was murdered by Uhtred the Bold's son, Ealdred?"

"I believe he is."

"Was the man he murdered one of his killers?"

"Edward of Billingham was killed for a golden torc that belonged to King Aelle of Deira. There was no honour in the murder." He looked relieved. "You and your men had better eat. It would look strange if you were waiting outside your homes. We will watch." He nodded, "Remember, I do not want you in danger. You and your men should just prevent their escape."

Left alone with my men I said, "Haldir, Aed and Ragnar, stand behind that dwelling there." I pointed to the first house on the east side of the settlement. "Karl and I will stand there. Wait for me to move. Just back me up."

"We will."

Karl and I moved to the first house on the west side. It was nearer to Thord's and meant that when I emerged, Haldir and the other two would be slightly behind them and able to hinder any attempt to escape.

The Sword of Cnut

"Karl, we must be certain that these are the men. Much depends on you. If we attack the wrong men then it is we who will be guilty of a crime."

"Do not worry, Eorl, their faces are etched in my mind. I will not forget them." The evening became darker as the sun set behind the mountains to the west. "What will become of Billingham, my lord?"

"What?" My mind was still on the job at hand and I had not thought that far ahead.

"All Edward of Billingham's family are dead. There needs to be a hand that rules. Will that be you?"

"Ultimately, yes, but you are right and when this business is done I will have to put my mind to that. King Cnut has charged me with ensuring his land prospers and that means in times of peace as well as war."

The hoofbeats in the distance told us that someone was coming. I did not wear my helmet and I had my shield across my back. I drew Oathsword. There was no need to alert Haldir, he had sharp ears. Karl drew his own sword and kissed the hilt. He was a Christian. The hoofbeats came closer and they were slow ones. I peered from behind the house. As the form of the horses became clearer, I saw that they were being led. That made sense. The horses had been ridden hard for forty miles. One clearly limped. The brief glimpse I had told me that the men were mailed and that, in many ways, identified them. The only ones who rode mailed were those intent on violence, as we were.

"Karl, is that them?"

His head darted out and after a few heartbeats he withdrew it and he nodded, "It is. Thurbrand leads them."

I used all my experience to time my movement. I had to hope that Thord and his men had heard the hoofbeats and were doing as I had asked and got around the rear of the warriors. I stepped out and Karl followed me. I was just ten paces from the men when I was seen. Their hands went to their swords as soon as we appeared.

"I am Eorl Sven Saxon Sword and I am here to arrest you for the murder of Edward of Billingham and his men."

Thurbrand of Settrington looked around and he gave me a cruel smile, "There are two of you and even though you have a Dragon Sword, Eorl, I think that the odds of five to two means that I shall own your sword this night."

I had intended to tell them that I was not alone even as Haldir, Aed and Ragnar slipped from the building, but Thurbrand dropped his reins and shouted, "Kill them!"

The Sword of Cnut

The murderer was right in one respect, five against two meant that we would have to fight for our lives until my men could enter the fray. Drawing Norse Splitter I said, "Karl, guard my left."

Thurbrand and a man I took to be a bodyguard came at me, while another bodyguard launched himself at Karl. It was clear who the sons were for they hung back. I blocked the blow from Thurbrand with Oathsword and tried to use Norse Splitter to slow the swipe from the bodyguard's blade. I managed to slow it a little, but the sword still cracked against my ribs. If one bodyguard was a good fighter then the other would be too and Karl would be in trouble.

"Haldir!" I needed my ex-pirate. My son-in-law and Aed could handle the sons.

I stepped back to gain time and the bodyguard came on. Thurbrand did not advance. This time, when the bodyguard swung at me, I was able to use the flat of Oathsword to block it and Norse Splitter flashed at the bodyguard and pierced the mail and found flesh. It was then that Thurbrand swung his sword at me for he thought me committed to the blow. I was but I had quick reactions and Oathsword blocked the strike. I had wounded the bodyguard but he was a veteran. I heard a cry from Karl as he was wounded. The clash of arms ahead told me that my men were engaged. My plan was unravelling fast. The Norns had spun.

It was Thurbrand's eagerness to kill me and have a legendary sword as well as the torc that saved me. He drew his own dagger and lunged at me. It was at the same moment that his bodyguard had raised his sword to strike at my unprotected head. He could not as his master was in the way. Norse Splitter blocked the dagger and then I turned it and pressed it at Thurbrand's middle. In his haste to stab me, he had moved forward and his momentum enabled my blade to stab him. He reeled back and the bodyguard came at me. I knew that he was a powerful man. His first blow had swept Norse Splitter away and as the sword came down to cleave my skull in two, I raised my two blades and held the sword between the two weapons. I brought up my knee and rammed it between his legs. I have yet to meet a man who can endure such a blow and he was no exception. He doubled up and I pushed my two blades at his neck. They both bit into his flesh and the gushing blood and his sagging body told me that he was dead.

"I will see you in Valhalla."

I looked around and saw that Haldir had slain the second bodyguard. Aed and Ragnar were standing over the two sons. One lay dead while the other was wounded. Karl was hurt, "See to Karl!" I looked around and saw that a wounded Thurbrand was trying to escape. He was running, as fast as his wound would allow, to his horse.

The Sword of Cnut

I was not hurt and I ran after him. I was on him within a few strides, "You cannot escape, murderer. Turn and die like a man. Your murdering days are over." He whirled and I swung Oathsword at head height. Thurbrand wore mail and a helmet but his neck was bare. His throat sliced, his corpse fell at my feet.

It was then I saw Thord, his sons and his men behind the horses with drawn swords. I was pleased that they had obeyed me and not had to kill. Justice had been served by Cnut's Sword and his men. "Guard the prisoner." I turned and went to Karl. Maeve and Haldir were tending to him.

Haldir looked around and smiled, "He tried his best but that bodyguard knew his business. The sword almost cut to the bone. Maeve is sewing it."

I looked down at Karl, "Thank you, Karl, you did your duty."

He lay on the ground and smiled, "And Lord Edward is avenged. The training on Sunday paid off, my lord, but I fear that my days in the shield wall are done."

"Aye, but men will honour your name."

I walked back to the prisoner. Aed had bound the wound to his arm. "What is your name?"

He gave me a surly look, "I am Thurbrand son of Thurbrand of Settrington and grandson of Thurbrand the Hold, and you are nothing more than a killer yourself, Sven Saxon Sword."

Ragnar smacked him hard in the side of the head, "He is Eorl so mind your manners, or we shall save a length of rope."

It was only then, I think, that the young man realised his fate. "Rope?"

I nodded, "Aye, for we shall bind you this night and on the morrow ride back to Billingham. There Lord Edward of Billingham's people shall see at least one of his killers hanged."

"But I..."

"Silence! There can be no excuses and even if others struck the fatal blows you were part of the murders. You tried to kill me here. There is nothing that you can say that will save your life. I will let my priest hear your shrift and that will be the only gift I give you. Bind him."

Thord approached, "We did nothing to help. I am sorry."

I waved an arm at the bodies, "These were armed, mailed men and you had no defence. Take the mail and arms from the dead bodyguards. The next time you need to draw a weapon then there will be a defence for you. We will take Thurbrand's mail back to Norton. Take two of the horses too. We will leave in the morning."

The Sword of Cnut

Maeve was good with a needle and one of the other women was a volva. She gave Karl a potion that helped him to sleep. We took it in turns to watch in the night. I did not want to return without some evidence for the people of Billingham of Cnut's justice.

We left the next day with Thurbrand of Settrington's body draped over one horse and a bound prisoner on another. Karl was able to ride although it was a difficult ride. We reached the river in the early afternoon and passed Norton at Nones. As we rode across the causeway people gathered. Aed had ridden ahead and as we neared Billingham, I saw Father John waiting. We had planned what to do on the way home and after we had dismounted, Haldir and Aed threw two ropes over the gatehouse beam.

Ragnar and I propelled Thurbrand son of Thurbrand forward and I shouted to the crowd who had gathered, "People of Billingham. We have taken those who murdered your lord." I held up the torc which we had found, along with the other things they had stolen, in a hessian sack, "They came for this but it was not worth the lives of those they killed." I nodded at Haldir who put a rope around Thurbrand of Settrington's bloody neck and hauled the corpse to swing beneath the fighting platform.

It was then that his son began to struggle and to weep, "No, I beg of you, mercy!"

"And did you show mercy to those you slew?" His head bowed, "Father John."

The priest came over and put his head close to the killer. Ragnar and I stood apart. The man's hands were bound. He was going nowhere. Father John made the sign of the cross, stepped away and nodded.

"Karl." Karl had dismounted and now he limped over to put the rope around the man's neck. That done he went to join Aed and Haldir. I nodded and said, "Thus is murder avenged." The three of them pulled on the rope. They gave him a quicker death than he deserved. His body twisted and jerked for a few moments and then became still. It was over.

The Sword of Cnut
Epilogue

My wife was glad when, after three days, the two bodies were removed and thrown into the river where they would be taken to the sea. Unlike Edward, Osgar, Edgar and Ethelred, there would be no graves to remember them and their heinous act was punished in the most appropriate way. Of course, I realised that I had incurred the enmity of Thurbrand of Settrington's brothers but Ealdred was higher up the list than I was. I thanked Ragnar before he left for his home. He had come of age both in the war and in the hunt for the killers. He and I were closer now and that was good for he was the father of my blood kin. Haldir too had shown me that when the Norns had spun at Hwitebi, it had been for our good. He would never be hearthweru, but I now had someone to replace, in some part, Gandálfr. No one would ever truly take his place but I was now an eorl and I would have to lead armies from the wapentake.

Bersi and Haldir ate with us that night. I had washed the blood from me and changed into better clothes but I still felt the stain of battle upon me. I was hungry but did not feel like eating. Osgar had fought alongside me and whilst Edward and his sons were no warriors, they had been men I liked. In many ways, Edward was more like Siggi. A man who shunned war and embraced farming.

The others were largely silent too until Mary spoke, "What of the torc? Where will it lie?"

"I do not want it to draw others here. I will visit Dun Holm and ask the bishop to keep it there. God can protect it."

The answer pleased Mary who beamed, "And Billingham?"

I realised that I had not told her all that had happened in Roskilde. "King Cnut rewarded me with the power to give away land. I think that Bersi would make a good hersir and he will not live as far away as Steana. What say you, son? Can you be the Lord of Billingham?"

"Do you think I am ready?"

"I believe you are, but the real question is do you think that you are ready?"

He looked at Seara and she put her hand on his and nodded, "I think I am. I have much to learn but I have one close by to whom I can look for advice and example, the man the king calls, Cnut's Sword."

"Then all is good and you will carry on, as Osgar and Edward did, guarding and protecting the land."

The Sword of Cnut

I was happy for I did not want another son to be separated by a sea. I wanted to see him often and watch my grandchildren grow. I had left Denmark and like my grandchildren, I would now be English.

The End

The Sword of Cnut

Norse Calendar

Gormánuður October 14th - November 13th
Ýlir November 14th - December 13th
Mörsugur December 14th - January 12th
Þorri - January 13th - February 11th
Gói - February 12th - March 13th
Einmánuður - March 14th - April 13th
Harpa April 14th - May 13th
Skerpla - May 14th - June 12th
Sólmánuður - June 13th - July 12th
Heyannir - July 13th - August 14th
Tvímánuður - August 15th - September 14th
Haustmánuður September 15th-October 13th

Canonical Hours

Matins (nighttime)
Lauds (early morning)
Prime (first hour of daylight)
Terce (third hour)
Sext (noon)
Nones (ninth hour)
Vespers (sunset evening)
Compline (end of the day)

The Sword of Cnut

Glossary

Acemannesceastre - Bath (aching men's city- a reference to the springs.)
Bagsheta - Bagshot
Beardestapol – Barnstaple
Beck - a stream
Beohyll – Beal (Northumberland)
Blót – a blood sacrifice made by a jarl
Bondi - Viking farmers who fight
Bjorr – Beaver
Breguntford - Brentford
Brycgstow - Bristol
Burgh/Burh - King Alfred's defences. The largest was Winchester
Byrnie - a mail or leather shirt reaching down to the knees
Cantwareburh - Canterbury
Cent – Kent
Chape - the tip of a scabbard
Corebricg – Corbridge
Cuneceastra – Chester Le Street
Dorchestershire- Devon
Deoraby – Derby
Din Guardi - Bamburgh
Drekar - a Dragon ship (a Viking warship) pl. drekar
Dudecota - Didcot
Dun Holm - Durham
Dyflin - Old Norse for Dublin
Eoforwic - Saxon for York
Føroyar - Faroe Islands
Fey - having second sight
Ferneberga – Farnborough (Hants)
Firkin - a barrel containing eight gallons (usually beer)
Fret - a sea mist
Fyrd - the Saxon levy
Galdramenn - wizard
Gegnesburh – Gainsborough (Lincolnshire)
Gesithas – a Saxon bodyguard, hearthweru
Gighesbore – Guisborough
Gippeswic - Ipswich
Gleawecastre – Gloucester

The Sword of Cnut

Hamtunscīr - Hampshire
Hamwic - Southampton
Heiða-býr – Hedeby in Schleswig - destroyed in 1066
Herepath - the military roads connecting the burghs of King Alfred
Herkumbl - a badge on a helmet denoting the clan
Hersir - a Viking landowner and minor noble. It ranks below a jarl
Herterpol – Hartlepool
Hnefatafl – a Viking game a little like chess
Hoggs or Hogging - when the pressure of the wind causes the stern or the bow to droop
Hremmesgeat – Ramsgate
Hringmaraheior – Ringmere
Hrofescester - Rochester, Kent
Hundred - Saxon military organization. (One hundred men from an area led by a thegn or gesith)
Isle of Greon - Isle of Grain (Thames Estuary)
Jarl - Norse earl or lord
Joro - goddess of the earth
kjerringa - Old Woman - the solid block in which the mast rested
Knarr - a merchant ship or a coastal vessel
Kyrtle - woven top
Ligera Caestre – Leicester
Lincylene – Lincoln
Lydwicnaesse - Breton Point, Exmouth
Mast fish - two large racks on a ship designed to store the mast when not required.
Meðune – River Medina in the Isle of Wight
Mere lafan – Marlow Bucks
Midden - a place where they dumped human waste
Miklagård - Constantinople
Northwic - Norwich
Njörðr - God of the sea
Nithing - A man without honour (Saxon)
Northantone, - Northampton
Ocmundtune - Oakhampton
Odin - The 'All Father' God of war, also associated with wisdom, poetry, and magic (The Ruler of the gods).
Østersøen – The Baltic Sea
Otorbrunna – Otterburn
Oxnaford - Oxford
Persebrig – Piercebridge

The Sword of Cnut

Ran - Goddess of the sea
Roof rock - slate
Saami - the people who live in what is now Northern Norway/Sweden
Sabrina - The River Severn
Sandwic – Sandwich (Kent)
Scorranstone - Sherston (Wilts)
Scree - loose rocks in a glacial valley
Seax – short sword
Sennight - seven nights- a week
Shamblord - Cowes, Isle of Wight
Sheerstrake - the uppermost strake in the hull
Sheet - a rope fastened to the lower corner of a sail
Shroud - a rope from the masthead to the hull amidships
Skáktafl - Chess
Skald - a Viking poet and singer of songs
Skeggox – an axe with a shorter beard on one side of the blade
Skumasþorp- Scunthorpe
Skreið- stockfish (any fish which is preserved)
Skjalborg- shield wall
Snekke- a small warship
Snotingaham - Nottingham
Stanford - Stamford
Stad- Norse settlement
Stays- ropes running from the masthead to the bow
Strake- the wood on the side of a drekar
Suindune - Swindon
Swynfylking – a series of small wedges.
Tarn - small lake (Norse)
Teignton - Kingsteignton
The Norns - The three sisters who weave webs of intrigue for men
Thing - Norse for a parliament or a debate (Tynwald in the Isle of Man)
Thor's Day - Thursday
Threttenessa- a drekar with 13 oars on each side.
Thrall- slave
Trenail- a round wooden peg used to secure strakes
Tresche – Thirsk
Ubbanford – Norham
Úlfarrberg- Helvellyn
Ullr-Norse God of Hunting

The Sword of Cnut

Ulfheonar- an elite Norse warrior who wore a wolf skin over his armour
Verðandi -the Norn who sees the future
Volva- a witch or healing woman in Norse culture
Walhaz -Norse for the Welsh (foreigners)
Waite- a Viking word for farm
Wiht -The Isle of Wight
Windles-ore - Windsor
Witan- Saxon Parliament
Withy- the mechanism connecting the steering board to the ship
Wintan-ceastre -Winchester
Woden's day- Wednesday
Wyrd- Fate
Wyrme- Norse for Dragon
Yard- a timber from which the sail is suspended

The Sword of Cnut
Historical Notes

The Dragon Sword is a blade of my own imagination, although King Alfred did give a sword to the illegitimate son of Prince Edward, the king's son. Æthelstan became the first king accorded the title King of England. As readers of my books will know, swords are always important. This series will reflect that.

A word about Denmark, the maps and the place names. If you look at a map of modern Denmark, you will see that Ribe is not where I place it. Names change over the years and you will see, as the series progresses, the reason for some of the changes. The Heiða-býr of King Sweyn is also no longer there. It was destroyed sometime after King Sweyn died. There are some ruins where it once was but as the Danes built using wood, they are not as substantial as the Roman ones would have been.

Excavations of battlefields have shown that the Viking warriors had a high proportion of young men. Many were barely teenagers. This was a time when boys became men quickly. It was the same with women. As soon as a girl was able to bear children she might be married. Shakespeare's Juliet was barely 13 when she was married and that was five centuries later.

The names of the places around Norton are based on the names I found on the 1866 map. Rus' Worthy is Roseworth and Ragnar's Worthy is Ragworth. Pers' Track is Portrack and Stockadeton is Stockton. Fulthorpe is the name of a farm close to Thorpe Thewles.

The treachery of the period beggars belief. Eadric Streona changed sides as often as a weathervane turns yet Cnut, Æthelred and Edmund continued to believe him. The challenge from Edmund to Cnut was real. At Assundun Cnut stayed in the rear while Edmund fought in the front rank.

The death of Edmund has four reported versions. One suggested that he died of wounds received at Assundun. The other three all have similar threads. One was that when he was on the privy a hook was inserted into his bowels and that is how he died. I dismissed that one as clearly improbable. A second was that a crossbow was fired into him. That too seemed unlikely as it did not guarantee death. The one I took was a spear. Streona claimed it was he who did the deed but he seems to me to be too cowardly to do such a thing and I used the evidence that it was his sons. He did admit to the deed to Cnut and was executed as I

The Sword of Cnut

said. There were rumours that Cnut put Streona up to it. He may have done so. He was a far more ruthless man than history suggests.

Tyr was a god, the son of Odin and he had a sword that was deemed to be magical. Legend has it that the sword passed to Attila the Hun who conquered Rome with it. The sword in the Branstock is a legend of a one-eyed man (possibly Odin) who enters a hall at a wedding and rams the sword into an oak tree (the Branstock). He said that whoever could pull the sword from the oak would be unbeatable in battle. It is a variation of the Excalibur legend.

Until 1752 when the Gregorian calendar was adopted, the New Year traditionally began on Lady Day (March 25th). It was adopted officially in 1155 but was celebrated before that date. Although a Christian celebration, the pagans celebrated Eostre and the rebirth of the land at that time as the new growth would appear. After 1752, the April Fool began as people clung on to the old New Year.

Battle of Helgeå caused me problems as the two sources I used, Bartlett and the Anglo-Saxon Chronicles disagreed. The battle, according to the Anglo Saxon Chronicles, was fought at sea, close to Kristiansand. As Kristiansand is some way from the sea that is a problem. Bartlett talks of a land battle. What is certain is that the Swedes dammed a river and then released the water. The Chronicles say that killed many men but as the Danes had six hundred ships and the Swedish Norse force four hundred and fifty, then it begs the question how did the flood kill men on the Danish fleet and not the Swedish Norse one? That the Danes won the sea battle is proven by the fact that the Norse fleet was destroyed and many men died in the four-hundred-mile walk back to Norway. This was the high water mark for King Olaf.

There is also an issue with Jarl Ulf. That he was murdered on the orders of King Cnut the day after the return from the battle is documented as it happened in a church, but Jarl Ulf, like Thorkell the Tall, is problematic. I came to the conclusion that Ulf sided with the Swedes but when they failed to win the Battle of Helgeå tried to return to the Danish court. In terms of a story, I think that my version works. The game of chess (Skáktafl) and the murder of the jarl by Ivar White are documented in the Anglo-Saxon Chronicles.

Eirík of Lade did go on pilgrimage and died of some illness. Earl Godwin went with King Cnut to make war on the Wends and was mentioned as having led a night attack on a Wendish camp. Uhtred's sons murdered Thurbrand and the blood feud continued. I made up the story of King Aelle's torc. Thurbrand of Settrington was one of the killers of Uhtred the Bold. I added the torc and the plot to give Uhtred some justice.

The Sword of Cnut

Sven Saxon Sword is an invention of mine. He helps to put flesh on the historical bones. The story will continue.

- **King Cnut- W B Bartlett**
- **Vikings- Life and Legends -British Museum**
- **Saxon, Norman and Viking by Terence Wise (Osprey)**
- **The Vikings (Osprey) -Ian Heath**
- **Byzantine Armies 668-1118 (Osprey)-Ian Heath**
- **Romano-Byzantine Armies 4th- 9th Century (Osprey) -David Nicholle**
- **The Walls of Constantinople AD 324-1453 (Osprey) -Stephen Turnbull**
- **Viking Longship (Osprey) - Keith Durham**
- **The Vikings- David Wernick (Time-Life)**
- **The Vikings in England Anglo-Danish Project**
- **Anglo Saxon Thegn AD 449-1066- Mark Harrison (Osprey)**
- **Viking Hersir- 793-1066 AD - Mark Harrison (Osprey)**
- **National Geographic- March 2017**
- **British Kings and Queens- Mike Ashley**
- **Norse Myths and Tales**

Griff Hosker January 2024

The Sword of Cnut

Other books by Griff Hosker

If you enjoyed reading this book, then why not read another one by the author?

Ancient History

The Sword of Cartimandua Series
(Germania and Britannia 50 A.D. – 128 A.D.)
Ulpius Felix- Roman Warrior (prequel)
The Sword of Cartimandua
The Horse Warriors
Invasion Caledonia
Roman Retreat
Revolt of the Red Witch
Druid's Gold
Trajan's Hunters
The Last Frontier
Hero of Rome
Roman Hawk
Roman Treachery
Roman Wall
Roman Courage

The Wolf Warrior series
(Britain in the late 6th Century)
Saxon Dawn
Saxon Revenge
Saxon England
Saxon Blood
Saxon Slayer
Saxon Slaughter
Saxon Bane
Saxon Fall: Rise of the Warlord
Saxon Throne
Saxon Sword

The Sword of Cnut

Medieval History

The Dragon Heart Series
Viking Slave *
Viking Warrior *
Viking Jarl *
Viking Kingdom *
Viking Wolf *
Viking War
Viking Sword
Viking Wrath
Viking Raid
Viking Legend
Viking Vengeance
Viking Dragon
Viking Treasure
Viking Enemy
Viking Witch
Viking Blood
Viking Weregeld
Viking Storm
Viking Warband
Viking Shadow
Viking Legacy
Viking Clan
Viking Bravery

The Norman Genesis Series
Hrolf the Viking *
Horseman *
The Battle for a Home *
Revenge of the Franks *
The Land of the Northmen
Ragnvald Hrolfsson
Brothers in Blood
Lord of Rouen
Drekar in the Seine
Duke of Normandy

The Sword of Cnut

The Duke and the King

Danelaw
(England and Denmark in the 11th Century)
Dragon Sword *
Oathsword *
Bloodsword *
Danish Sword
The Sword of Cnut

New World Series
Blood on the Blade *
Across the Seas *
The Savage Wilderness *
The Bear and the Wolf *
Erik The Navigator *
Erik's Clan *
The Last Viking

The Vengeance Trail *

The Conquest Series
(Normandy and England 1050-1100)
Hastings
Conquest

The Aelfraed Series
(Britain and Byzantium 1050 A.D. - 1085 A.D.)
Housecarl *
Outlaw *
Varangian *

The Reconquista Chronicles
Castilian Knight *
El Campeador *
The Lord of Valencia *

The Anarchy Series England

The Sword of Cnut
1120-1180
English Knight *
Knight of the Empress *
Northern Knight *
Baron of the North *
Earl *
King Henry's Champion *
The King is Dead *
Warlord of the North
Enemy at the Gate
The Fallen Crown
Warlord's War
Kingmaker
Henry II
Crusader
The Welsh Marches
Irish War
Poisonous Plots
The Princes' Revolt
Earl Marshal
The Perfect Knight

**Border Knight
1182-1300**
Sword for Hire *
Return of the Knight *
Baron's War *
Magna Carta *
Welsh Wars *
Henry III *
The Bloody Border *
Baron's Crusade
Sentinel of the North
War in the West
Debt of Honour
The Blood of the Warlord
The Fettered King
de Montfort's Crown

The Sword of Cnut

The Ripples of Rebellion

Sir John Hawkwood Series
France and Italy 1339- 1387
Crécy: The Age of the Archer *
Man At Arms *
The White Company *
Leader of Men *
Tuscan Warlord *
Condottiere

Lord Edward's Archer
Lord Edward's Archer *
King in Waiting *
An Archer's Crusade *
Targets of Treachery *
The Great Cause *
Wallace's War *
The Hunt

Struggle for a Crown
1360- 1485
Blood on the Crown *
To Murder a King *
The Throne *
King Henry IV *
The Road to Agincourt *
St Crispin's Day *
The Battle for France *
The Last Knight *
Queen's Knight *
The Knight's Tale

Tales from the Sword I
(Short stories from the Medieval period)

Tudor Warrior series
England and Scotland in the late 15th and early 16th century

The Sword of Cnut
Tudor Warrior *
Tudor Spy *
Flodden

Conquistador
England and America in the 16th Century
Conquistador *
The English Adventurer *

English Mercenary
The 30 Years War and the English Civil War
Horse and Pistol

Modern History

The Napoleonic Horseman Series
Chasseur à Cheval
Napoleon's Guard
British Light Dragoon
Soldier Spy
1808: The Road to Coruña
Talavera
The Lines of Torres Vedras
Bloody Badajoz
The Road to France
Waterloo

The Lucky Jack American Civil War series
Rebel Raiders
Confederate Rangers
The Road to Gettysburg

Soldier of the Queen series
Soldier of the Queen
Redcoat's Rifle
Omdurman

The British Ace Series

The Sword of Cnut
1914
1915 Fokker Scourge
1916 Angels over the Somme
1917 Eagles Fall
1918 We will remember them
From Arctic Snow to Desert Sand
Wings over Persia

**Combined Operations series
1940-1945**
Commando *
Raider *
Behind Enemy Lines
Dieppe
Toehold in Europe
Sword Beach
Breakout
The Battle for Antwerp
King Tiger
Beyond the Rhine
Korea
Korean Winter

Tales from the Sword II
(Short stories from the Modern period)

Books marked thus *, are also available in the audio format. For more information on all of the books then please visit the author's website at www.griffhosker.com where there is a link to contact him or visit his Facebook page: GriffHosker at Sword Books or follow him on Twitter: @HoskerGriff or Sword (@swordbooksltd)

216

Printed in Great Britain
by Amazon